The doors opened wide. The interior of the barn glowed with the light of the kerosene lantern. Three mounted men. Pernot, Lowe, and Crackley. Crackley had the shotgun. They started to exit the horses from the stable at a walk, none of them able to see the deputy waiting for them in the dark driveway.

Creed turned sideways, leveled the Colt's at Crackley, cocked the hammer, and waited another second for the riders to come a few feet closer . . .

CREED

ARKANSAS RAIDERS

BRYCE HARTE

BERKLEY BOOKS, NEW YORK

For my sister
Dayna
because I love her

ARKANSAS RAIDERS

A Berkley Book / published by arrangement with
the author

PRINTING HISTORY
Berkley edition / June 1993

ISBN: 0-425-13809-7

A BERKLEY BOOK ® TM 757,375
Berkley Books are published by The Berkley Publishing Group,
200 Madison Avenue, New York, New York 10016.
The name "BERKLEY" and the "B" logo
are trademarks belonging to Berkley Publishing Corporation.

PRINTED IN THE UNITED STATES OF AMERICA

10 9 8 7 6 5 4 3 2 1

REAL HISTORY

Every Western historian has heard of Judge Isaac Parker, the famous hanging judge of the federal court at Fort Smith, Arkansas, in the 1880's, but ask those same historians to name one judge who preceded Parker in that post and few, if any, could name one. Few could pinpoint the year when the court was moved from Van Buren, Arkansas, to Fort Smith.

As in all of the books of the Creed series, a vast majority of the characters were real people, and they are portrayed as accurately as possible.

Also, all geographical features mentioned in the story are accurately detailed for the time period. This includes towns and other historical places.

The expository details of the characters are real history, and the history of Van Buren, Crawford County, the Indian nations, and the state of Arkansas is depicted as accurately as the existing records will allow.

For additional reading, the author recommends *Fort Smith, Little Gibraltar on the Arkansas* by Edwin C. Bearss and A. M. Gibson; *Law West of Fort Smith* by Glenn Shirley; and *Old Cattle Brands and Lost Trails* by Ivan Denton.

ACKNOWLEDGMENTS

The author wishes to express his gratitude to Donna Young of *Especially Arkansas,* Van Buren, Arkansas, for all her assistance in gathering research materials for this chapter in the life of Slate Creed.

Also, the author wishes to thank Dr. Louis Peer of Van Buren, Arkansas, for his contributions to the research. Dr. Peer heads up the restoration group that is presently turning back the clock in Van Buren and bringing history alive again. Every visitor to Arkansas should make Van Buren a must stop on the family travel agenda.

PROLOGUE

Nobody was more surprised to see Creed and Little Bee again than Louise Thayer was, and nobody was more surprised that Creed was asking her to take Little Bee than she was.

"I'm glad to see that you finally came to your senses," she said rather haughtily.

"It's only temporary," said Creed.

They—Creed, Little Bee, and Louise—were standing apart from the others. Tyler and Drake were tending to the animals, while Reverend Thayer and Faye slept restlessly in their beds.

"Only temporary?" queried Louise. "What do you mean by that?"

"I mean, I'll be back for him," said Creed. He put his arm around Little Bee's shoulders and hugged the boy to him. "Isn't that right, son?"

"I rather doubt that you'll ever come near him again," said Louise, "once you ride out of here."

"Is that right?" said Creed.

"Yes, it is," said Louise.

"Well, let me set you straight on that, Miss Thayer," said Creed. "You're wrong. You see, I'm a Texan, and Texans keep their word." He smiled and added, "Because if they don't, they know that's a surefire way to get a one-way ticket straight to hell." He turned serious again. "I gave Little Bee my word that I'd be back for him just as soon as I get things set straight on my mother's ranch. I gave him my word just the same as I gave his mother my word a month ago up in the Cherokee Nation, and I don't think I have to say anything more about that."

"Well, we'll just have to wait and see what happens in the future, won't we?" said Louise.

"Yes, we will, won't we?" he said. "In the meantime, you can see to it that he learns to read and write and cipher real well because I don't want to come back here and find out he's still some kind of uneducated Hoosier." He looked at Little Bee,

1

hugged him again, and said, "You understand that, son?"

"Sure, Slate, I understand," said the orphan.

"You needn't worry about his education," said Louise. "I'll see to it personally. That *much* he can depend on."

Creed had had enough of this woman's attitude. "Will you excuse us for a minute, Little Bee?" he said.

"Sure, Slate," said the youngster. He walked away to visit with Drake and Tyler.

"All right, Louise," said Creed. "Let's have it."

"Have what?" she queried.

"Let's have it out. I want to know what it is about me that you detest so much that you have to speak to me like I'm so much horse dung stuck to the heel of your shoe."

"It isn't only one thing, Mr. Creed. It's *everything* about you that I detest. From the crown of your hat to the toes of your boots, I loathe everything about you."

For an instant, she lowered the veil of her soul and allowed Creed to see into her heart. Her lips might have been speaking hateful words, but she was feeling just the opposite.

"You're a liar," he said.

"What?" she gasped.

"You heard me. You're a liar."

"How dare you call me a liar!" she snapped. She raised her hand to strike him, but he caught her arm and twisted it downward. Even so, she remained defiant, gritting her teeth and saying, "You're hurting me."

"Not as much as you're hurting yourself, Louise."

Her face scrunched up with confusion. "What?" she rasped.

Creed released her and said, "You're hurting yourself by not being honest, Louise. You're not being honest with yourself or anybody else. You aren't fooling anybody with this bit of playacting that you're doing."

"Playacting? What does that mean?"

"You know perfectly well what that means." He chuckled, then said, "You've been playacting since the moment I met you. Probably before that, too. You've probably been playacting for years. Probably so long that you don't even know that you're doing it anymore. You'd better stop it, and stop it soon, or you just might miss out when the right man for you comes along."

"The right man? Someone like you, I suppose."

"Maybe."

"Don't flatter yourself, Mr. Creed."

"No, don't you flatter yourself, Louise. Do you remember what I told Faye when I said good-bye to her on the Muddy Boggy River?"

"I wasn't listening."

"There you go again. Lying. You've got to stop that, Louise, and start being honest. If you don't, you'll wind up either as an old maid or as a very unhappy woman with a man that you really will detest."

Creed had finally struck the right nerve. She winced, being taken aback by his statement; but she recovered immediately. "Just who do you think you are to talk to me this way?" she said fiercely.

"I'll give you your choice on that one," said Creed. "I'm either a man who feels sorry for you because you're pathetic or I'm a man who cares about you, a man who would come a-courtin', if things were different with the rest of my life. But things aren't different with the rest of my life, so let's just say I'm someone who cares about you and I don't want to see you unhappy for the rest of your life.

"Now, I've already seen that you've made up with Faye," he continued, "and I see that you're getting along better with Drake and your father. But what I don't see is you getting along with yourself. Until you start doing that, you'll be unhappy, and worse than that, you'll wind up making everybody around you just as unhappy as you are. Do you really want that, Louise?"

"No," she said softly, "of course not."

"Then you'd better start being honest with yourself," he said, "and start letting your feelings out. Your true feelings. Not what you think everybody expects from you, but what you really want to feel and say and do. Once you start doing that, you won't have to look for happiness, Louise. It'll find you." He turned to walk away, then stopped, standing sideways to her. "I didn't mean to preach to you like that, but you just bring that out of me, I guess."

"No," she said rapidly, urgently, "it's all right." She sighed, then continued. "I guess you really do care. About me, I mean."

Creed's smile spread across his face. He shook his head and said, "You really do catch on quick, don't you?"

Louise lowered her eyes and said, "Yes, I suppose I am a little slow sometimes." Looking up again, she asked, "Did you really mean what you said about courting if things were different in your life?"

He smiled and said, "You caught that part, did you?"

She smiled back at him and said, "Yes."

"Well, let me put it this way," said Creed, "I told Faye that the only woman who could ever tie me down would have to be part wildcat, part mule, and part cottontail with just a tiny bit of alley cat thrown in to make her real interesting. She doesn't have that alley cat in her. But you do." He tipped his hat and said, "I'll be going to say good-bye to Little Bee now." He turned and walked away toward the meadow where the animals were staked out.

Louise watched him go, wishing that he would come back and take her into his arms and never leave again. But she knew that couldn't be. Not now, anyway. Maybe when he came back for Little Bee, whenever that should be. She could wait until then, or so she told herself.

Creed caught up to Little Bee, Drake, and Tyler in the meadow. "I'm going now," he said. "I just came to say good-bye." He offered his hand to the ex-slave. "Mr. Tyler, I hope we'll meet again one day, and the next time we do, we can get off to a friendlier start."

Tyler shook his hand and said, "I think I'd like that, Mr. Creed. You watch out for yourself now."

"Write me a letter, Mr. Tyler, and let me know if you find your family. I'd like to meet them someday."

"I'll do that," said Tyler. He released the grip.

Creed turned to Drake. "You had a hard lesson about guns, Drake," he said, "but I think you learned it well." He offered his hand to young Thayer. "You hurry up and get that education back in Kentucky and get back here. This country needs more people like you and your father. Peaceful folks. Good men to lead the way."

"Thank you, Slate," said Drake. He finished the handshake and walked off with Tyler so Creed could say his farewell to Little Bee.

"I'm going to miss you, son," said Creed.

Little Bee threw his arms around Creed's waist, squeezed him as tight as he could, and said, "Please take me with you, Slate."

Creed held the boy close to him and said, "We've already talked this out, Little Bee. I won't go into it again. You're going to stay here like we agreed. And I'll come back for you as soon as I can."

"When?" cried the orphan.

"As soon as I can," said Creed. He squeezed his eyelids tight, trying to hold back the tears. "I'll tell you what, Little Bee. When I come back, we'll go look for my Grandpa Hawk, and we'll stay with him so he can teach you how to be a real Choctaw warrior. How would that be, son?"

Misty-eyed, Little Bee looked up at Creed and said, "I'd like that, Slate."

"Then it's a promise," said Creed. "I give you my word that's what we'll do when I come back for you. Texan's honor."

August 3, 1866—Creek Nation

"And don't come back looking for no handout," said the trail boss.

"Don't you worry none," said Crackley bitterly. "We won't be wanting nothing you got."

"That's right," said Lowe. "Just see if you can get those cattle to Kansas without us."

"Yeah, just see," said Crackley. "You'll be sorry you fired us, Millett. You just wait. You'll be sorry."

"Yeah, you'll be sorry," said Lowe.

Captain Eugene Millett didn't hear them, couldn't hear them, didn't want to hear them. He'd heard enough of them ever since they'd left Guadalupe County, Texas, three weeks earlier. I never should have hired those two, he told himself as he rode away to rejoin the herd and the good drovers that he'd hired for this drive.

Crackley and Lowe watched Millett ride away. Neither one of them had a clue about why they'd been fired from the trail crew. As far as they were concerned, Millett was picking on them. Hell, it wasn't their fault those cows had run off that bluff and broke their legs like that. Stupid critters. Everybody knows cows are stupid, that's how Crackley and Lowe saw it.

"What are we gonna do now, Harry?" asked Lowe once Millett was out of sight. Blue eyes, ruddy complexion, brown hair, Lowe had been Crackley's shadow since childhood.

"Hell, I don't know," said Crackley. Brown hair, brown eyes, freckles, and big teeth marked his features. He was smarter than Lowe, but that wasn't saying much; so was a rock. "Let's just ride off that way and see what's down that road." He pointed toward the trail that led to the east. "Maybe there's a town or something that way. I heard old hard ass Millett say that some place called North Fork Town was near here. Maybe we can find it if we go that way."

"Well, I'm with you, pard," said Lowe.

They nudged their horses into motion and headed down the

two-track to the east, neither of them realizing that North Fork Town lay to the northeast, the direction that Millett and the herd had taken. In an hour they came to a farm where they saw a man picking corn in a field.

"Hey, Lowe, lookey there," said Crackley. He pointed toward the farmer. "There's a nigger out there picking corn. Let's go see if he's got any food at his house. I'm sure hungered."

They rode past the field toward the house.

The farmer saw them pass by, and it worried him. His young wife and their infant were at the house without anybody to protect them. He dropped his sack of corn ears and ran toward the house to intercept them.

"Hey, Lowe, look at that nigger run. Fast son of a bitch, ain't he?"

Lowe giggled like a giddy little girl and said, "Yeah, he sure is."

"He must have something important up at that house of his," said Crackley. "Let's get up there ahead of him and find out what it is."

They spurred their horses into a gallop and won the race to the cabin on the knoll overlooking the cornfield.

The farmer's wife saw them coming. She ran inside and barred the door behind her.

The farmer ran up to Lowe and Crackley as they climbed down from the saddle. "What you gentlemen want here?" he asked breathlessly. He eyed the six-guns stuck inside their waistbands.

"Don't know yet, nigger," said Crackley. "What you got that's worth anything to a white man?"

"We ain't got nothing, sir," said the farmer. "We's just poor colored folks here. We ain't got nothing."

"You're lying, nigger," said Crackley. "Every nigger I've ever knowed was a liar. Niggers is born that way. Ain't that right, Davy?"

"Sure is," said Lowe.

"Honest, sir, we ain't got nothing worth nothing," pleaded the farmer.

"What's your name, boy?" demanded Crackley.

"Slater, sir."

"Well, nigger Slater, let's just go inside that cabin and see if you're lying or telling us true."

"Ain't nothing in there, sir, 'cept my wife and child. Honest, sir."

"You got food in there, ain't you, boy?" insisted Crackley.

"Yes, sir, we does, and you is welcome to share with us, sir. Both of you gentlemen. We'd be most happy to share our food with you."

"Well, let's just go in there and see what else you've got to share with us, nigger Slater," said Crackley.

"Yes, sir, you do that," said Slater. "Open the door, Hester. We's coming in."

Slowly, the door opened, and Hester peeked out. She held her three-month-old daughter in her arms.

"You first, nigger Slater," said Crackley.

"Yes, sir," said Slater nervously. He stepped onto the small porch.

Crackley drew his Remington and shot Slater in the back.

The farmer fell forward, landing facedown in the doorway.

Hester screamed and tried to close the door. She couldn't; her husband's dying body blocked the way.

A few hundred yards away on the other side of the knoll from Slater's cabin Sergeant Timothy Aloysius McGuire rode on the seat of a wagon filled with a squad of infantrymen. He heard the shot that Crackley fired into Slater's back and ordered the driver to halt the four mules pulling them up the hill.

Crackley stepped up to Slater's dying body, put the muzzle of his revolver close to the back of Slater's head, and fired a second shot.

McGuire heard that one clearly. "Gunfire," he announced to the men. "Handgun. Get your weapons out, boys. We got trouble up ahead."

Hester screamed and ran for a corner of the cabin. Her baby bawled with fright.

"Let me shoot him, too," said Lowe.

"Go ahead," said Crackley, "but it don't make no difference nohow. He's already dead."

"Aw, shucks, Harry, you never let me have no fun."

"You're wrong, Davy. I'm gonna let you have some fun right now."

"You are?"

"That's right," said Crackley. He eyed Hester evilly. "I ain't never had me a nigger bitch before. How about you, Davy? You ever humped a nigger bitch before?"

"No, I ain't, Harry. Are we gonna hump this one?"

"I am," said Crackley, "then you are."

Hester was terrified. "Lordy, don't hurt my baby," she begged. "Please don't hurt my baby."

"Put the brat down," said Crackley, "and we won't hurt it none. Then get that dress off and get in that bed."

Tears streaming down her cheeks, Hester cooed, "It's all right, sugar, it's all right," as she put the crying child in the crib. "It's all right, sugar. You just quiet down now. It's all right," She turned away from the crib, removed her dress, and lay down naked on the bed.

When the wagon came around the bend in the road, McGuire saw the horses in front of the little cabin on the knoll. "Stop here, Buckner," he said to the driver.

Buckner reined in his mules, bringing the wagon to a complete halt.

"Dismount, men," said McGuire. He alit as the twelve soldiers obeyed him without question. "All right now. There's something wrong at that cabin. Eagan, you take five men and circle around to the back of the place and wait for my signal to close in. The rest of you men follow me around to the front. Buckner, you stay here with the wagon. All right now, let's go."

The soldiers followed orders perfectly. McGuire brought his men around to the front of the cabin. He saw Slater's body lying in the doorway, and he could hear Hester and the baby's cries within the house. Then he heard Crackley slap Hester and yell, "Shut up, bitch!"

"The saints preserve us!" gasped McGuire. "Come on, boys. We're gonna rush the place." He raised his hand to signal Corporal Eagan to do the same, and altogether, the soldiers ran toward the house.

McGuire was the first man onto the porch and through the door. He saw Crackley atop Hester, and the sight sickened him. He burst past Lowe, knocking the idiot to the floor. "You filthy bastard!" he screamed at Crackley as he grabbed him by the hair and jerked his head back, nearly breaking the rapist's neck and wishing he had. He pulled Crackley off Hester, slammed him against a wall, and proceeded to beat him senseless. He would have killed the villain, if Eagan hadn't stopped him.

The soldiers buried the dead farmer, and they arrested Crackley and Lowe for their crime. At North Fork Town, they turned the two outlaws over to the United States Deputy Marshal who took them to Van Buren, Arkansas, to stand trial for their crime.

1

In the early days of the Choctaw Nation West, a small trading post was set up near Little Sandy Creek about a mile from where a much-used trail crossed the Washita River. The store remained unnamed until a band of Cherokees, who were driven out of Texas shortly after the Texas Revolution, settled in the vicinity, building houses and carving farms from the wilderness. The trading post with its blacksmith shop became known as Cherokee Town, and the ford across the Washita River was named Cherokee Crossing.

Cherokee Town was situated at the junction of two roads: the east-west route from Boggy Depot to Fort Cobb and the south-north route from Red River Crossing to the Seminole Agency above the South Fork of the Canadian River. In time, a few typical stores, another blacksmith shop, a livery stable and barn, and a few dozen log and slabwood houses were erected in the community. The village remained small, but it was large enough to be the commercial center for hunters, trappers, and Plains Indians as well as the local farmers. It became the best known place west of Fort Washita until Fort Arbuckle was built in 1851.

Prior to the War Between the States, Confederate General Albert Pike met with the Plains chiefs at Cherokee Town and asked them to align themselves with the Confederacy against the Union. Pike's only achievement was to alert the wild Indians to the weakness of the settlers in the area, and the Comanches, Kiowas, and Prairie Apaches used this knowledge to turn the region into a bloody war zone known as "Scalp Alley" among the Nations.

With the end of the War Between the States and the return of Union soldiers to Fort Arbuckle, Fort Cobb, and Fort Washita, the Plains Indians were driven back and their depredations along the lower Washita River ceased. Those people who had moved away to avoid the savage attacks of the untamed Indian bands to the west started coming back to their homes and farms as early as the spring of 1865. It was this restoration of peace and tranquillity that

9

Reverend David Thayer had hoped to abet with the establishment of a mission and school at Cherokee Town; thus, his reason for choosing this locality.

The village was only slightly changed since Creed's last visit there in April. Prosperity was returning ever so slowly. It showed in that the village was cleaner, more orderly with less livestock roaming free, and some of its buildings boasted a fresh coat of whitewash, spread over clapboard walls sometime during the past six months. Also, some new buildings had been erected. Among these, and most prominent, was Reverend David Thayer's Presbyterian Academy, a one-room log structure with a belfry at one end and a stone and mud chimney at the other. The building doubled as a church on Sundays.

Having already bid farewell to his guide, George Bent, at the center of town, Creed drove his covered wagon to the Thayers' mission, where he reined in the mules, set the wagon brake, and parked at the end of the pathway to the front door of the school. "This is it," he announced to his two passengers, his sister-in-law, Hannah Slater, and his nephew, Warren Denton Slater, III. He wrapped the reins around the brake handle and jumped down from the seat. He faced the wagon to help his sister-in-law alight.

Hannah remained seated, staring at the schoolhouse with apprehension. Is this our new home? she wondered as she held her son close to her bosom. Although the building's logs were new, they were still logs, very rough logs, which more than likely meant dirt floors within them as well as everything else that could be crude in a frontier structure. This is better than a saloon in Denver? she wondered.

"Slate!"

Hearing a familiar voice behind him, the Texan spun around to see Little Bee Doak burst through the school's front doorway, bound down the four porch steps, and dash toward him along the path to the road.

"Slate!" cried Little Bee.

Although he was surprised by the lad's appearance, a broad smile spread across Creed's face as he felt the joy of seeing his little friend again. Little Bee's golden skin glowed with the same happiness that the Texan remembered, and his black hair glistened in the sunlight just as it had the last time he saw the youth. It was Little Bee's attire that threw Creed off the mark. The boy wore a boiled shirt, suspenders, black homespun trousers whose legs only went to the middle of his calves, and shoes with black knee stockings.

Little Bee jumped into Creed's waiting embrace, and he locked his arms around the Texan's neck.

Creed rotated a turn and a half as he hugged the boy to him and said joyously, "Hello, Little Brother."

"You came back, Slate. You came back for me."

Creed put Little Bee on the ground between him and the wagon and said, "Didn't I say I would?"

"Yeah, you did," said Little Bee, his smile out of control as he buried his face into Creed's chest and hugged him around the waist.

The Texan nudged Little Bee away from him, and holding him at arm's length, he said, "Let me look at you, Little Brother." He gave the youth a good scan, then pronounced, "You've grown some. A little taller to be sure, but you've filled out a lot. Miss Louise's vittles must agree with you pretty good."

"Yeah, she sure can cook, Slate."

Creed's grin faded. "Can she teach as well as she can cook?" he asked, his back to the school.

"Maybe you should ask her that question," said Little Bee. He nodded toward the academy.

Creed looked over his shoulder to see Louise Thayer standing in the doorway, arms folded beneath her breasts as she watched the man and boy with agitated interest. He turned all the way around for a better view.

Attractive, tall, blond, blue eyes, high cheekbones, twenty-one, wearing a brown dress of homespun cloth and a yellowed white apron, Louise Thayer stared at Creed with scorn and disapproval. She didn't approve of her pupil leaving the classroom without her permission. She didn't approve of Little Bee's public display of affection for Creed, and she didn't approve of Creed in general.

A wry smile curled Creed's lips. What other kind of reception should I expect? he asked himself.

Louise looked past Creed and Little Bee to Hannah and Little Dent. Her aspect softened as she unfolded her arms, lifted her skirt a few inches, and descended the porch steps. She released the dress and marched down the path toward Creed. "How nice to see you again, Mr. Creed," she said perfunctorily as she came close to him.

The Texan tipped his hat and replied, "Nice to see you, too, Miss Thayer."

Louise nodded, said, "Thank you," and breezed past Creed and Little Bee to the wagon. She smiled up at Hannah and said, "You must be Mrs. Slater." Her face glowed with charm and grace. "And that bundle must be Little Dent. Mr. Creed wrote me about you two. I am Louise Thayer. Welcome to Cherokee Town."

"How do you do, Miss Thayer?" said Hannah as politely as she could. "Clete has told me so much about you, too."

"Yes, I suppose he has," said Louise dryly.

"Oh, it was all good, Miss Thayer, I can assure you. Clete thinks very highly of you."

Louise's brow furrowed. "That's the second time you've called him Clete. I thought his name was Slate Creed." She emphasized the surname, as if she thought Hannah was corrupting it into Clete.

Hannah bit her lip and looked at Creed for assistance. She didn't know that Louise and her family were unaware of Creed's real name. When he didn't make an immediate attempt to help, she said anxiously, "That's right. His name is Slate Creed. Cletus Slater Creed. He goes by Slate now, but I always knew him as Clete when we were growing up, and I guess it's hard to change old habits."

Satisfied with Hannah's explanation, Louise smiled and said, "Yes, I suppose it is. Could I hold your baby for you while you get down?"

"Thank you, ma'am," said Hannah. She handed Little Dent to Louise.

Creed came to Hannah's aid, helping her alight from the wagon seat.

"Thank you, Clete," said Hannah.

Louise smiled lovingly at Little Dent, and the child cooed at her. "Isn't he just precious?" said Louise.

"Thank you, ma'am," said Hannah.

"No, please address me as Louise, and may I call you Hannah?"

"Yes, of course, you can," said Hannah. She looked at Creed with delight. "You were right about this lady, Clete. She is color-blind."

Louise glared at Creed. "Color-blind?" she queried. "What's that supposed to mean, sir?"

Before Creed could answer, Hannah explain, "It means you don't see the color of a person's skin when you meet them. You only look into their eyes and into their hearts to find out what kind of person they are. Isn't that the way you told me she was, Clete?"

Creed blushed with mild embarrassment and said, "Something like that, Hannah."

Louise was speechless for the moment as she studied Creed for any sign of guile. Seeing none, she said, "I had no idea you thought of me that way, Mr. Creed."

Recovering, Creed said, "Well, now you do. Does this mean we have to be friends now?"

Louise regained her posture and said, "Not necessarily, sir." She turned to Hannah. "Come, let's go inside out of the sun." She glared at Little Bee and said, "Elbie, you return to your seat this minute."

"Elbie?" queried Creed. "What's that, Little Brother?"

"I got tired of being called Little Bee," said the boy, "so I decided to change my name. Miss Louise suggested that I go by my initials, so now everybody calls me Elbie."

Creed nodded his approval and said, "Elbie? I like it. It fits you, Little Brother. Or should I call you Elbie now?"

"You can call me anything you want, Slate," said Elbie.

"Then Elbie it'll be," said Creed.

"Call him what you will," said Louise, "but later. Now he's got some arithmetic to finish."

"Aw, gee, Miss Louise."

"You heard the teacher," said Creed. "School. We can talk later."

"Yes, we must talk later, Mr. Creed," said Louise. "Right now, I've got a class to teach. I'll take Hannah and Little Dent inside and have Faye take them to our house behind the academy. You can put your wagon and team in the corral out back, then come into the house. Father and Faye will be glad to see you, I'm sure."

2

As he unhitched the mules from the wagon and put them in the corral, Creed wondered why Louise was behaving so belligerently toward him. The way he recalled it they had parted on more cordial terms back in April. So why was she taking this attitude with him? Who knows? he thought. After all, she is a woman, and didn't Grandpa Hawk always say that women are the second greatest mystery in life?

Reverend Thayer came out to greet Creed as he was closing the corral gate. The clergyman's appearance wasn't exactly as Creed remembered. Thayer's thick lips, heavy jowls, and girth had diminished considerably, and his collar of whiskers that still hid a pair of chins and a thick neck was more gray than black now. Two things that hadn't changed were his bald pate and his green eyes. The lines in his face had deepened and multiplied making him look much older than forty-nine.

"Mr. Creed, how good to see you again!" said Thayer with genuine exuberance.

"Thank you, Reverend," said Creed, meeting the parson's enthusiasm equally. He offered to shake hands as he added, "It's good to see you again, too. You're looking fit, sir."

Thayer shook Creed's hand and said, "Thank you, sir." He gave a short, nervous laugh. "Quite frankly, we didn't expect to see you ever again, Mr. Creed, which should tell you how surprised we were to receive your letter a few weeks back. Knowing how slow the mails can be, we've been looking for you to arrive almost every day since. We were beginning to think that some tragedy had befallen you, what with you having to cross the Plains among all those wild Indians."

"The Army delayed us in Colorado Territory," said Creed. "They've got a military order about small parties crossing the Plains, and we were about as small a party as there could be. So they held us up until we could hook up with a larger outfit heading east."

"I see," said Thayer. He slapped Creed on the shoulder and

14

added, "Sounds to me like you had an adventure of sorts. Come inside and tell us all about your journey and what you've been doing since we saw you last."

Creed walked beside Thayer to the double log cabin where he renewed his acquaintance with the minister's younger daughter at the doorway. "Hello, Faye," he said with a smile and a tip of his hat, which he removed after entering the home.

"Hello, Slate," said Faye. Like her sister, she was tall and blond, although Louise's hair was a shade darker than hers. Also possessing blue eyes and high cheekbones, she was two years younger than Louise. Her beauty had blossomed even more since Creed had last seen her. She appeared to be more mature, in full bloom, ready to meet the demands of marriage and parenthood. "It's nice to see you again," she added with an inflection that was closer to her father's greeting than Louise's.

"It's nice to see you again, Faye," said Creed. He glanced past her to see Hannah sitting at the table holding Little Dent on her lap.

The room was spacious, taking up most of this wing of the house, a small bedroom occupying the remainder. Six chairs sat around the table to one side of the kitchen, while an iron cookstove and counters filled the other.

"Sit down at the table, Mr. Creed," said Thayer. "Would you like something to eat? I believe we have some biscuits and cold meat in the larder. Faye, get Mr. Creed something to eat."

"No, that's not necessary," said Creed. He sat down. "We had a meal on the trail only a few hours ago. I'm just fine. How about you, Hannah?"

"Nothing for me, thank you," she said.

"Then something to drink?" queried Thayer. "Cider? Water? Coffee? Faye could make some coffee for you, if you like. Faye, make some coffee for Mr. Creed."

"No, that's not necessary, Reverend," said Creed. "A drink of water will do just nicely."

"Faye, fetch Mr. Creed a drink of water," said Thayer, then he sat down opposite Creed.

The daughter obeyed her father.

Elbie burst into the room, and Louise entered a moment later.

"School all over for today?" asked Creed.

"There was little sense in continuing," said Louise, "once you showed up. Elbie couldn't pay attention, and the rest of the class has a tendency to follow his lead. Thus, I saw no use in continuing for today."

Faye returned with two porcelain cups and a pitcher of cool water. She filled the cups for Creed and Hannah, then set the ewer on the table between them.

"Thank you," said Creed.

"Well, I'm glad you dismissed your class," said Thayer. "Now Mr. Creed can tell us all about his adventures since leaving us last spring."

"Yeah, Slate, tell us what you've been doing," said Elbie eagerly. He pulled out a chair and sat down. "Have you had any more shoot-outs with outlaws since you killed Ed King?"

Louise remained standing.

"Killing another man is nothing to boast about," said Creed sternly, "no matter how much he deserves being killed. Always remember that. I don't like killing anybody. I'd rather do things the way the Lord taught us when he said, 'Blessed are the peacemakers.' "

"Amen!" interjected Thayer firmly.

"But sometimes those bad men won't listen to anything except a ball whistling through their heads," said Creed.

A brief silence intervened until Thayer said, "You said in your letter that you found Mrs. Slater in a place called Denver. How did you come to be there?"

Creed heaved a sigh, then said, "I might as well start at the beginning when I left here last spring."

"Yes, please do," said Louise dryly. "We're all very anxious to hear your stories."

After shooting an annoyed look at Louise, Creed began his tale, telling them of how he went to Texas first to see his mother and stepfather and how he fell in with Clay Allison along the way when Allison was scorned by Belle Shirley and a fight was avoided with Cole Younger. "Something tells me," he editorialized, "that we've not heard the last of those people. Clay, Cole, and Belle gave me the impression that they're gonna butt heads with fate and maybe come out on the short end of things."

The next chapter in his story concerned his parents and how he and Allison went to work on their ranch, helping them to get back on their feet financially. "My stepfather's cousin is Oliver Loving," said Creed. "I suppose that name doesn't mean much to you folks, but down in Texas he's well-known as a great cattleman. We teamed up with him and his partner, Mr. Charles

Goodnight, and we trailed a herd of cattle to New Mexico Territory. We sold part of it there, then took the rest north to Colorado Territory where we sold the balance to a man named Iliff. Mr. Goodnight didn't go to Colorado with us. He took the money we'd made in New Mexico and went back to Texas to get another herd. I haven't heard whether he made it back or not, but my guess is he did. Mr. Loving took the other men back to New Mexico to meet Mr. Goodnight. I stayed in Denver, and that's where I came across Hannah."

Quite intentionally, Creed left out all the parts about Nance Hill, Nance's mother and brother, and his shoot-out with four teenagers down in Parker County, Texas. However, he did mention being attacked by Comanches while they were gathering cattle. Another intentional oversight was the fact that Hannah was working and residing in a saloon in Denver. It would never do to tell the Thayers about that part of her life at this time; better that they got to know her and accept her before revealing that detail.

"We left Denver the first week of September," said Creed, "as you already know by my letter. We spent a week on the road to a place called Pueblo where we joined the Santa Fe Trail and turned east along the Arkansas River. We got to Fort Lyon, and the Army held us there until we could hook up with a bigger outfit crossing the Plains to the east. We went as far as the cutoff to Chouteau's Island, then George Bent, the son of William Bent and a Cheyenne woman, guided us here. George left us this morning and headed back to Kansas to rejoin his father and brother Robert who were leading their own wagon train to Missouri when we left them."

Hannah knew that he was leaving out a lot of the story, especially everything concerning the two plainsmen, Gaspard LeFleur and Jefferson Soutell; but she said nothing to embellish his review of their journey.

"You've been on the trail for seven weeks," said Thayer. He clucked his tongue. "Such a long time for a woman with a small child at her breast."

"It wasn't so bad," said Hannah. "We stayed at Fort Lyon for a couple of weeks, and a soldier there was real nice to us." Tears welled up in her eyes as she recalled Corporal Holloway and the way he died.

"Is something wrong, Hannah?" asked Louise with genuine concern for the young mother.

"Corporal Holloway was killed by a bad man on the Santa Fe Trail," said Creed. "He was part of a group of soldiers being mustered out of the Army, and they were traveling with our party when it happened."

"What happened to the bad man?" asked Thayer. "Did he get away?"

"No, he paid for Corporal Holloway's death with his life," said Creed.

Hannah sobbed.

"There, there," said Louise, trying to comfort her.

"I think we've spoken enough about that unfortunate time," said Creed.

"Yes, of course," said Thayer.

"Would you like to come to my room and lie down for a spell?" Louise asked Hannah.

Hannah nodded.

Louise helped Hannah to her feet, then led her to a bedroom in the other wing of the house.

Creed decided that a change of subject was necessary. "So, Reverend, tell me what you folks have been doing since I was here last," he said.

"Nothing as exciting as you've been through, I assure you," said Thayer. "As you can see, we've built this cabin and the church."

"The church?" queried Creed.

"The school," interjected Elbie.

"Yes, the school," said Thayer. "It serves as our church on Sundays. We don't have much of a congregation yet, but it is growing. New souls coming to us every week."

"Our school is also growing," said Faye. "We started out with just Elbie, and now we have all the children within walking distance coming here for lessons."

"Yes," said the parson, "and we're looking into building two dormitories for those boys and girls who live too far away to attend school here regularly."

"That's wonderful," said Creed. "So what about Drake? Did he go back to Kentucky to school?"

"Yes, he did," said Thayer proudly. "He left here just a few days before we received your letter. He's written to us regularly since then, telling us about his journey to Louisville and how he arrived there safely. His latest letter tells of how much he's enjoying his classes at the college there."

"That is good news," said Creed. "Drake will be good at whatever he decides to become."

"He's thinking of taking up medicine," said Thayer. "After Faye's unfortunate experience with the rattlesnake and my collision with a bullet, he felt this country needed more doctors than lawyers or ministers." He smiled and added, "I can agree with the former, but the latter? I'm not so sure."

"I'm sure Drake will make a fine doctor," said Creed, "and I know he's already a good Christian."

"Thank you, Mr. Creed," said Thayer. "I think the same of my son. He will do well, I'm sure."

"Yes, he will," said Creed. "So tell me about Mr. Tyler. Did he go back to Texas to look for his family?"

"Mr. Tyler stayed on with us until we had our cabin built," said Thayer, "then he took his leave and rode off to Texas to look for his family. We received a letter from him a few weeks before yours came, and he said that he was in Texas in the vicinity of Nacogdoches. He hadn't found his family as of that writing, but he had hopes of finding them soon. We haven't heard anything from him since then."

"Well, I hope he has better luck than Hannah had," said Creed. "She left Texas last year to look for her family up in Kansas, and she didn't even find Kansas."

"Speaking of Mrs. Slater," said Thayer, "you wrote that she's your sister-in-law. How is that, Mr. Creed? I mean, she is a Negro, isn't she?"

"Some of her ancestors came from Africa, that's true, but some of them also came from Europe. In fact, her father was a white man. So was her mother's father. So what does that make Hannah? White or black?"

"Well, she's a mulatto, isn't she?"

"She's just a person," said Louise as she returned to the kitchen. "She's no different than any of us, Father. She's a person whose ancestors came from two different continents. In my estimation, she has a greater heritage than we do because our ancestors came only from Europe."

"That was not my point, Daughter," said Thayer. "I was wondering how she became Mr. Creed's sister-in-law."

"My brother married her," said Creed.

"Yes, I assumed that much," said Thayer, "but her name is Slater and yours is Creed. How is that?"

Creed cleared his throat and explained. "My given name is Cletus McConnell Slater. When I came home from the war, I was informed that I'd been disinherited by my grandfather. Since

I was no longer a Slater by name, I decided I could still live by the family creed. The Slater Creed, if you will, and that became my name, Slater Creed, which I shortened to Slate Creed."

"What is this Slater Creed?" asked Louise.

"Steadfast in honor and loyalty and justice," said Creed. "I try to live by those words every waking moment."

"An admirable aim, Mr. Creed," said Thayer.

"Yes, very admirable," said Louise, "but how successful have you been living up to it?"

"That's not for me to determine," said Creed. "That's up to the Lord when I meet Him on Judgment Day."

"Amen, Mr. Creed," said Thayer.

"But you said that your brother married Hannah," interjected Faye. "Is that right?"

"I don't know how they did it," said Creed, "but they did it. Hannah said so, and that's good enough for me. I have no reason to doubt her word on that, especially when I know that her baby is my brother's child. I don't know that their marriage is legal under the laws of Texas, but I know that it's legal in the sight of God, and that makes it all right with me."

"Amen again, sir!" said Thayer vehemently.

"If I'm to understand your letter correctly," said Louise, "You're asking us to take Hannah in to live with us until such a time that she and her child can come to live with you in Texas. Is that correct?"

"Well, mostly," said Creed. "Everything up to that part about her and Little Dent coming to live with me."

"That's what I thought," said Louise with fire in her eyes. "You're planning on leaving them with us just like you left Elbie with us. Abandoning them just the same as you abandoned Elbie."

"He didn't abandon me here," said Elbie.

"You stay out of this, boy," said Thayer.

Surprised by Louise's sudden onslaught, Creed retaliated without thinking first. "What's eating you, lady? You've been surly with me ever since we got here. What's wrong, Louise? Are you still playacting with yourself or something?"

"Well, isn't that what you're planning to do?" she spat back at him.

"No, it's not," said Creed. "I'm taking Little Bee with me now—"

Louise interrupted him. "I seriously doubt that."

"I'm taking Little Bee with me to my folks' ranch in Texas," said Creed evenly, regaining control of his temper, "and then I'm going back to Lavaca County to marry my sweetheart. Then we're gonna go live with my folks on their ranch until we can get a spread of our own, and as soon as we do, I'll be back to get Hannah and Little Dent so they can come live with us."

"I doubt that as well," said Louise. "You won't be taking Elbie with you when you leave here, and you won't come back for Hannah and her child either. You'll ride out of here and never come back."

"Now why wouldn't I ever come back here?"

"Because the Army will probably hang you first."

3

Louise's bombshell stunned everyone into silence, including Creed. How did she know that the Army wanted him? How did she know about the noose hanging over his head? How did she know anything about him that he didn't tell her himself? These questions and more went through his mind as he tried to remain outwardly calm.

"What nonsense is this, Louise?" demanded Thayer.

"It's not nonsense, Father," said Louise. "Mr. Creed is a wanted criminal."

"What's all this about, Mr. Creed?" asked Thayer. "I don't think I understand what's happening here."

"That makes two of us, Reverend," said Creed. "Suppose you might tell us about it, Louise?"

"Why don't you tell us instead?" She smirked.

Creed considered the question for a moment, then said, "All right, but first you have to answer a few questions for me."

"Such as?"

"Such as how do you know that I'm wanted by the Army?"

Without hesitation, she reached into her apron pocket and pulled out two letters. "These came for you last week," she said. "They were addressed care of me, so I took the liberty of opening and reading them." She held them out to Creed who took them tentatively.

"You read Mr. Creed's mail?" gasped Thayer. "Why would you do such a thing, Daughter?"

Louise didn't answer; she was too busy watching Creed.

The Texan examined the crinkly envelopes. Both had been opened; both were addressed to Mr. Slate Creed care of Miss Louise Thayer of Cherokee Town, Chickasaw Nation, Indian Territory. One came from Colonel John C. Burch, Attorney-at-Law, Nashville, Tennessee; while the other had Texada's return address on it: T. Ballard, Oakland Post Office, Lavaca County, Texas.

Excited with joy and fear, Creed found himself in a quandary over which to open and read first. He opted to put business ahead of his heart. He removed Colonel Burch's letter and read:

Nashville, Tennessee   *1 October 1866*

Dear Slate,

Allow me to begin by relating how happy I am to hear that you are still safe and in good health, especially after your trials and tribulations in Missouri. That was a most unfortunate business which I am happy to learn you survived in one piece.

Secondly, I am very surprised to learn that you have gone from Texas to Colorado Territory and are now returning to the Indian Territory.

Thirdly, I am delighted that you found Marshall Quade and that you were able to obtain a confession from him. However, I do not believe that it will be sufficient evidence to gain you a new trial or a pardon. The words of a dying man, although witnessed by several reliable observers, may not carry enough weight with a military court to get the previous trial and sentence set aside and get a new trial in a local court granted to you.

It is my opinion that you will have to find another witness to corroborate Quade's confession and thus prove your innocence in this affair. One living witness and Quade's confession recanting his earlier testimony should be enough to get a new trial if not a full pardon.

I replied to your letter of 23 May, but I take it that you never received my response because I sent it to you care of your stepfather, Howard Loving, of Weatherford, Texas, and according to your most recent missive, you haven't been there since early June. In that earlier letter, you asked if I had received any word from General Canby concerning your case. Yes, I have received word from his office, from a Colonel Walter Peck, who states that a new trial is out of the question, that you have been convicted and condemned, and that I am to reveal to him any information that I might possess concerning your whereabouts so the Army might recapture you and carry out its sentence to hang you. I invoked my attorney-client privilege of confidentiality and wrote him that he would learn nothing from me concerning you or your whereabouts.

As for Quade's confession, I assume that you are carrying it on your person at all times now. That may

*not be wise; therefore, I suggest you leave it with
somebody trustworthy or in a bank vault in a large town or
city. I would suggest that you send it to me for safekeeping,
but as the mails are unsafe these days, I retreat from that
notion.*

*I will try again to contact General Canby concerning
your case, and if my next attempt ends as the first, I
will write to General Grant in Washington and request
that he review your case. If I cannot obtain a hearing
through him, I will approach the President as I stated
once before.*

*Write to me as soon as you receive this letter so that I
might know that you have arrived safely in the Indian
nations. Until then, I am*

*Your obedient servant,
John C. Burch*

Colonel Peck again, thought Creed. Why am I beginning to think
that he's the real villain here? He shook his head, replaced the
letter in the envelope, then opened Texada's letter and read:

30 September 1866

My dearest darling Clete,

*Your letter of 3 September has brought me great joy. The
news that you have Marshall Quade's confession is
almost too good to be true. To know that you will soon
be able to clear your name and return home as a free man
is such wonderful news. I have missed you so very much.
This has been the longest year of my life. I love you, my
darling.*

*The news about Hannah and your brother Dent is very
surprising. Rumors had circulated through the county
about them while you were off fighting the war, but nobody
ever thought that matters were so serious between them. It
is very shocking to learn that Dent considered a darkie to
be his wife. I am not certain why you are going to such
lengths for Hannah and her baby, but I am certain that
you have good reasons.*

It is just as well that you will no longer have to search for the other men who blamed you for their foul deed. Dick Barth, Dick Spencer, Jonas Burr, and Jasper Johnson were gathering cattle west of the Lavaca River this past summer. Barth and Johnson signed on for the trail drive to Missouri, but Burr and Spencer stayed here in the county. News came recently that the trail crew ran into a difficulty in the Indian nations, and either Barth or Johnson was arrested and sent to jail in Arkansas. I do not know for certain which one was arrested because neither of them has returned here yet.

Jack Blackburn was seen in Hallettsville recently. I have heard that he is now living in DeWitt County.

Of course, you know that Malinda and her Yankee have left the county and are now living up north near your mother. Markham was sent to command a new fort that is being built up there. The new commander here is Major Phineas Stephens.

Jake and the boys gathered a herd to take to New Orleans like you did last year, but they came up short as very little went right for them on the trail. A new man in the county is talking about taking a herd to New Orleans next year. Oddly, his name is also Ballard. He hails from Kentucky, but he fought for the Union and was an officer. Even so, he's a decent sort, and Cousin Peggy is partial to him.

The Golihars are still running with the Thicket Gang. Rumors abound about them. Some say they are leading the gang. Others say they are responsible for the raids on some freight caravans coming up from Indianola. No one knows for certain.

I am so glad that all this business between you and the Army will soon be finished. I miss you so much, my darling. My heartache is greater now than during the war when I thought you were dead. Then I had resigned myself to the fact that you would never come back to me. Now I live on hope which I think is much more difficult.

I love you so much, my darling. I wish we could be

together right this very minute, but, alas, we cannot.
Until we can, I am

> *Your ever loving,*
> *Texada*

Creed continued to stare at the page as his mind tried to deal with the ache in his heart. Slowly, he replaced the letter in its envelope, refusing to look up at the others in the room as he did. Finally, he heaved a sigh and faced them, beginning with Elbie because he appeared to understand the least and to fear the worst.

"What some of Louise says is true," he began, "but not all of it because she doesn't know the whole story." He looked straight into Louise's eyes. "It's true that I'm wanted by the Army and that I'm under a sentence to hang. However, I was tried and convicted for a crime that I had no part in." He reached into his coat and removed Marshall Quade's confession. "This is proof that I'm innocent, but my attorney says it may not be enough to clear my name."

"Innocent or guilty, it's all the same," said Louise. "Either way, you're running from the law, and you've made us criminals as well just by being here."

"That's one way of looking at it," said Creed.

"And another way is you're a liar, Slate Creed or Clete Slater or whatever your name is today," said Louise. "You've been lying to us all along. All of us. Father, Faye, me, and especially Elbie. You've lied to each of us and all of us." She folded her arms over her breasts with a great deal of self-satisfaction. "And you once accused me of being a liar. The nerve!"

Creed frowned at Louise, then shifted his view to Elbie. "What do you think, Little Brother?" he asked. "Do you think I've been lying to you?"

Elbie swallowed hard and said, "No, but you didn't tell us any of this stuff before, and I don't understand why you didn't."

"Without this paper," he said, holding up Quade's confession, "would you have believed me to be innocent if I had told you everything about this business with the Army?"

"I would have," said Faye.

Creed nodded at her and said, "Thank you, Faye. I knew I could count on your support."

"That still doesn't change the fact that you're a wanted criminal," said Louise.

"Wanted, yes," said Creed, shifting his view to the older sister, "but I'm no criminal. I've never knowingly broken the law. Every man that I've ever killed I killed in battle or in self-defense. I've never robbed anybody in my life, and I've never abused a woman."

"I believe you, Mr. Creed," said the reverend. He turned toward Louise. "And I think you should believe him, too, Daughter. This man saved our lives on more than one occasion, and he's trusted us with caring for Elbie and now with caring for his sister-in-law and nephew. Are these the actions of a criminal?"

"No, Father, but the Army—"

"Hang the Army!" snapped Thayer. "The Army is not infallible, Daughter. They make mistakes just the same as other men do, and I believe Mr. Creed in this matter that the Army has convicted an innocent man. And doesn't he have proof of it?"

"I'd like to see that proof," snarled Louise.

Creed offered the paper to her. "Here. Read it yourself."

She took it and read aloud:

"To all who read these last words of mine, I, Marshall Quade, swear on my death that Cletus Slater had nothing to do with the raid on the Army wagon train down in Mississippi back last year after we were all paroled for fighting for the Confederacy. The only men involved in that raid whose names I care to mention here were Jack Blackburn, Jonas Burr, Jasper Johnson, Dick Barth, Dick Spencer, and myself. There were others, but they ain't been caught yet, and I ain't going to tell on them now. Just know that Clete Slater had nothing to do with that raid or any other raid that I know about. As God is my witness and my judge, I swear this to be a true and lawful statement.

"It's dated 1 September 1866," said Louise, "and witnessed by several people, including a policeman and a doctor who wrote this for Marshall Quade who made his mark over his name."

"He made it with his own blood," said Creed.

"I see," she said, handing the document back to the Texan.

"Even so, I'm afraid it's not enough proof that I'm innocent," said Creed. "My attorney, Colonel Burch, says I still need a live witness to testify to my innocence if I'm to be granted a new trial or a pardon."

"So what does that mean?" Louise asked snidely.

"Well, I'm not exactly sure yet," said Creed.

"I'll tell you what it means," said Louise. "It means you'll be leaving here without Elbie."

His eyes filling with tears, the boy shot a pained look of fear at Creed.

The Texan met Elbie's gaze. "I gave you my word," he said, "that when I came back here I'd take you with me to live with me and my folks. I'm still planning to keep my word to you, Little Brother."

"No, you're not," spat Louise, pointing an accusing finger at Creed. "You're lying to him, and you're lying to yourself, Slate Creed. You can't take him with you, and you know it."

"And I know it, too," said Elbie suddenly, surprising everybody, "but it's all right, Miss Louise." Refusing to look away from Creed, he added, "I know Slate will come for me one day. As soon as he gets this business with the Army cleared up. Isn't that right, Slate?"

The youngster's maturity stunned Creed, and it shut Louise's mouth.

"Yes, that's right," said Faye, anxious to salve the moment. "Isn't it, Slate?"

"Yes, of course, it is," said Creed. He stood up, facing Elbie. "I didn't think you'd understand, Little Brother, but you do, don't you?"

Elbie nodded, jumped to his feet, came around the table, and threw his arms around Creed's waist, hugging him as tightly as he could.

Creed reciprocated. "Just like I told you the last time," he whispered into the lad's ear, "I'll come back for you, and we'll go find Grandpa Hawk together. I promise, Little Brother."

4

Texada had written that either Dick Barth or Jasper Johnson had run afoul of the law while trailing cattle through the Indian nations. She wasn't sure which one found trouble there, but she did write that he was sent to jail in Arkansas. That was all Creed needed to be told to know where to start looking for either or both of them.

Before departing Cherokee Town, Creed took care of some important business. He wrote to Texada and to Colonel Burch to tell them of his plans.

Cherokee Town, Chickasaw Nation   *23 October 1866*

My darling Texada,
   Your letter arrived here before I did. I was so happy to read it. It was good to hear news from home, even if it was not all good.
   I also received a letter from Colonel Burch, my lawyer in Nashville. He gave me some bad news. He wrote that Marsh Quade's confession is not enough to clear my name. He tells me that I still need a living witness to clear my name. Because of this, I will not be returning home just yet. I am going to Van Buren, Arkansas, to see about Dick Barth and Jasper Johnson. I am not sure what I can do should I find one or both of them. I suppose I will cross that bridge when I get to it.
   I miss you, and I love you, my darling. I dream about you almost every night, and I think of you every day. I want nothing greater than to be with you for the rest of my days. Until then, I am

                          Your ever loving,
                               Clete

Cherokee Town, Chickasaw Nation   *23 October 1866*

Dear Colonel,
      *Your letter arrived here before I did. I was distressed
to read that Marsh Quade's confession is not enough
evidence to clear my name. However, I am glad that I
learned this before returning to Texas and falling into
the hands of those who would see me dead.*
      *I am going to Van Buren, Arkansas, from this place because
I received word that one or two of the men who put their
crime on my shoulders might be there in the federal jail for
some trouble in the Indian nations. You may write to me
there. I would prefer to meet you there so I could give
you Marsh Quade's confession for safekeeping, but I
suppose that is out of the question. Somehow I will see to
it that it gets into your hands.*
      *I did not tell you this before because I did not think it
to be important until you wrote to tell me that Colonel
Peck has become involved in my case. Marsh Quade told
me that Colonel Peck told him and Blackburn and the
others to put the blame for their crime on my shoulders.
He did not write that in his confession, but he did say it
to me. I offended Colonel Peck in New Orleans when I
came in for my parole. Of course, he deserved offending,
but I had no idea he would hold a grudge against me. I
think you would be wise to go around him in this matter.*
      I will write from Van Buren. Until then, I am
                                          Your obedient servant,
                                          Slate Creed

Creed posted the letters, and alone, the day after arriving in
Cherokee Town, he took his leave of Reverend Thayer, his daugh-
ters Louise and Faye, Elbie, Hannah, and Little Dent. He rode
southeast toward Boggy Depot, retracing his steps of the previous
spring when he resumed his journey to his parents' ranch in Texas.
He arrived at the old trading post two days later, but unlike the
earlier trip, he turned to the left at the river crossing and proceeded
to the northeast along the old Butterfield Stagecoach Road. Six
more days and nights of cautious travel brought him to Fort
Smith, Arkansas, where he stayed the night at the LeFlore Hotel.
Ironically, the hostelry's name reminded him of Gaspard LeFleur,

the man whose tragic death he'd witnessed just a month earlier several hundred miles up the Arkansas River where it passed through the prairies of Kansas.

The next morning, now nine days after departing Cherokee Town, Creed rode five miles across the river bottom flats to a ferryboat landing, paid the ferryman six bits to take him and his horse across the Arkansas River, and before noon, he led Nimbus onto the dock below Van Buren, the seat of Crawford County, Arkansas.

President Thomas Jefferson purchased Louisiana from Napoleon and France in 1803, and part of the land transferred to the United States of America was a vast area known only as Missouri. The southern portion of this territory was a mountainous region known as Arkansas. Jefferson felt confident that this country would be the ideal place for the civilized Indian tribes of Appalachia to relocate their nations.

At the close of Jefferson's administration, a council was held with the Cherokees in regard to their separation into Eastern and Western Nations. Jefferson told this august body of Cherokee headmen: "The United States, my children, is a friend to both parties and as far as they reasonably can are willing to satisfy both parties. Those who wish to remove are permitted to send an exploring party to reconnoiter the country on the banks of the Arkansas and White rivers; and the higher up the better as our settlements will begin at the mouths of those rivers." Such was the promise of the president of the United States in 1809.

In 1817, the first treaty was entered into between the United States and the Cherokees, according to Jefferson's word eight years earlier. Many of the Western Cherokees had already relocated in the country between the Arkansas and White Rivers. They were allowed to remain there for eleven years before the United States began to renege on its word.

In 1819, the Territory of Arkansas was carved out of the Territory of Missouri for the purpose of admitting Missouri as a slave state to balance the admission of Maine as a free state. This new official territory included all the lands already relegated to the Western Cherokees and their neighbors and archenemies, the Osages, who had been dispossessed of their hunting lands without being consulted by either the United States or the Cherokees. The two tribes had been at war with each other since the first Cherokee hunting party was detected by an Osage hunting party and a fight ensued. As part of the treaty of 1817, the Cherokees demanded protection from the aggressive Osages, and the United

States complied by building Fort Smith on Belle Point, a thumb of land between the Arkansas and Poteau Rivers at the western most edge of the Western Cherokee Nation. The establishment of this post led to the two tribes burying the hatchet in 1825, creating an everlasting peace between them.

Three years later the United States and the Western Cherokees made another treaty in which the Cherokees traded their lands between the Arkansas and White Rivers for even more land to the west with a perpetual outlet that bordered on the Mexican province of Texas. The Cherokees moved again, and they were joined by hundreds of their eastern brothers who decided the time had come for them to leave their homeland in the southern Appalachian Mountains.

In 1836, Arkansas was admitted to the Union, and all Indians were ordered out of the state by the government. At the same time, President Andrew Jackson had begun the forced removal of all eastern tribes to the Indian lands west of the Mississippi River.

Prior to these moves, the Twenty-third Congress of the United States passed the Intercourse Law, which placed many restrictions on the relations between Americans and Indians. It was titled, "An Act to Regulate Trade and Intercourse with the Indian Tribes and Preserve Peace on the Frontiers." It described the Indian country as "all that part of the United States west of the Mississippi and not within the States of Missouri or Louisiana or the Territory of Arkansas, also that part of the United States east of the Mississippi and not within any state, to which the Indian title has not been extinguished," and provided "that for the sole purpose of carrying this act into effect, all of that part of the Indian country west of the Mississippi River that is bounded north by the north line of the lands assigned to the Osage Indians, produced east to the State of Missouri; west by the Mexican possessions; south by the Red River; and east by the west line of the Territory of Arkansas and the State of Missouri, shall be and hereby is, annexed to the Territory of Arkansas; and that for the purpose aforesaid, the residue of the Indian Country west of the Mississippi River shall be and hereby is annexed to the judicial district of Missouri; and for the purpose aforesaid, the several portions of the Indian Country east of said river shall be, and are hereby severally annexed to the Territory in which they are situated." These lands became a part of the Western District of Arkansas for judicial purposes, and "so much of the laws of the United States as provides for punishment of crimes committed within any place within the sole or exclusive jurisdiction of the United States shall be in force in the Indian Country. Provided, that the same shall not extend to crimes committed by one Indian against the person or property of another Indian."

When Arkansas became a state, it was made into one federal judicial district with one judge who held court in the state capital of Little Rock twice a year. The next year Congress approved an act giving the Court of the United States for the District of Arkansas "the same jurisdiction and power in all respects, whatever, that was given to the several district courts of the United States, by an act of Congress entitled, 'An Act to Regulate Trade and Intercourse with the Indian Tribes and Preserve Peace on the Frontiers' " and provided that "the courts of the United States in and for the District of Arkansas be and hereby are vested with the same power and jurisdiction to hear, try, determine and punish all crimes committed within that Indian Country designated in the twenty-fourth section of the act to which this is a supplement, and therein and thereby annexed to the Territory of Arkansas as were vested in the courts of the United States for said territory before the same became a state. And for the sole purpose of carrying this act into effect all that Indian Country hereunto annexed by the said twenty-fourth section of the act aforesaid to the Territory of Arkansas be, and the same is, annexed to the State of Arkansas."

By an act approved March 3, 1851, Congress divided Arkansas into two districts, the Western District embracing nine Arkansas counties, and "all that part of the Indian Country within the present judicial district of Arkansas." The court seat was at Van Buren, the seat of Crawford County, five miles down the Arkansas River from Fort Smith.

The court remained at Van Buren until the opening of hostilities between the North and South in 1861. It ceased to exist throughout the duration of the War Between the States and was reopened in 1865, at first under the direction of the local military commander at Fort Smith, then later under the auspices of a grand jury led by a committee of commissioners. It was to this court that white men who committed crimes in the Indian nations and Indians who committed crimes against whites were remanded for trial.

Creed learned this last bit of information during his last passage through the Indian nations when the outlaw Ed King was arrested by the Army for attempting to rob Reverend Thayer's party as they traveled through the Creek Nation. King never reached Van Buren, instead escaping from the Army and having his life ended

by Creed at Cherokee Town a few weeks later. This fact—King's
ability to avoid incarceration—caused the Texan to wonder if
Barth or Johnson ever made it to jail. Only one way to find out.

Van Buren, like so many towns, began as a farming settlement along a major river. Thomas Martin, a squatter, resided on
the land in the earliest days, and in the late 1820's, the James
Phillips family arrived to purchase the town site and establish a
steamboat dock that became known as Phillips Landing. In 1831,
upon application for a post office, Thomas Phillips, James's son,
was appointed postmaster for Van Buren, named for Martin Van
Buren, then Secretary of State under President Andrew Jackson. A
rival community named Columbus grew up a mile down the river,
paralleling Van Buren's development until 1838 when the seat
of the county government was moved to Van Buren, effectively
putting an end to Columbus as a separate town. Since that time,
Van Buren continued to grow until its population surpassed the
2,500 mark just prior to the War Between the States. The number
of residents fluctuated with the fortunes of war, but after the
cessation of hostilities, the census returned to its pre-war level.

With federal troops stationed at Fort Smith, the Army felt a
garrison would be unnecessary at Van Buren; thus there was an
absence of blue uniforms on the streets as Creed sought out the
federal court that sunny November day. Few citizens manned the
streets this day because it was Friday, the day before market for
the rural folks.

The ferry landing was situated at the foot of Main Street. Ware-
houses dotted the area between the river and Water Street. Houses
and businesses lined both sides of Main for the first two blocks,
but this didn't hold true with the third as the right side of the
town's central thoroughfare between Columbus and Thompson
streets was all business and the left mostly residential. The fourth
block to the right was occupied by the county courthouse, while
businesses and homes made up the left. Beyond this area was the
main business district of Van Buren.

Creed would see the rest of the town later. Now he had business
at the courthouse because it was the most likely place to start
looking for his man.

The Crawford County Courthouse was built fifty feet on a side
with walls twenty inches thick, a stone foundation two feet thick
beneath the surface of the ground and laid in good lime mortar.
The building was red brick with four pilasters on each side, three
feet wide, projecting four inches, and sitting on a water table
of cut stone. Not including the cellar, the whole height of the

building rose to thirty feet with a cornice, a copper gutter laid in the cornice all around the eaves, and a hipped roof covered with tin and topped with an octagonal dome. Including the spire on the dome, the total height reached to seventy-five feet. Twenty-three windows with twenty-four panes each provided natural light from outside.

Creed alit and tied Nimbus to a hitching post on the street. Well aware that he was about to confront the law, he made certain that his Colt's was well concealed beneath his coat. Confident that the gun wouldn't be seen, he walked up the brick path to the front steps, ascended to the upper level, and entered the courthouse through the front door. Inside, he found a staircase leading up to the second story and down to the cellar at the far end of the hall. Two rooms opened to each side of the hall. The sign over the door of the second one read: E. G. Whitesides, Crawford County Sheriff; over the first read: Samuel Hays, U.S. Marshal, Western District of Arkansas. The marshal's door was open, so Creed went inside.

A counter and gate divided the room into work space and visitor area. Beyond the barrier at the only desk sat a stout, gray-mustached, gray-haired gentleman in a gray and black pinstripe suit, boiled shirt, black tie, and starched collar. He looked up at Creed with friendly gray-blue eyes set wide in a ruddy, fleshy face. A sign on the desk read: Samuel Hays, U.S. Marshal.

"Help you, stranger?" he asked.

Creed tipped his hat politely and said, "Yes, sir. My name is Slate Creed from Lavaca County, Texas, and I'm looking for an old acquaintance of mine." He studied the lawman's reaction to his name and his home county, and when he saw that they made little impression on him, he added, "I received a letter from my sweetheart back home telling me that he might be in jail here in Van Buren."

"What's his name?" asked the marshal.

Creed grinned sheepishly and said, "Well, it could be Jasper Johnson, or it could be Dick Barth. I am acquainted with both men. You see, sir, my sweetheart wrote that they were both part of a trail crew moving a herd of cattle through the Indian nations this past summer, and one of them got into a tight spot with the law and was brought here, but she didn't know which one of them it was because neither of them had returned to Texas yet."

The lawman's head bobbed slowly as he listened to Creed.

When the Texan finished his explanation, the marshal said, "You say this fellow is a friend of yours?"

"No, sir, I said both of them were acquaintances. We're from the same vicinity down in Texas, and we served together in the war for a short time."

"Which side?"

"Confederate," said Creed without flinching.

"Figures," grunted Hays. "What's your interest in this here acquaintance of yours, Mr. Creed?"

"Not much, Marshal," said Creed with a shrug. "Just one Texan looking out for another, I guess."

"Uh-huh," muttered Hays. He scratched the nape of his neck, crooked his head to the right, and said, "Well, I got a Dick Barth locked up downstairs, and he says he's from Lavaca County, Texas. You said these acquaintances of yours were named Dick Barth and Jasper Johnson, didn't you?"

"Yes, sir, I did."

Hays nodded and said, "Well, this Barth was riding with a fellow named Johnson when my deputy caught up with him. Reckon that was your other acquaintance?"

"More than likely. They were always pretty close, if I recollect rightly."

"Well, they should have stuck closer because this here Barth fellow shot an Indian pony over in the Cherokee Nation, and he pistol-whipped a colored man who was riding him. He claimed the darkie stole the horse from their trail herd, and he was only trying to stop him when he shot the horse by mistake. Mad that he'd killed the horse, he took it out on the darkie until another darkie came along and put a stop to it. This Johnson fellow came along about then and got Barth free from the darkies before they did him harm. This colored fellow—name was Vann—he looked up my deputy over to Fort Gibson and told him that Barth had whipped him and killed his horse. He produced a bill of sale to prove that he'd bought the horse from a Cherokee named Alberty, so my deputy rode out and arrested Barth and brought him here for a hearing before the grand jury. That was back in August. The grand jury met in September, and they held him over for trial." He smiled and added, "You came along just in time. Court goes into session on Monday. His trial should come up by the end of the week."

"I see," said Creed. "If he's found guilty, what's the worst that can happen to him?"

"A year in prison for the assault and a fine for killing the horse, if he's got the money. If not, then he'll probably get another year in the penitentiary."

"I see," said Creed.

"He could get off, too," said Hays, "if this colored fellow don't show up to testify against him. That being the case, the judge will have to throw it out of court and dismiss the charges, and I'll have to set him free. And there's a good chance of that happening, too. I ain't seen this colored fellow in town yet. He's supposed to come by the courthouse to let me know he's available to testify, and he ain't come by yet. Of course, it's only Friday. He could still show up today or tomorrow or Sunday. We'll just have to wait and see."

"What did you say this Negro's name was, Marshal?"

"Vann. Willie Vann. Turns out he's got a place on the other side of the Grand River on Brushy Creek. Little settlement of darkies there. Him and a few others and their families. Freedmen." Something occurred to the lawman. "Say, how come you want to know this darkie's name? You ain't aiming to help your friend downstairs by scaring off this colored fellow, now are you? Because if you are, I'll have to do something about that."

"No, Marshal," said Creed, shaking his head, "that thought never entered my mind. It's just that I met a man named William Vann when I was passing through the Nations last spring. He was a decent man, and he had a nice family. I was just wondering if this Vann that you spoke of might be the same fellow, and I guess he just might be because the William Vann I met had a place near Brushy Creek."

"Say, you don't talk like that white trash I've got locked up downstairs," said Hays. "How come? Didn't you say you were from Texas and that you fought for the Confederacy?"

"Yes, sir, I did," said Creed.

"Then how come you talk nice about coloreds?"

"Let's just say I had my eyes opened a while back, and I started seeing folks for what's inside them instead of what's on the outside of them."

"Now you talk like one of them Indians over in the Nations. Like a Cherokee or a Choctaw or one of them others."

Creed felt a pride glow inside him, but he knew better than to tell Hays that half of his ancestors had been Choctaws and Cherokees. "Well, I learned a little something from those people, too," he said.

"Uh-huh," said Hays, less suspicious of Creed now. "I guess you'll be wanting to see Barth now, right?"

"Well, not now, Marshal," said Creed. "It's near noon, and I was thinking about getting something to eat before deciding whether I should stay around here for Barth's trial or go on my way back to Texas. Could you recommend a good place to eat?"

Hays stood up and said, "Come on, Mr. Creed, and I'll show you where you can get the best fried catfish in town."

5

Hays grabbed his hat and took Creed to the Brodie Hotel on Water Street.

From the earliest days of Van Buren, the building had been a hotel serving passengers of steamboats, flatboats, and stagecoaches passing through the town, It was known as the Mansion House when John Bostick owned it. He sold it to George Gross who sold out to John Brodie at the conclusion of the War Between the States. When Butterfield's Overland Mail Company was still in business and its stagecoaches passed through Van Buren, this hostelry served as their stage stand. Smaller, localized lines also employed the inn as their depot because of the restaurant's widespread reputation for serving good food for reasonable prices and because it was the closest hotel to the ferry crossing of the Arkansas.

The dining room touched on the elegant. Hardwood floor; papered walls with a flowered print of green, yellow, and soft orange on white; varnished hardwood wainscoting; molded ceiling with Ionic cornices; kerosene lamps in sets of four on two wheels suspended from the ceiling; large double windows with southern exposure overlooking the river; square tables and straight-backed chairs of oak; checkered cloths on the tables; pewter dishes; porcelain cups; silver flatware; and cloth napkins.

Customers sat at nearly all the tables when Creed and Hays entered. They consisted of the usual assortment of professionals and businessmen, who didn't work out of their homes, as well as the hotel's guests and residents. Hays scanned the cast of patrons until he saw two gentlemen seated at a corner table. "There we go," he said. He waved at them, then turned back to Creed and said with a mischievous smile, "I hope you don't mind eating with a couple of lawyers, Mr. Creed."

"I've dined with lesser creatures, sir," said the Texan with a precocious grin.

Hays chuckled and said, "I didn't know such varmints existed." He slapped Creed on the shoulder jovially. "Come along, Mr. Creed. I think you'll fit in nicely with this crowd."

Creed followed Hays to the table in the corner where two men wearing black suits, vests, and watch chains sat sipping coffee as they waited for their food to be brought to them.

"Gentlemen," said Hays, tipping his hat at the men, "I'd like you to meet Mr. Slate Creed of Lavaca County, Texas. Mr. Creed, allow me to introduce Mr. John B. Ogden and the Honorable James W. Sangster, our county judge."

Both men stood up and offered to shake hands with Creed; Sangster first.

"Your Honor," said Creed as he removed his hat with his left hand and shook the man's hand with his right. He met the judge's blue-eyed gaze straight on.

"How do you do, Mr. Creed?" said Sangster who was short, wide, bearded, balding, and graying.

"Mr. Ogden," said Creed, shaking hands with the lawyer.

"It's a pleasure, Mr. Creed," said Ogden who was medium in height, width, and facial features from his average nose, lips, chin, and eyebrows to his bland blue eyes.

"May we join you?" asked Hays.

"Of course, of course," said Sangster. "Please sit down, Mr. Creed." He pointed to the chair to his right.

"Thank you," said Creed, He looked around for a coatrack to hang his hat on, saw the pegs on the wall near the door, then looked at Hays and said, "Let me hang up your hat for you, Marshal."

"Thank you, sir," said Hays, handing the black peak hat to Creed. As the Texan hung up the hats, Hays pulled out a chair and sat down.

Ogden and Sangster sat down again.

"Did I hear you right, Sam?" said Ogden conspiratorily. "Did you say Mr. Creed is from Lavaca County, Texas?"

"That's right, I did," said Hays, "and to answer your next question, yes, he does know that Texan I'm holding for trial. That's what he's doing here."

Creed returned to the table and took his seat with the others, having missed the short exchange between Ogden and the marshal.

"You're not a lawyer, are you, Mr. Creed?" asked Sangster.

Creed shook his head and said, "No, sir, I'm not. I'm a cattleman. I have a stake in a place down in Lavaca County, Texas, and another in Parker County, Texas. I was on my way home from Colorado Territory when I heard about an old acquaintance getting himself into a fix that landed him in jail here."

"Colorado Territory?" queried Sangster. "What were you doing out there?"

"I helped trail a herd of beeves from Parker County through New Mexico Territory and up to Colorado this past summer," said Creed.

Eyebrows rose all around the table in surprise and respect for such a feat.

"You don't say?" said Ogden. "I've heard of cattle drives going from Arkansas to California in the past. Back in '52 or '53, a couple of fellows up to Fayetteville took a herd out there."

"I remember that," said Sangster. "Shores and Carter were their names. They'd gone out for the Gold Rush of '49, then came back here for a drove of cattle in '52. They were buying all sorts of cattle, I remember, trying to get up a herd of a thousand head. I don't know if they ever made it or not."

"Now I recollect that we had a couple of boys take herds west back in '49, I believe," said Hays. "The Clarksville Mining Company took a herd out, and so did a fellow named Hackett, and John Johnston and his son took a herd out, too."

"Yes, but that was later," said Sangster. "Hackett went out in '53, and Johnston went out in '54."

"That's right," said Ogden.

A waitress stepped up to the table. Tall, thin, middle thirties, brunette hair tied in a bun with a black ribbon, brown eyes, sallow complexion, wearing a dark blue dress and white apron, she carried a coffeepot and two cups. "Coffee, Marshal Hays?" she asked.

"Yes, thank you, Ellen," said Hays.

She placed a cup in front of the lawman and filled it with the aromatic dark brew. "How about you, sir?" she asked Creed.

"Yes, ma'am, I'll have some, too," he said.

She put a cup in front of Creed and poured coffee into it. "Would you like cream or sugar with that, sir?" she asked.

"Sugar would be nice, thank you."

"I'll bring the bowl," said Ellen. "I suppose you're thinking about having catfish today, Marshal?"

"That's right, Ellen. How was Rafe's luck this morning? Anything of size on his line?"

"He brought in three over thirty inches," said Ellen. "Cut those up into steaks. We still got a few left, or you can have a couple of the smaller fryers whole."

"How small?" asked Hays.

"Eighteen, twenty inches."

Hays looked at Creed. "How's that sound to you, Mr. Creed?" he asked. "Steaks or fryers?"

"Both are making my mouth water so much that I can't make up my mind," said Creed. "You choose, Marshal, and I'll take the other."

"Fair enough," said Hays. "Ellen, divide those steaks betwixt Mr. Creed and me and put a whole fryer on for each of us as well."

"Hush puppies or corn bread?" she asked.

"Corn bread for me," said Hays.

"Me, too," said Creed.

"Be back with your dinners in a minute, Judge, Mr. Ogden." She left the men to their conversation again.

"You say that you went through New Mexico Territory to get to Colorado, Mr. Creed?" queried Ogden.

"Yes, sir. Parker County lies in the northern part of Texas. My stepfather's cousin, Mr. Oliver Loving, and his partner, Mr. Charles Goodnight, thought about going north through the Nations, but they were concerned about the wild Indians on the Plains. So they chose to follow the old Butterfield Stagecoach Road southwest to the Pecos River, then north along the Pecos to Fort Sumner where the Army has the Navajos penned up. From there, Mr. Loving and I took some of the crew and what was left of the herd after the Army bought what it wanted, and we trailed them up to Colorado where we sold the cattle to Mr. John Iliff who was trying to stock his range along the South Platte River north of Denver. I had business in that city, so I remained in Colorado for a time, while Mr. Loving and the other drovers returned to New Mexico to meet Mr. Goodnight who had gone back to Texas for another herd. My business in Denver caused me to return through the Indian nations instead of rejoining Mr. Loving and Mr. Goodnight in New Mexico."

"So how did you hear about this acquaintance of yours being in jail here?" asked Sangster suspiciously.

"I received a letter from my sweetheart through some friends at Cherokee Town," said Creed, "and she told me about Dick Barth being in a fix with the law."

"I see," said Sangster. "The reason that I asked you if you were a lawyer, Mr. Creed, is if you were, then you'd understand without question that I can't discuss Barth's case with you."

Creed's face scrunched up with intentional perplexity as he said, "Why would I want to discuss Barth's case with you, Judge? I thought Marshal Hays said you're the county judge here."

Sangster looked at Hays. "You didn't tell Mr. Creed that I'm the acting judge for the federal court, Sam?"

"No, I didn't, Jim," said Hays.

"And I suppose you didn't tell him that I'm the prosecutor in Barth's case either," said Ogden.

Hays shook his head and said, "Nope, John, I didn't. I didn't think it mattered any."

Creed smiled and said, "Gentlemen, allow me to put your concerns to rest. My only interest in Dick Barth is as a neighbor from down home who served with him in the war. Like I told Marshal Hays already, I hardly know the man. I just thought I'd see if I might be able to do him some kindness, such as take a message to his family or something of that kind."

Ogden and Sangster glanced at Hays for confirmation, and the marshal said, "That's right, boys. That's pretty much what he told me in my office not more than an hour ago, and I believe him."

"Then that's good enough for me," said Sangster.

"Same here," said Ogden.

Ellen returned with a sugar bowl for Creed and put it down in front of him. "More coffee, Judge?" she asked.

"Yes, Ellen," said Sangster.

"How about you, Mr. Ogden?"

"Yes, thank you, Ellen," said Ogden.

The waitress departed to get the pot.

"Did I hear you correct a minute ago, Mr. Creed?" asked Sangster. "Did you say that you were in Cherokee Town when you received news about Barth being in jail here?"

"Yes, sir, I did," said Creed. He dipped a spoon into the sugar bowl, scooped out a spoonful of the sweetener, poured it into his coffee, and stirred the brew absently as he concentrated on the conversation at hand.

"Well, Cherokee Town is in the Chickasaw Nation, isn't it?" said Sangster.

"Yes, sir, it is," said Creed, removing the spoon from the coffee and setting it on the table beside the cup.

"That seems to me to be a pretty fair piece to go just to be neighborly to a fellow that you barely knew in the war," said the judge.

"I was on the road nine days coming here," said Creed without batting an eyelash at the magistrate's insinuation. "Just goes to show how far one Texan will go for another when he's in need."

"I see," said Sangster.

Ellen brought Ogden's and Sangster's meals and placed them in front of them.

"Jim, I think you're barking up the wrong tree here," said Hays as soon as Ellen left them again. "Mr. Creed is acquainted with the man that Barth pistol-whipped over in the Cherokee Nation, and from what he's told me, I'd have to say that Mr. Creed would be more disposed toward the colored than he would be to Barth."

"You know Barth's accuser, Mr. Creed?" queried Ogden.

"I do if he's the same William Vann that I met last spring in the Cherokee Nation."

Ellen returned with the coffeepot, refilled Ogden's and Sangster's cups, then left them again.

"Wait a minute, Mr. Creed," said Sangster. "I thought you said you were gathering cattle last spring in Texas."

"I did," said Creed. "I passed through the Nations last March and early April on my way home to Texas. I crossed the Red River at Colbert's Ferry on April 18, and after that, I was busy gathering cattle for the trail drive to New Mexico."

"How do you know the exact date?" asked Sangster, still suspicious of Creed.

"I keep a journal," said Creed. "Besides that, I'd been away from Texas for several months, and I was glad to be home again. The day has stuck in my memory, Judge."

"Yes, I know what you mean," said Sangster. "I remember the exact day that the Union army recaptured Fort Smith and occupied Van Buren. That was an important day to me. September 1, 1863. General Blunt captured Fort Smith, and the next day Union soldiers arrived in Van Buren. That was the end of the Confederacy in this county, Mr. Creed. I'll never forget it."

"I'll never forget it either," said Hays.

"I wasn't here then," said Ogden, "so the date means nothing to me."

"John served the Confederacy," explained Sangster. "Sam and I were among the few who remained loyal to the Union throughout the war."

"The war is over now," said Ogden, "and we've put it behind us here in Van Buren."

"Not all of us," said Hays. "There's still some who would—"

"That's neither here nor there," interjected Sangster with annoyance. "We're talking about the present situation, Sam, not something in the past that needs to remain in the past forever. We're talking about why Mr. Creed went so far out of his way for this outlaw you've got locked up in the jail."

Ellen brought two plates of catfish fried to a golden crisp, red beans boiled with bacon, and corn bread for Creed and Hays. "Eat hardy, gentlemen," she said.

"Thank you, ma'am," said Creed.

"Thank you, Ellen," said Hays.

The waitress left them.

"Judge," said Creed, "I don't blame you for being suspicious of me. If I was in your shoes, I guess I'd be wondering about a stranger like me coming in here from way off to see a fellow that he hardly knows. I'd be wondering what sort of cards he's got up his sleeve, if you know what I mean."

"Yes, I do know what you mean, sir," said Sangster.

"Well then, Judge," said Creed, "let me put your fears to rest." The Texan opened his coat to expose the butt of his revolver.

All three older men spotted the gun and recognized danger. Ogden and Sangster shrank away with fright. Hays dropped his fork, tried to stand up quickly without sliding his chair back first, and almost succeeded in upsetting the table.

"Easy, gentlemen," said Creed firmly, evenly, as he steadied the table.

Hays stopped in mid-rise.

"I mean no harm here," said Creed, meeting the marshal's glare eye to eye. He pulled the Colt's from his waistband with his left hand and offered it butt first to Hays. "I'm just trying to show you that I'm exactly what I've said I am. Marshal, I surrender my weapon to you for as long as I'm in your town."

6

Wide-eyed with surprise and with a shaky hand, Hays accepted the Colt's from Creed and sat down again.

"It's against the laws of this state, this county, and this town to carry sidearms in public, Mr. Creed," said the judge, shaking his finger at the Texan.

Creed donned his Choctaw-Cherokee warrior's face and looked the magistrate straight in the eye as he said, "Every man has the right to defend himself, Judge, and having just ridden through the Indian nations, I believe I'm more aware of that fact than any of you gentlemen."

"He's right," said Ogden, coming to Creed's defense. "Every man does have the right to bear arms. The Constitution guarantees us that much."

"That was only meant in the olden days when our forefathers had to contend with the British," argued Sangster. "Times are different now."

"Are they, Judge?" queried Hays as he placed Creed's gun on the corner of the table between him and Ogden and covered it with his napkin. "Didn't we just go through a war where neighbor fought neighbor? And aren't some of those neighbors still fighting each other for the same stupid reasons that they fought each other during the war?"

"That's right, Jim," said Ogden. "There's still folks fighting each other up in Missouri and around here as well. I see all sorts of bad things happening around us because the Yankees want to punish us for leaving the Union."

"They don't want to punish me," said Sangster. "I didn't leave the Union."

"I didn't either," said Hays, "but I still see the Yankees as bringing us a lot of grief. Just look at what's happening in the Nations. Outlaws everywhere you go. Isn't that right, Mr. Creed?"

"Yes, sir," said Creed. "I met more than my share of bad men in the Nations, but I met a few up in Missouri, too, and they were

46

in Colorado, and we've got them down in Texas." He shifted his weight and leaned his elbows on the table. "I can tell you firsthand, gentlemen, that the recent war has made a lot of men into outlaws, and being one of those who fought on the losing side, I can tell you that many of those on the winning side don't wish to let bygones be bygones and allow us to live in peace. Let me tell you about some of the horrors I've seen in the past year and a half since the war ended.

"I witnessed the murder of a preacher up in Missouri last winter—a preacher, gentlemen, a man of the cloth—shot in the head at point-blank range with his wife sitting next to him on the seat of their buggy. And why? Because he espoused the cause of the Confederacy instead of the Union. This was in February, gentlemen, of this year. Almost a year after General Lee surrendered at Appomattox.

"And that wasn't the only incident I've been a witness to. There was a shoot-out up in Platte City, Missouri, a month after the parson's murder, where some Union men wanted to murder a man who fought for the Confederacy just for that reason and no other. They wanted him to leave town because of his loyalties during the war, and knowing that he wouldn't go voluntarily, they came after him prepared to lynch him with a rope. The result was the killing of two men who would have been better off if they'd simply done what the Bible tells us about forgiving and forgetting.

"Out in Colorado I came across some Yankees from Indiana who wanted to string up every man in the territory who fought for the South. Why? Because a few men who had fought for the Confederacy—and I emphasize the word few here, gentlemen—a few Southern men were robbing and killing peaceful folks.

"From what I've seen since the war ended last year, gentlemen, there are a lot of Union men who don't want the war to end until every man who fought for the Stars and Bars is dead and buried. We've already had some hard times in Texas, and from what I've seen in other parts of the South, times are only going to get harder before they get better because the Union men who stand to profit from our suffering want us to continue to pay for the war in one way or another. I believe that, gentlemen, because of everything I've seen in my travels. Now you can believe what you want, but I'm here to tell you that the war isn't over. Not by a long shot, gentlemen."

Creed inspected the three faces staring back at him with incredulous expressions, and he realized that he'd stepped into the pulpit again. When am I gonna learn? he wondered. As a way of smoothing over the effects of his lecture, he added, "You'd better eat your catfish, gentlemen, before it gets cold."

The quartet ate without conversation for the next several minutes until the marshal broke the interlude, saying, "I don't doubt a word of what you've told us, Mr. Creed. You've only confirmed what I've been suspecting for some months now. I think you may be the first man to come to this town who can appreciate the problems of my office, sir. As you know, I am the United States Marshal for the Western District of Arkansas, and that territory includes all the Indian nations. I don't have but a handful of deputies to cover all that country. Of course, the Army helps us, but not all that much. Word has it that General Sherman is reducing the size of the Army, and that means they'll be pulling troops out of Fort Smith and Fort Gibson and just about every other place east of the Plains. Once they do that, there won't be much law between here and the Rocky Mountains."

"Sam's right," said Sangster. "Before the war, the biggest problem the federal court had here was keeping whiskey peddlers out of the Nations. The Indians pretty much took care of themselves with their own laws and lawmen. If some white man caused them trouble, they just turned him over to the Army, and they just escorted him over the border and sent him on his way. If his crime was serious enough, he was sent here for trial, and he usually got a few years in prison. Some killers were even sentenced to hang, but the war saved most of them."

"I believe we hung two of them," said Hays.

"That's right," said Ogden. "The others had their sentences commuted, or they were released for one reason or another."

"That's neither here nor there," said Sangster. "My point is this. Crime is growing at a very rapid rate in the Nations because men who are wanted for some crime here in the States are hiding there." He shifted his piercing look at Hays. "What's that fellow's name that you've got locked up in jail, Sam? The one who stole some cows over in the Cherokee Nation a few months back."

"Wilson?" queried Hays.

"Yes, that's the one," said the judge. "Sinker Wilson. He was a 'Mountain Reb' during the war, and now he's an outlaw. He was probably an outlaw before the war, but now he's a little more open about it because the Indians can't do anything to him and the

Army isn't gonna bother with a mere cattle thief who's stealing from the Indians. That leaves it up to Sam and his deputies to deal with his kind."

"And there's not enough of us to do the job right," said Hays. "Sure, we might catch an outlaw now and then, but bringing him in is another matter altogether."

"And even when they get him here," said Ogden, "there's no guarantee that we'll get a conviction because too often the witnesses against the villain don't show up in court to testify, and the judge is forced to release the vermin."

"When we do get a man before the bar," said Sangster, "and the witnesses testify against him, he gets convicted and sent to prison where he belongs. Those instances are too few, unfortunately."

"So now, Mr. Creed," said Hays, "you must see why we're so concerned about who visits with our prisoners."

"Yes, sir, I do," said Creed, "and I can't say that I blame you for being nervous about a stranger like me." He snickered and added, "I know I'd be worried about another Texan riding in here. We're a pretty rowdy bunch, Marshal."

"Don't I know it, though," said Hays. "Dick Barth isn't the only Texan I've got locked up in my jail. There's two others who robbed and killed a colored man in the Creek Nation this past summer. Noisy, foulmouthed sons a bitches. They give you Texans a bad name, Mr. Creed."

"What part of Texas are they from, Marshal?" Creed asked casually before taking another bite of catfish.

"Some place called Guadalupe County," said Hays. "Do you know it?"

Creed swallowed and said, "No, I don't."

"Well, these two fellows were part of a trail crew driving a herd of cattle to Kansas," said Hays. "They were fired by their boss while they were moving through the Creek Nation. With little money in their pockets, they went looking for trouble and found a colored named Slater—"

The hairs stood up on the back of Creed's neck.

"—and they robbed and killed the poor fellow and abused his woman. Some soldiers came along while these vermin were in the midst of mistreating the woman, and they put a stop to that and arrested them for killing her man. The Army turned the killers over to my deputy at North Fork Town, and he brought them here."

"We'll get a conviction against those two," said Ogden. "The sergeant who commanded the soldiers who caught them is here to testify against them. His word should—"

Sangster raised his hand to stop Ogden from saying anything further about the case, saying, "Hold it right there, John. I can't be hearing any of this now. You know that."

"My apologies, Your Honor," said Ogden with a touch of sarcasm. He turned back to Creed. "Anyway, these two killers will be properly dealt with when the time comes."

Sangster pulled his watch from its pocket and said, "It's time I went back to the courthouse, gentlemen." He replaced the watch, wiped his mouth one more time with the napkin, pushed himself away from the table, stood, and said, "If you'll excuse me, gentlemen? Mr. Creed, it was a pleasure to meet you. I hope we shall meet again."

Creed stood and said, "The honor is all mine, Judge. Until we meet again. . . ." He offered to shake hands.

Sangster shook his hand and departed.

Creed sat down again. He wanted to make further inquiries of the marshal and prosecutor about the murder victim named Slater in the worst way, but he feared that expressing an interest in that case might arouse their suspicions all over again. He would wait to ask the marshal when a better opportunity presented itself.

"Mr. Creed," said Hays, "I don't believe I need to keep your gun while you're here in Van Buren, but please do me a favor and don't carry it on your person while you're in town." He uncovered the gun and slid it across the table to the Texan.

"I'll do just that, Marshal," said Creed. He picked up the Colt's, stuck it inside his waistband, and closed his coat over it again. He finished his meal and wiped his mouth. "Well, Marshal, now that I've eaten I think I'd like to see Dick Barth, if that's all right with you."

7

As he walked back to the courthouse with Hays and Ogden, Creed wondered if the murder victim named Slater might be one of his grandfather's former slaves, and if he was, then which one. How do I find out? he asked himself. Before climbing the steps to the county building, an idea came to him.

The trio passed the length of the hall to the stairways at the far end where they paused.

"It was a pleasure to make your acquaintance, Mr. Creed," said Ogden as he extended his hand to the Texan.

"The honor was mine, Mr. Ogden," said Creed as he shook with the lawyer. Without thinking about it, he looked at his fingers when they finished the grip.

"Don't worry, Mr. Creed," said Ogden. "They're all there. I didn't take any."

"Don't be so sure about that," said Hays.

Creed realized how he must have appeared to the attorney, bringing a blush to his face as he said, "My apologies, Mr. Ogden. I meant nothing—"

Ogden's laugh interrupted the Texan. The lawyer slapped Creed on the shoulder and said, "Think nothing of it, sir. I'm accustomed to it. I'm a lawyer."

"Yes, sir," said Creed.

"I'll visit with you later, Sam," said Ogden. He turned away and headed up the stairs to his office.

"The jail's downstairs, Mr. Creed," said Hays. "Come on. I'll take you down and tell our jailer to let you see Barth."

"Thank you, Marshal," said Creed.

They descended the steps to the jailer's room. A single door was in the rear of the cubicle. The area beneath the stairs was a caged room with a small desk and two chairs, ostensibly a meeting room for lawyers and their imprisoned clients. High up on the wall beneath the stairway a window provided light from outside. In the main room, another small desk with a single chair behind it occupied one side of the space, and two chairs stood against the

51

opposite wall. A shotgun stood ominously in the corner. Sitting at the desk was the jailer, a thickset fellow with closely cropped brown hair, brown eyes, heavy eyebrows, a bulbous nose, and thick lips.

"Afternoon, Marshal," said the jailer. "Got another one for the cage?" He eyed Creed with a smugness that annoyed the Texan.

"No, Jake," said Hays. "This gentleman is Mr. Slate Creed from Texas. This is our jailer, Jake Blodgett."

Creed and Blodgett exchanged nods.

"Mr. Creed has come to see Dick Barth," said Hays. "You let him in so he can visit with the prisoner."

"Sure thing, Marshal," said Blodgett, coming to his feet. He took a ring of keys from a peg in the wall behind the desk, then moved toward the door. "Right this way, Mr. Creed," he added with a bit more respect than when he thought Creed to be a criminal beneath his contempt.

"Jake will take care of you for now, Mr. Creed," said Hays. "I've got some paperwork to tend to upstairs. Stop in when you're finished here, and I'll point you to the right place to stay in town. If you're planning to stay long, I mean."

"Thank you, Marshal," said Creed. "I'll be sure to do that when I'm done here."

Hays ascended the stairs.

Blodgett unlocked the door to the cell block, and Creed followed him through the doorway into a long hall that ran the length of the basement and dead-ended against the front foundation wall of the courthouse. The stench of human feces and the pungent scent of urine attacked his nostrils and actually made his eyes water.

"Pretty powerful stink, don't you think?" chortled Blodgett with a smirk that indicated he reveled in visitors' revulsion of the foul odors.

"Powerful isn't the word for it," said Creed as he wiped the involuntary tears from his eyes. "How can you stand it?"

"You get used to it," said Blodgett.

Yeah, I'll bet you got used to it with no trouble at all, thought Creed. Damn! Not me.

A single lamp at the far end of the corridor provided some light, but more illumination came through the doorway behind them as they passed by the first two doors, one to each side, and stopped at the second on the right. Grunting and heavy breathing came from behind the opposite door.

"Got two fellows in there," said Blodgett. "Sounds like the one's buggerin' the other. Dirty sons a bitches! I can't wait till they hang that pair."

"Are those the two outlaws who killed a Negro over by North Fork Town?" asked Creed.

"Yeah, that's them. Why?" asked Blodgett, squinting at the Texan with suspicious eyes.

"The marshal told me that the man they murdered was named Slater, and I knew some slaves named Slater once. I was just wondering if the Slater they killed might have been somebody I once knew."

"Marshal Hays didn't tell you the nigger's first name?"

"No, I didn't get the opportunity to ask him. You wouldn't happen to know it, would you, Jake?"

"No, but I can ask those two in there for you." He stepped across the hall, slid back a peephole door, put his face up to the opening, and said, "Hey, Crackley?"

"What the hell do you want?" groused Crackley from within the darkened cell.

"Fellow out here wants to know the name of that nigger you murdered over in the Nations," said Blodgett.

"Tell him to go screw himself," said Crackley. "I ain't tellin'."

"Now that's no way to be, Crackley," said Blodgett. "You wouldn't want me to separate you and your honey in there, would you now?"

A few seconds of silence was followed by some panicked whispering, which was in turn followed by Crackley saying, "His name was Slater."

"What was his first name?" asked Blodgett.

"Lucius," said Crackley.

Lucius? pondered Creed. Didn't we have a field hand named Lucius? I'll ask Hannah next time I see her. At least, his name wasn't Gabe. Thank God! That would break Hannah's heart to hear that her brother was murdered in the Nations.

Blodgett noted the quizzical expression on Creed's face. He turned back to the window and said, "Are you sure?"

"That's what the nigger bitch called him."

Blodgett glanced at Creed who nodded that he heard and accepted the reply. "Thank you, Crackley. You can go back to diddlin' your sweetie in there now."

"Screw you, Jake."

"You'd like that, wouldn't you, Crackley?" giggled Blodgett

just before he closed the peephole door. Looking at Creed again, he said, "Their kind makes me sick."

Creed wondered if Blodgett really meant that or not. For certain, he was reviled by Crackley's sort. Abusers, that's what they were to Creed. He'd known a few of them in the war. They'd abuse young recruits when no women were available to abuse. He recalled one incident in particular.

His company was raiding in a Unionist part of Tennessee in '63 when they came across a farmhouse where only the woman and her teenage son were at home. After watering their horses and taking feed for them, Creed ordered his men to leave the place. A mile down the road he paused to make certain that all the men had rejoined the outfit. A quick count revealed three were missing. He ordered his sergeant to keep the column moving, while he went back to the farm to look for the stragglers. A hundred yards from the house he heard a woman's screams. He rode up to the house, jumped down from Nimbus, revolver in hand, burst through the open doorway, and saw one man raping the woman, another doing likewise to her boy, while the third watched. Without hesitation, Creed shot the voyeur through the head. The two rapists stopped, begging for their lives. The Texan paid them no heed. He shot and killed both of them. The mother and son embraced, fearing he would shoot them as well. He didn't; instead, he left without saying a word. He rode off into the woods, dismounted, and vomited.

Although he had killed those men in cold blood and without a trial, Creed had never regretted it, reasoning that people who violate other people in that manner have made their lives forfeit just the same as a murderer has. The laws of God, man, and Nature said so.

Blodgett slid back the peephole door of the cell across the hall from Crackley's compartment, put his face up to the opening, and said, "Barth, you got a visitor. Get up to the door." The jailer stepped back and faced Creed. "You can talk to him through here, Mr. Creed. When you're done, close the window and come back to the door at the end of the hall, and I'll let you out."

"Thank you, Jake," said Creed.

The jailer returned to his room.

Creed stood up to the cell door and looked through the peephole. The foul odor in the corridor blew worse from the cell, forcing Creed to step back. He blinked away the tears this time and focused on the dark, dirty, unshaven face that appeared in the door's window.

"Who the hell are you?" asked Barth. He leaned forward for a better look at Creed, giving the Texan a better view of him. Aquiline nose; dusty, brown, wispy beard and mustache; greenish-gray eyes; narrow face; large ears; turkey-necked; dirty, yellow teeth with wide gaps and some missing.

"My name is Creed," he said evenly.

"I don't know anybody named—"

He doesn't recognize me, thought Creed. Well, I'll be!

"Wait a minute," said Barth. "Did you say Creed?"

Now he knows me, thought Creed. "That's right, Dick," he said. "Slate Creed."

"Clete Slater, you mean," interjected Barth. "You're Clete Slater, aren't you?"

"I was till—"

"But you're supposed to be dead." Fear of the unknown raised his voice an octave. "You're supposed to be dead and buried up in Missouri somewheres." More fright. "Kindred said you were dead. He said he saw you hung by a lynch mob."

"He did," said Creed.

"Then you're dead, Slater."

"No, Dick, I'm not dead, but Clete Slater is dead because you and Blackburn and those other bastards killed him when you blamed him for your crime and stole his name."

A moment of silence followed as Barth tried to figure out what was happening here. As soon as he had the answer, he said, "You would have done the same thing to save your neck, if you'd been us, Slater."

"First off, Dick, let's get a few things straight. My name is Slate Creed until you or one of those other bastards sets the Army straight on who really led that raid in Mississippi last year, and secondly, I'm not here to do you any harm. I need you alive, Dick, and I need you out of here. Is that much understood?"

"Eat shit, Slater. Blackburn told us what you'd do if you ever caught up with any of us,"

"He did? And what did he tell you, Dick?"

"He said you'd shoot us for telling the Yanks that it was you who led us on that raid. That's what he said."

"And you believe him, Dick?"

"Hell yes, I believe him. That's what I'd do to you, if the shoe was on the other foot. I'd shoot your ass off in a minute, and never give it a second thought. Hell yes, that's what I'd do."

"Well, Dick, I'm not you, and if you knew me better, you'd know that I wouldn't come gunning for you or Blackburn or any of the others because what you've done to me can be fixed. Now, I'll admit that if there was no way of fixing things, then I'd shoot you down like a dog for ruining my life. But I don't have to do that, Dick, because it's not too late to fix what you boys did to me."

"Is that right?" asked Barth sarcastically. "Well, let me tell you something, Slater—"

"The name is Creed," interrupted the Texan.

"All right." He sneered. "Creed." He mocked the name. "Let me tell you something, Mr. Creed." He mocked the man. "If you think I'm gonna tell those Yanks that you had nothing to do with that raid and put my ass in the fire again, you got another thing coming, because I ain't gonna get hung just to save your ass. You got that, Mr. Creed?"

"What if I told you that I already got Marsh Quade to confess that you boys did the raid without me?"

"I'd say you were a liar because Marsh would never spill his guts for you, asshole."

"Well, that goes to show you how little you know about Marsh Quade," said Creed. "Marsh did the honorable thing by me before he died."

Barth didn't respond immediately as he mulled over Creed's words in his mind. "Marsh is dead?" he asked at last.

"Sad to say, yes, he is dead."

"You killed Marsh, you son of a bitch?"

"No, I didn't kill him. He took a bullet for me in a saloon in Denver, Colorado," said Creed slowly. "He saved my life."

"You're lying, you son of a bitch! Marsh ain't dead. You're lying to me."

"Stop loud-mouthing me, Dick, and start using your head. Would I be here talking to you if Quade was alive?"

"Sure you would because you're lying about the whole thing. Marsh is alive, and you're lying about him being dead just so you can get me to confess to the raid and save your ass for you."

Creed put a hand inside his coat. "Can you read, Dick?" he asked. He pulled out Quade's confession.

"Sure, I can read. What of it?"

"Then look at this paper," said Creed. He held the document

up to the window for Barth to see. "This is Quade's confession. He made it just before he died, and he made his mark on it with his own blood. Can you see that, Dick? Can you see his mark there near the bottom?"

"Sure, I can see it," said Barth softly.

"Now do you believe me about Quade being dead?"

With angry resignation to the fact, he said, "Yeah, I believe you."

Creed recognized the sadness in Barth's tone, and he allowed the man a moment to mourn his friend.

"You say Marsh took a bullet that was meant for you?" asked Barth finally.

"That's right, he did," said Creed.

"Why did he do that?"

"I can't say. Who knows why a man does a thing like that? All I know is I'm here talking to you, and he's buried up in Colorado Territory."

"What was he doing with you in the first place?"

"He was gonna go back to Texas with me to tell the truth about that raid, Dick."

"Why would he risk that, Creed? Did you threaten to kill him or something?"

"No, I saved his life from a lynch mob," said Creed. Quickly, he told the tale of how he and Chief Ouray broke Quade out of jail in Central City, and how the three of them escaped to Denver where Quade stepped between Creed and the business end of a derringer. "If I ever have a son," he said in conclusion, "I'm gonna name him after Marsh so the whole world will remember the man who saved my life that day."

"That would be damn decent of you, Creed," said Barth. He thought about it for a second, then asked, "So what are you gonna do for me after the Yanks hang me for telling the truth about that raid?"

"Do you mean you'll confess?"

Barth burst out laughing as he said, "Hell no, I ain't gonna confess. Do I look stupid or something?"

I should have known better, thought Creed. "No, I guess not," he said. "Look, Barth. You're in a world of hurt here. I met the federal prosecutor, and he's planning on sending you to prison for what you did in the Cherokee Nation."

"Prison? You're fooling me, Creed. I ain't going to prison for whuppin' a nigger." He laughed. "Who ever heard of such a thing?

A white man going to prison for whuppin' a nigger. Who are you fooling, Creed?"

"You better look around, Barth. You're already in jail, and next week you're going to trial for beating William Vann and killing his horse. Do you think that Unionist judge is gonna let you go free for doing that?"

"I got a lawyer," said Barth. "I'll take my chances with the judge."

Creed shook his head with frustration. "I can get you out of this, Dick," he said.

"How? By having me tell the Yanks that you had nothing to do with that raid in Mississippi?"

"That's right, Dick."

"Go to hell, Creed! I already told you. I ain't gonna put my head in a noose for you or nobody else. Now leave me be."

"Well, you just keep thinking about it, Dick. I'm gonna stay around here until you've had your trial. If the judge lets you go, then we'll talk again. Somewhere away from the law. And if the judge decides you should pay for beating William Vann, then we'll still talk again. Right here, before they cart you off to the penitentiary. I'll see you at the trial, Dick."

8

Marshal Hays took Creed to Mrs. Levi Chapman's Boardinghouse Hotel, a large two-story, frame building located on the northwest corner of Strokes and Jefferson Streets. He introduced the Texan to the lady of the house, recommending the visitor to their town as a guest for her establishment.

Blond hair, blue eyes, rosy cheeks, attractive, and a form that hinted at being matronly and yet enticing like *les femmes fatale de Rue Bourbon* in New Orleans, Sarah Ann Chapman peered quizzically through spectacles at the bareheaded stranger standing before her on the porch of her home. She wore a navy-blue dress that was highlighted with lace at the high collar and long sleeves. "You say you're from Texas, Mr. Creed?" she asked sternly.

"Yes, ma'am," said the Texan, holding his hat along his left thigh.

"May I assume that you did your duty for the Confederacy in the late war, sir?" she asked.

"Eighth Texas Cavalry," said Creed proudly.

Her aspect brightened. "Well, if Marshal Hays says you're a respectable gentleman," she said, "then that's good enough for me. Welcome to my home, Mr. Creed." She smiled and offered to shake hands.

Creed took the lady's hand, bowed from the waist, and kissed it.

"Oh, my!" gasped Mrs. Chapman with delight.

Creed straightened again. *"Merci beaucoup, madame. L'honneur est tout le mien."*

The lady smiled sweetly. "Oh, you speak French, too. *Tres bien, monsieur.*"

"I've spent a little time in New Orleans, ma'am," said Creed. "I wouldn't say that I speak French, but I do know a few appropriate phrases."

"Well, you speak them quite well, sir. Won't you come inside?"

"Thank you."

59

"Seeing that you're in capable hands, Mr. Creed," said Hays, "I'll be returning to my office now. If there's anything I can help you with while you're in Van Buren, just give me a holler, and I'll see if I can't accommodate you." He turned to the landlady. "Miz Chapman?" He tipped his hat to her.

"Good afternoon, Marshal," said the landlady.

Hays left, and Creed followed Mrs. Chapman into the foyer of her home. Before closing the door behind them, she noted the gray Appaloosa tied to the post in front of her gate. Turning to Creed, she asked, "Is that your horse out front, Mr. Creed?"

"Yes, ma'am. That's Nimbus. I rode him all through the war."

"He looks like a magnificent animal. I'll have a boy put him in our barn in the back. Do you have traveling bags on your saddle?"

"Yes, I do," said Creed.

"I'll have the boy bring them to your room."

"I've also got a rifle and scabbard on my saddle. I'd like those brought inside, too, if it's in accordance with the rules of the house, Mrs. Chapman."

"It's acceptable, Mr. Creed. I'll have the boy bring them as well. Now if you'll follow me, I'll show you to your room."

Straight ahead of them, an open, wide stairway climbed to a middle landing, then turned to the right behind a wall, where the stairs continued up to the second story. To the right, a pair of sliding doors opened to the parlor, and beneath the staircase, another door led to the kitchen in the rear of the house.

Mrs. Chapman lifted the skirt of her dress and ascended the stairs with Creed two steps behind her. "We have rooms for single gentlemen," she said over her shoulder, "as well as more commodious accommodations for married couples. We even have two adjoining rooms for a small family. Back before the war, we had a family living with us. A druggist named Jonathan Eno and his wife Ellen and their little girl Clara." They reached the middle landing where the stairs turned to the right. "Mr. and Mrs. Eno came here from Connecticut. They were fine people. Mr. Eno was so highly regarded that he became our postmaster for three years. They moved to Greenwood in Sebastian County for a few years, then returned here just as the war began." They arrived in the hall at the top of the stairs where Mrs. Chapman halted in front of the first door around the corner. "Mr. Eno contracted pneumonia and died in the first winter of the war, and Mrs. Eno, who wasn't a well person at all, took her little Clara back to Connecticut the next autumn. She writes that her health is not good and that she doesn't expect to live to see her daughter reach her majority." The lady sighed wistfully. "The poor dear. I pray for her to recover, but I think the Lord needs her more than we do." She heaved another sigh, shook the blues gently from her countenance, forced a smile, and said, "Here we are, Mr. Creed." She opened the door to the room. "Usually, I reserve this room for a lady," said Mrs. Chapman, remaining in the hall, "but all the rooms I keep for single gentlemen are presently occupied."

Creed stepped inside and viewed salmon-pink walls, a white ceiling, a single window overlooking the street, a single poster bed with carved headboard of walnut wood, a dressing table of oak, a nightstand of pine, a ladder-back chair with cushioned seat, a flowered maroon carpet, curtains that matched the carpet, and a shade to keep the morning sun from invading too early in the day. "It suits me fine, Mrs. Chapman," he said, returning to the doorway. "I'm sure I'll be perfectly comfortable here."

"Breakfast is served at seven," she said. "Dinner at noon, and supper at seven. The room and all meals, whether you dine with us or not, will be a dollar a day, six dollars by the week, or twenty-five dollars by the month. In advance, if you please."

Creed dug into his trouser coin pocket and removed six coins: two silver dollars, three silver half-dollars, and a gold half eagle. He offered the gold piece and a silver dollar to the landlady. "I'm not sure that I'll be staying a whole week," he said, "but just in case." He placed the money in her hand.

"Thank you, Mr. Creed. I'll have a boy tend your horse and bring your things up here immediately."

Creed held out another silver dollar to her. "For boarding Nimbus," he said. "Is a dollar enough?"

She blushed and said, "Yes, of course. I nearly forgot to charge you for your horse." She cleared her throat and added, "Actually, Mr. Creed, I'll need another dollar for your horse."

Without hesitation, Creed gave her the money and asked, "Would you happen to have a library, Mrs. Chapman? I find myself with time on my hands, and there's nothing like reading a good book to make leisure time enjoyable."

"You continue to surprise me, Mr. Creed," she said with a warm smile. "I would have thought that being a Texan you would wish to spend your free time in the company of other men in a saloon imbibing beer and whiskey."

"Possibly at some later hour," said Creed, "but only if the company is desirable and the saloon serves something besides alcoholic beverages."

"You are a teetotaler, sir?"

"Not exactly, ma'am. Let's just say that I prefer to keep a clear head and a steady hand at all times."

"A wise philosophy, Mr. Creed. To answer your earlier question, yes, I do have a modest library, and you are more than welcome to select a book and read it there or in the parlor or in your room. But, please, when you've finished the book, return it to the shelf where you found it."

"Yes, of course."

"If you'd like, I'll show you the library now."

"That would be nice, ma'am."

"The key to your room is in the top drawer of the dresser, Mr. Creed. Although I've never had a theft within these walls, I believe an ounce of prevention is worth a pound of cure."

"A wise philosophy, Mrs. Chapman."

"Thank you. Shall we go?"

"After you, ma'am."

Creed followed her down the stairs to the foyer where she opened the doors to the parlor, a very spacious room with two brocaded sofas, matching wing chairs, and a mahogany coffee table as a centerpiece. A Persian carpet covered the hardwood floor. A fireplace dominated the most interior wall, and a large window looked out on the porch and street. A door to the left side of the fireplace led to the kitchen, and a second on the right led to the dining room. A third door in the wall opposite from the foyer opened into the library.

"I am more fortunate than most here in Van Buren, Mr. Creed," said Mrs. Chapman as they passed through the parlor to the library. "When the Yankees came, their officers chose my home for their residence, and this prevented their rabble from searching my home and stealing from me like they did to so many others in town." She paused at the doorway. "The terrible things they did to us, sir. If only we had been properly protected by our army, none of the atrocities committed against our persons and property would ever have occurred. We suffered greatly, sir, at the hands of the Union Army. If not for decent men like Sam Hays and Judge Sangster, I am certain our circumstances would have been much worse."

"Let us pray that those times are behind us forever," said Creed.

"Yes, of course." She turned into the library with Creed behind her. "This is my collection of books, Mr. Creed."

The wall to the left of the door contained a built-in bookcase that went from floor to ceiling, and every shelf contained books of all sizes, colors, and descriptions from the novels of Cooper and Dickens to biographies of kings and presidents. Two long windows, one each in the wall opposite the door and the wall to the front of the house, provided light from without. A writing desk filled the outside corner, while two winged easy chairs to each side of it offered comfort for the reader.

"I'm impressed by it," said Creed.

"Captain Chapman, my husband, brings me books every time he returns from a trip down the Arkansas, even if he only goes as far as Little Rock. He says they're meant to occupy my time while he's away from me."

"Another wise philosophy, I'm sure," said the Texan.

"Thank you, Mr. Creed. I will accept that as a compliment to myself as well as to Captain Chapman."

"Just as it was intended to be, ma'am."

Mrs. Chapman stepped back through the doorway to the parlor with Creed a step behind her. "You have the run of the library and the parlor, Mr. Creed," she said. "The dining room is through there." She pointed at the appropriate door. "I ring a dinner bell five minutes before meals are served. Please do not be late for grace."

"No, ma'am."

"Oh, and one last item. The privy is in the rear of the house out by the barn. There is a stairway at the end of the upper hallway that leads to the backyard. Please use that entrance when you are in the need. If you are downstairs at such a time, go through the kitchen. There." She pointed at the other door beside the fireplace.

"Yes, ma'am."

"I hope you enjoy your stay here, Mr. Creed."

"I'm sure I will, Mrs. Chapman."

"Now if you'll excuse me, I must send the boy to attend your horse and belongings. Good afternoon, sir."

Creed gave her a half bow and said, "Good afternoon, ma'am."

With the landlady departed through the kitchen door, Creed crossed the parlor to the foyer again. He would go back upstairs and wait for the servant to bring his things to his room, and he would write to Texada, Colonel Burch, and the folks back at

Cherokee Town to inform them that he had arrived safely in Van
Buren and that he had learned it was Dick Barth who had fallen
on the wrong side of the legal fence and had landed in jail.

As he reached the middle landing of the stairway, the doorbell
rang. Should I answer it? he wondered. No, this is not my house.
He took the first step to the upper hallway but halted on the second
as he heard Mrs. Chapman come from the kitchen into the foyer
by way of the door beneath the staircase.

"Now who could that be?" she grumped because she was called
away from supervising the preparation of supper.

Out of sight behind the wall of the upper section of the stairway,
Creed rigidized, listening to the conversation below.

Mrs. Chapman opened the door and faced a young woman in
tattered but clean clothes. "Yes, may I help you?" she asked.

"Afternoon, ma'am," said the girl, hardly glancing at the landlady. "Would you be Miz Chapman?"

"Yes, I'm Mrs. Chapman, and who might you be?"

Gaunt, pale, shadows beneath chestnut eyes, long dark hair,
she wore a butternut dress, black shawl, brown sunbonnet, and
a man's shoes. She carried a few meager possessions in a burlap
bag that was closed with a draw string. "My name is Sukey
Ann Rogers," she said with a mild stutter. "My daddy was Jim
Rogers, and my granddaddy was Ben Rogers whom the Unionists
murdered during the war. I was told by Miss Rachael Couch over
at the Farris Grove settlement that you might have some work
for a girl who comes from a family that was loyal to the South
throughout the war."

"Miss Rachael Couch from Farris Grove, you say?"

"Yes'm."

"I know Miss Couch, but how do you know her?"

"She took care of Mr. John Brodie during the war when he was
hurt in the neck by a Yankee ball, and Mr. Brodie told me about
her when he came by our house during the war. I came down
from the mountain hoping to find some work so I can make me
some money to feed my kinfolk this winter, and I went by Miss
Couch's family's place first, and they gave me some food and a
place to stay for a few nights, but they ain't got no work for me.
So they said I should come over here to Van Buren and see you
because you're a real Southern lady who takes care of those in
need. They said I was to tell you that Miss Couch sent me."

"I see," said Mrs. Chapman. "I take it you walked here from
Farris Grove this morning. Is that right?"

"Yes'm, it is."

"Then you must be very tired, child."

"Oh, no'm, I'm not," said Sukey Ann eagerly. "I'm ready to go to work right now, if you got any work for me to do. I'm ready and rarin', Miz Chapman."

The landlady frowned and said, "I don't have anything steady for you, Miss Rogers, but I—"

Sukey Ann stared at Mrs. Chapman with disbelief and said, interrupting her, "Miss Rogers? Why, ain't nobody ever called me that before, Miz Chapman. Miss Couch said you was a real lady. I guess she wasn't foolin' none about that."

"As I was saying, Miss Rogers, I don't have anything steady for you now, but I can let you do some odd jobs around the house for a few days for meals and lodging. And in that time, we just might find a place for you elsewhere in town where you can live and work."

"That's real nice of you, ma'am. I thank you kindly for your generosity."

"Yes, yes, of course. Come inside now, and let's get you situated, Miss Rogers."

"Thank you, ma'am, but please call me Sukey Ann. If somebody who knows me was to hear you call Miss Rogers, they might think I was puttin' on airs or something, and that wouldn't do, what with me being from the mountain and all."

"Yes, of course," said Mrs. Chapman. She closed the door behind Sukey Ann. "Follow me, Sukey Ann."

Creed continued to listen to their footsteps until Mrs. Chapman closed the kitchen door behind them. Then he resumed ascending the stairs to his room, thinking, That's quite a lady down there. It's not every woman who would give a helping hand to a stranger like that. And such a nice girl, too. Willing to work to feed her kinfolk in the mountains. Those people must really have problems, if they have to send a girl to town to make money so they can eat. And I think I've got troubles.

9

After writing to Texada and the folks in Cherokee Town, Creed decided against a letter for Colonel Burch. While walking to and from the Brodie Hotel with Marshal Hays, Creed had noticed a telegraph wire strung pole to pole along Main Street, culminating at a small office next to the hotel. Instead of a much delayed letter, he would send a telegram to the attorney.

Having paid Mrs. Chapman most of the cash that he carried on his person and needing money to pay for the telegram and postage, Creed went down the backstairs to the barn to retrieve additional coin from his secret hiding place. After making certain that no unwanted eyes were prying into his business, he found his saddle and its blanket draped over a stall wall. He picked up a horseshoe nail from the dirt, used it to break a few carefully placed stitches in the blanket's hem, and removed two double eagles that were sewn within. One more look around to be certain that nobody had seen him do this, and he left the barn, ostensibly for the house. He ascended the backstairs, stepped inside the second-story doorway, closed the door behind him, then reopened it a mere inch to watch the barn for anybody entering it too soon after his departure. After a few minutes of fruitless observation, he concluded that the remainder of his hidden money was safe, and he returned to his room for the letters and the telegraph message for Colonel Burch.

Letters and message in hand, Creed locked his door behind him and went downstairs to the parlor in search of Mrs. Chapman. Not finding her there, he peered into the library, but he didn't find her there either. Thinking that the kitchen was off-limits to guests except as a passageway to the back door and the privy outside, he knocked on the door and called out, "Mrs. Chapman, are you in the kitchen?"

"Yes, Mr. Creed," she called back.

"Could I speak with you, ma'am?"

"One moment, and I'll join you in the parlor."

Creed returned to the living room and waited for the landlady. Less than a minute passed before she came from the kitchen.

"Yes, Mr. Creed, how may I help you?"

He held up the letters and said, "I would like to post these as soon as possible, Mrs. Chapman. Could you tell me where the post office is located?"

"Yes, of course. It's at Mr. Bushong's drugstore on Main Street, just two blocks over from here, between Strokes and Perry. You can't miss it."

Creed nodded and said, "Thank you, ma'am."

"Be certain to return in time to wash up for supper, Mr. Creed. It's already half past four."

"Yes, ma'am," said Creed as if he were acknowledging an order from his mother or a schoolteacher.

Mrs. Chapman returned to the kitchen, and Creed exited the house for the post office then the telegraph office.

The streets of Van Buren appeared to be busier than earlier in the day when Creed first arrived in town. More wagons, more buggies, more surreys, more carriages, more single horses, and certainly more pedestrians moved about the dusty, narrow thoroughfares. The noise level had increased dramatically as well with the rattle of wheels, axles, and buckboards; the protests of horses; the snapping of whips and reins; the thumping and thudding of horses' hooves; and the loud chatter of people attempting to be heard over everything else. For sure, it was Friday, but most towns didn't know such business except on Saturdays, market day for rural folks. This many people on a Friday afternoon? It was perplexing to Creed as he deposited his letters with Mr. Bushong at the post office window in the rear of the drugstore.

Returning to the street, Creed turned south along Main Street to walk the three blocks to the telegraph office. He chose to walk on the east side of the street, which took him directly past the courthouse steps.

"Mr. Creed!" John Ogden hailed him from the courthouse landing.

The Texan turned to see Ogden waving at him. He reciprocated in kind, intending to keep moving along, but he saw Ogden excuse himself from talking to a gentleman in a gray suit and hurry toward him. Creed had no choice except to stop and converse with the lawyer.

"How nice to see you again, Mr. Creed!" said Ogden enthusiastically. "Sam told me that he got you settled into Mrs. Chapman's boardinghouse."

"Yes, sir, he did."

"Good for you," said Ogden. "A fine place to be staying, and with a real lady of a hostess."

"Yes, I agree," said Creed.

"Out sight-seeing, are you?"

"No, actually. I was just on my way to the telegraph office to send a wire to my attorney. Business, you know?"

"Yes, of course. Mustn't let the mice play while the cat's away, right, sir?"

"Yes, of course."

Ogden scanned the street. "The town's already filling up," he said. A glimmer of excitement danced in his eyes as he grinned. "There's nothing like a murder trial to bring extra business into town. It'll be standing room only in the courtroom when we put those two killers on trial next week. I can't wait to convict those bastards. Of course, they only killed a Negro in the Nations, but a conviction will certainly look good on my record, especially if the judge sentences them to hang. That'll make those Yankees in Little Rock stand up and take notice of me." He paused to enjoy the thought for a moment.

"You're positive that you'll get a conviction, Mr. Ogden?" queried Creed.

"As positive as the sun will rise in the east tomorrow morning. I've got two witnesses against them. The Army sergeant who caught them in the act of raping the woman and the woman herself who saw them murder her husband."

"But what good will the woman be as a witness, Mr. Ogden? She's a Negro, and the killers are white men."

"That was under the old laws," said Ogden. "Now there's something good that came out of that terrible war. She can testify now. The old laws have been done away with. This is a federal case, anyway, and under federal law, Negroes are allowed to testify against whites. Those two men are as good as hung, Mr. Creed. Bank on it."

"Well, I certainly hope so," said Creed. "Men like them don't deserve to live in this world with decent folks."

"I agree wholeheartedly, sir." Ogden surveyed the street again. "Yes sir, Mr. Creed. Lucky that you arrived when you did. All the hotels will be filled before tomorrow night, and those who can't find rooms will be camping on the courthouse grounds the way the soldiers did during the war. Yes, indeed. A murder trial sure can bring them in."

"When will their trial be held?" asked Creed.

"That depends on how fast the trials set before it take," said Ogden. "A trial list will be posted on the courthouse door, but I suspect it should be sometime by Wednesday. Thursday at the latest. It should all be over by Friday afternoon, and then we'll have a hanging to look forward to."

Creed thought about asking where Lucius Slater's widow might be found, but he reasoned that it would do him no good to have people wondering what his interest might be in this matter. Instead, he said, "Well, if you'll excuse me, Mr. Ogden, I must get to the telegraph office before it closes for the day."

"Oh, don't worry about that," said Ogden. "Dan Mobley never really closes down his telegraph. If he's not in the office, try knocking on the back door. He lives in a room in the rear."

"Thank you, I will," said Creed. He tipped his hat and moved along the street to the telegraph office.

Dan Mobley appeared exactly as Creed imagined he would. Thin, bald, pale, weak chin hidden by a salt-and-pepper beard, brown eyes, wearing a boiled shirt with no collar, vest, sleeve garters, and a visor. He took the message from Creed, counted the words quickly, and said, "That'll be three dollars, Mr. Creed."

"Three dollars?" queried Creed.

"Yes, sir. Ten cents a word. Thirty words. Three dollars. In cash."

Creed paid the money, and Mobley wired:

Colonel John C. Burch
Union and American Building
Nashville, Tennessee
    Arrived Van Buren. Barth in jail here. Waiting trial.
Unwilling to help. Advise.
Slate Creed
Chapman Boardinghouse
Van Buren, Arkansas

"If there's an answer," said Creed, "would you please deliver it to me at Mrs. Chapman's boardinghouse?"

"Glad to, Mr. Creed."

Creed returned to the boardinghouse in time to hear Mrs. Chapman ring the dinner bell. Not wishing to be late, he hung his hat on a peg in the foyer and hurried to the dining room. He was the first to arrive.

The table was set elegantly for ten people: Mrs. Chapman and nine residents. China dishes, silver flatware, crystal water glasses, yellow tablecloth, and centerpieces of dried flowers and autumn leaves.

Mrs. Chapman entered from the kitchen and stood behind her chair at the head of the table. "Mr. Creed, you will sit here to my left this evening. After this, you may choose to sit where you please or in whatever chair is available when you arrive at the table."

"Yes, ma'am," said Creed, moving to stand behind the chair that she had indicated until she sat or until grace was spoken, whichever should happen first.

"I will introduce you as soon as everybody is settled and the blessing has been asked," said Mrs. Chapman.

"Yes, ma'am."

Other people filtered into the room.

When everybody was in place behind a chair, Mrs. Chapman asked the blessing, then said, "Before everybody sits down, I wish to introduce our newest resident, Mr. Slate Creed, a cattleman from Lavaca County, Texas." Starting on her right, she named the other residents, and each exchanged a pleasantry with Creed.

"Mr. Leo Smith," a robust gentleman in a suit and tie with slicked-down red hair and whiskers that wrapped around his face from ear to ear over his lip but not his double chin; "Mr. Calvin Landon," a thin man in a black suit with a bald head, bushy black eyebrows, full black beard; "Miss Mary Steen," a young brunette woman whose plain looks said schoolteacher; "Mr. Lawrence Darrell," a nondescript fellow wearing a brown coat and gray trousers; "Mrs. Vivian Nance," a large lady of middle age wearing a high-collar white blouse adorned with crocheted roses; "Mr. Nelson Peterson," a very tall man with chestnut eyes and hair and appearing to be afraid of those around him; "Mr. Thomas Buckmaster," a very short man with a sharp nose, mousy eyes, and a thin, tight mouth; and "Miss Jennifer Nipper," a girl in her early teens with blond curls and blue eyes wearing a robin's egg blue pinafore over a pastel yellow dress.

"Now please be seated," said Mrs. Chapman. She rang a small table bell, and two young women, one a former slave, entered from the kitchen, the darker girl pushing a cart carrying a soup tureen and bowls. "Everybody, we have a new girl in the kitchen," said the landlady. "This is Miss Sukey Ann Rogers. She comes to us on recommendation from Miss Rachael Couch from over to Farris Grove."

So this was the girl at the door, thought Creed. She's so frail. I wonder how long it's been since she had three meals in a day. Poor thing!

As Mrs. Chapman named the residents for Sukey Ann's benefit, Creed noted that she studied each face and mouthed the name that went with it until she came to Buckmaster. Oddly, her lips didn't move with his name, and the look she gave him appeared furtive at best, almost as if she were afraid to recognize his presence. When the Texan was introduced to her, the girl's basically cool shyness vanished from her eyes, being replaced with an inviting warmth that said she liked what she was seeing.

The other girl ladled chicken and dumplings into the bowls, and Sukey Ann distributed them around the table, beginning with Creed and ending up with Mrs. Chapman. As soon as everybody had their supper, the servers were dismissed, but before exiting, Sukey Ann took one last peek over her shoulder at Creed.

Conversation commenced as soon as Mrs. Chapman picked up her soup spoon and began eating. Sitting in the second chair on the landlady's right, Buckmaster initiated the talk by asking Creed about whether the cattle business had brought him to Van Buren.

"No, I'm here on a personal matter," said the Texan. "A fellow from my county back in Texas has run afoul of the law, and I'm here to see if there isn't something that I can do for him."

"A federal prisoner?" queried Buckmaster.

"As a matter of fact, he is," said Creed. "His name is Dick Barth. Do you know him?"

"Not all that well," said Buckmaster. "He's retained me to represent him in court next week."

"I see," said Creed. "So you're a lawyer."

"Yes, I am," said Buckmaster, He reached inside his coat and took a business card from an inner pocket. "My card, sir." He stretched across the table to hand it to the Texan.

Creed accepted the card, reading the name and the man's address: Bentonville, Arkansas. "I take it that you're here for the federal court term, Mr. Buckmaster?"

"That's right," said Buckmaster, "I come down here for the federal court terms as soon as the Benton County court terms are finished in April and October. I manage to find a client or two in need of my services."

"And this time you found Dick Barth."

"Yes, sir."

"What do you think his chances are?"

"His chances?"

"In court."

"Oh, yes, of course," said Buckmaster. He cleared his throat, then added, "Quite frankly, Mr. Creed, I'm not at liberty to discuss my client's case outside the courtroom."

"Yes, of course," said Creed. "Is he your only client in the federal jail?"

"No, I also represent a few others. It might interest you that two of my other clients are Texans. Mr. Harry Crackley and Mr. David Lowe, Are you acquainted with them as well as Mr. Barth?"

"No, sir, I am not," said Creed coldly.

Buckmaster smiled, delighted with himself for getting under Creed's skin. "But you do know who they are?" he queried.

"Vaguely," said Creed. "I'm more acquainted with their crime."

"Alleged crime, Mr. Creed," said Buckmaster, his smile patronizing the Texan. "Every accused person is innocent until proven guilty, sir."

Creed noticed young Jennifer staring wide-eyed at him, listening to every word passing between him and Buckmaster. Acutely aware of her interest in the conversation, he said, "Perhaps we should postpone this discussion until a later hour, Mr. Buckmaster." He shifted his eyes at the girl, hoping the lawyer would perceive his meaning and cooperate without hesitation.

Buckmaster glanced at Jennifer and said, "Yes, of course, sir. Perhaps in the parlor after supper?"

"Yes, after supper," said Creed. Lawyers! he thought, and this one is short, too. A short lawyer. With a chip on his shoulder the size of Pikes Peak. Jesse and Alex James and those other bushwhackers used guns to hold up that bank in Missouri. This fellow uses a law book to rob people.

10

Creed had no real desire to debate the merits and the faults of the American legal system with Thomas Buckmaster after supper that evening. Even so, he kept the appointment made at the dining room table. For one simple reason: his curiosity drove him to do it.

Why did Sukey Ann Rogers mouth the names of the other residents at this table and look each person straight in the eye, but she hardly glanced at Buckmaster? Creed asked himself several times during the meal. He'd catch a glimpse of Buckmaster and ask himself, Does she know him? And what about him? He wouldn't look at her either. If they do know each other, why didn't they acknowledge the fact? Do they have something to hide? If they do, what could it be? Only one way to find out.

The ladies excused themselves from the company of the men as soon as the meal was completed. Mrs. Chapman invited them to bring their sewing to her quarters in the rear of the house. "We can take turns reading Mr. Dickens's *Great Expectations* while we sew," she said. "I'll have Sukey Ann bring us some cool apple juice, and Roberta will serve cider to the gentlemen in the front room."

The men retired to the parlor for the debate between Creed and Buckmaster. Smith, the portly Yankee banker, and Landon, the balding store clerk, sat on one sofa, while Peterson, the gangly bank teller, and Darrell, the bland mule skinner, stationed themselves on the opposite couch. Buckmaster chose one winged chair, leaving the other to Creed. Somewhat like duelists, they squared off for the verbal affray.

"As I was saying at supper, Mr. Creed," said the lawyer, taking charge of the informal discussion, "every accused person is innocent until proven guilty. That is the American system of justice, unlike those of Europe where a man is guilty until proven innocent, which I don't mind saying, doesn't happen very often when the accuser is a person of some social or noble rank and the accused is a common man. In this country, the theory is no man should be denied justice, no matter how poor he might be."

"The key word there, Mr. Buckmaster," countered Creed, "is theory. The theory is not always practiced, is it?"

"Quite right, sir," said Buckmaster. "It is unfortunate in this land that some people can't afford to employ an attorney and thus are forced to appear in court without legal representation. But, of course, that's only in civil matters and some minor criminal cases. If the case involves a capital crime, such as the one my two clients are accused of committing, then the court appoints an attorney to represent the accused."

"I see," said Creed. "That seems fair and just. But what if the accused is not a white man? Does he enjoy the same rights?"

"Of course not," said Buckmaster. "The law states very clearly that whites are superior to all others."

"All others being Negroes, mulattoes, Indians, breeds, and the like?"

"Precisely, Mr. Creed."

"And the law makes the distinction between whites and all others?"

"Yes, of course, sir. Whites are all white, and anybody who isn't all white is something else."

Roberta entered the room from the kitchen carrying a tray of glasses and a pitcher of cider. She set them down on the coffee table in the center of the room. "Would you gentlemens like me to pour your cider for you?" she asked.

"Yes," said Buckmaster.

"No," said Creed.

The lawyer frowned at the Texan.

"I'll do it," said Peterson.

"Let the nigger do it," said Buckmaster.

"I don't mind doing it," said Peterson.

Buckmaster frowned at him and said, "No, I suppose you don't."

"Thank you, Roberta," said Creed. "We'll take care of ourselves from here."

The serving girl curtsied to Creed and left the room.

Peterson filled the glasses with cider for all of them. As soon as every man had a glass of refreshment, he returned the tray and pitcher to the kitchen. He came back to the parlor just as Smith raised his glass to offer a toast. The others followed his example.

"To the lady of this house," said Smith. "A more gracious hostess than she does not breathe."

"Here, here!" said some of the other men in chorus.

"To Mrs. Chapman," said Buckmaster.

They each took a swallow of cider, then the debate resumed.

Creed placed his glass on one end of the coffee table, leaned forward in his chair, rested his elbows on his knees, and gestured with his hands as he spoke. "You were saying, Mr. Buckmaster, that to be white, one has to be all white."

"My precise words were," said the lawyer, also putting his glass on the table, " 'Whites are all white, and anybody who isn't all white is something else.' My precise words."

"I see, and because a man has one great-grandparent who isn't white, then he's not entitled to the same rights as the man whose great-grandparents were all white people. Is that correct, Mr. Buckmaster?"

"Quite correct," said the lawyer smugly. "The man whose ancestors are not all white has tainted blood, and that tainted blood denies him the rights reserved for white people."

"Tainted blood? Where is it written that the blood of Indians taints the blood of whites?"

Buckmaster waved his hands and said, "Mr. Creed, we're not here to discuss racial issues. We're trying to debate the law and a man's rights."

"Yes, you're right," said Creed, leaning back in his chair again. "As you were saying, a man is innocent until proven guilty. I agree with that, sir, but it's my understanding that your clients, the two Texans that you mentioned, were caught in the act of raping a woman after murdering her husband."

"A Negress, sir, and—"

Creed straightened up, cocked his head to one side, and interjected with a hint of anger, "What does her color have to do with anything, Mr. Buckmaster? She's still a woman, a human being, and no human being has the right or privilege to violate the body of another human being. Or do you disagree with that, too?"

"Like I was about to say, the woman was a Negress, and under the law, she has no rights."

"Under whose law, Mr. Buckmaster? Man's or God's? North or South?" When Buckmaster made no immediate reply, Creed continued. "And what about her husband? Are you gonna tell me that he didn't have the right to live just because he was Negro?"

"No, sir. Under the old laws as a slave, he would have had as much right to live as a man's horse."

Creed was incredulous, near to frustration. "A man's horse? We're talking about people here, Mr. Buckmaster. Not cattle or horses or chickens, but people. Every man and woman and child has the right to live, and that man that your clients murdered had his right taken away from him. For that, your clients deserve to die."

"But they only killed a Negro, Mr. Creed. What is the big deal about that?"

Creed threw up his hands and fell back in the chair. "I can see that I'm wasting my time talking to you about these matters, Mr. Buckmaster. You're never gonna see Negroes as people."

Buckmaster took offense. "I see them as people, Mr. Creed," he said. "Inferior people."

"Inferior? Inferior to what? To you because you're white?"

The lawyer snickered, feeling he'd won the debate. "Why, yes, of course because I'm white."

Got you, thought Creed. He leaned forward again and pointed an accusing finger at the diminutive attorney. "You're also short, Mr. Buckmaster. Does that make you inferior to me because I'm more than a head taller than you are?"

The lawyer bounced to his feet, jabbed a stubby finger at Creed, and said, "Hell no, it doesn't make me inferior to you, you ignorant Texas son of a bitch! I'm a lawyer, and that makes me—"

"A piece of horseshit," interjected Creed.

Enraged, Buckmaster jumped onto the coffee table that separated him from the Texan. "I'll whip your ass for that remark!" he spat as he leaped at Creed with both fists flailing the air.

Creed sprung out of his chair, reached out with both hands, caught the lawyer by his armpits, and squeezed them hard as he held the much smaller man at arm's length from him. When his attacker tried kicking him as well, the Texan dug his fingers into Buckmaster's soft flesh until the attorney screamed with pain.

The other men were too shocked at Buckmaster's sudden charge to react. None of them moved, but Roberta did. She'd been listening at the kitchen door, and as soon as Buckmaster attacked Creed, she ran to tell Mrs. Chapman that the "gentlemens is fighting in the parlor! You best come quick, Miz Chapman, or they gonna break everything."

"Put me down!" screamed Buckmaster just as Mrs. Chapman entered the room.

"Mr. Creed!" gasped the landlady. Mrs. Nance, the widow; Miss Steen, the schoolteacher; young Jennifer, the schoolgirl; and Sukey Ann and Roberta, the two serving girls; all huddled behind her.

Creed ignored her, knowing if he relaxed his hold on the lawyer that Buckmaster would take advantage and strike him with a fist or a foot.

"Put me down, you son of a bitch!" yelled Buckmaster.

That was a mistake.

"Mr. Buckmaster!" bellowed Mrs. Chapman. "I will not have that sort of language spoken in this house!"

Creed shook Buckmaster violently as if he were a rag doll and in spite of the increased torture to his own fingers. As soon as the lawyer went limp in his hands, the Texan threw him over the coffee table into the winged chair, which rocked backward from the impact but didn't fall over, coming back to balance in its original position with a decisive thud.

The action stunned the onlookers into a collective gasp.

Now in agony, Buckmaster reached for his armpits, thinking his own touch would relieve the piercing pain. He was wrong. His face twisted with suffering and rage.

Flexing his fingers in an attempt to restore their circulation and thus reduce the ache in them, Creed glared at Buckmaster and said, "I believe I've made my point, sir. I agree that being short makes you no less of a man than I am, any more than being dark-skinned makes an Indian or a Negro or a mulatto or a breed less of a man than you or I or anybody else in this room or in this world. God made us all different. Tall, short, fat, skinny, black, white, red, blond, brunette, smart, and stupid. But to Him, we're all the same. If we sin, He'll punish us for it. And if we're righteous, He'll reward us for it. It's only the color of our hearts that He's interested in, Mr. Buckmaster. Not the color of our hides."

"Here, here, sir!" said Smith.

Peterson also agreed. Although he spoke no words, the adoration in his eyes for Creed said volumes.

Creed turned to Mrs. Chapman and said, "My apologies for this disturbance, ma'am. If you wish, I will remove myself from the premises and seek lodging elsewhere."

"No," said the landlady instantly, fearfully. Then realizing how she must have sounded, she regained control and added, "No, that won't be necessary, Mr. Creed. No damage has been done."

"You assaulted me," growled Buckmaster.

"No, he didn't," said Peterson. "You attacked him. Isn't that right, gentlemen?"

"Yes, that's right," said Landon.

"You started the ruckus, Buckmaster," said Smith.

Darrell concurred, but nobody noticed.

The lawyer refused to surrender. "You started it when you called me a piece of horse—" He stopped himself from repeating the exact epithet, remembering the presence of the ladies. Instead, he said, "Dung."

"That's not true," said Peterson in Creed's defense. "You called him something much worse before that." He turned to Mrs. Chapman, as if she were judge and jury here. "He called Mr. Creed a name that was disparaging to Mr. Creed's mother."

"Yes, I heard Mr. Buckmaster use that word a moment ago, Mr. Peterson," said the landlady.

This was going too far, and Creed felt a need to bring the evening to a halt. "Mrs. Chapman," he said, "Mr. Buckmaster and I were debating a point, and I made a remark about his stature that caused him to lose his temper." He turned to face the attorney. "I did it intentionally to make my point, and since I've made it, I believe the discussion is closed. Am I right, Mr. Buckmaster?"

The lawyer's lips said, "Yes, Mr. Creed," but his evil eyes said, Not on your life, you son of a bitch! I'll have the last word and the last laugh. You've only begun to pay for this, Creed.

Somehow, the Texan knew that he'd opened a can of worms with this little bastard, and although he felt a twinge of guilt for thinking it, he wondered why Buckmaster's parents hadn't drowned this runt at birth.

11

Rising early the next morning, Creed joined the other residents for breakfast, which was less formal than supper had been the evening before. He sat in the third seat on Mrs. Chapman's right, flanked by Peterson and Jennifer, both of whom behaved as if they were enamored of him. Their syrupy-sweet attention flattered him on the one hand and discomforted him on the other. He humored them, feeling Jennifer's attitude was merely a schoolgirl's crush on an older man that she would outgrow soon enough and Peterson's solicitude was simply a display of hero worship by a young fellow who was impressed by someone who was more manly than he was.

Surprisingly, Buckmaster spoke to Creed civilly, although without any outward sign of friendliness. Smith and Landon greeted him warmly, and Darrell gave him a casual nod. The ladies, Miss Steen and Mrs. Nance, performed in a ladylike fashion as they bade him a good morning, and Mrs. Chapman was as friendly as ever.

Nobody mentioned the incident of the previous night, and this suited Creed just fine as he limited his conversation to one-word responses to small-talk questions about how he slept and the like and to requests to pass the salt or butter or whatever. He ate in relative peace, the repast consisting of bacon, fried cornmeal mush, biscuits, and gravy. He did observe that once again the lawyer and the serving girl, Sukey Ann, avoided making eye contact with each other whenever she was in the room. Why are they acting like this? he wondered. Why do I care? he chastised himself.

Excusing himself from the breakfast table and the company of the other residents, especially Jennifer and Peterson, the Texan repaired to the Chapman barn, saddled Nimbus, and rode him to a blacksmith shop he'd noticed the day before in the same block as the Brodie Hotel. He would have the stallion's feet examined for excessive wear and have pine tar applied to the hooves in order to hold the natural varnish that prevented cracking of the hoof wall.

79

While the Appaloosa was being tended, he took his saddle and harness to a saddle maker on Water Street to have the straps replaced with new leather. With those chores in the working, he opted to take a stroll along Main Street and see what the various stores had to offer.

While passing by Williams Mercantile on the corner of Columbus and Main Street, Creed caught a glimpse of his reflection in the store window. It disappointed him. His overall appearance was shabby at best. His coat and hat were torn, tattered, and threadbare. He needed new attire, and he saw the perfect place to do his shopping up the street a block on the corner of Perry and Main at Watson's Apparel Shop.

Creed found a nice charcoal-gray coat that was a little loose in the shoulders and waist, but that suited him just fine because the extra room would help to hide his Colt's whenever the occasion called for him to carry it. The wide brim of his grandfather's plainsman had become bent and torn, and its crown had some serious dents in it. The Texan had two choices: have the hat cleaned, repaired, and blocked or buy a new hat. He opted to do both. Although it would be cleaned, repaired, and blocked, the old plainsman was still brown, meaning it wouldn't go well with his new coat; but Creed couldn't bear to part with it because the hat was all that he had left of Grandfather Dougald Slater. A new plainsman the same color as the new coat would look good on him. He had the crown of the new hat creased to make it appear flat on top. His next purchase was a new boiled shirt with a cloth collar and a maroon tie to give it style. Because winter was close at hand with its chill winds from the north, Creed bought two pairs of heavy woolen socks and a cotton union suit to combat the cold.

Having finished his shopping, Creed returned to Mrs. Chapman's boardinghouse just in time for dinner. The only other residents at the meal were Buckmaster, Jennifer, Mrs. Nance, and Miss Steen. Mrs. Chapman explained that the other gentlemen took lunches to work with them or they dined at one of the many restaurants or saloons. Once again, Jennifer sat beside Creed and doted over him. Buckmaster treated the Texan civilly, and just like supper the night before and breakfast that morning, every time Sukey Ann Rogers entered the room the lawyer twitched nervously and did everything he could to avoid looking directly at her and she did likewise. Such strange behavior, thought Creed. These two must know each other, but why are they trying to hide it? Why do I care? I've got my own problems to think about here. Even so . . .

Sukey Ann served them roast beef, boiled potatoes, boiled carrots, stewed canned tomatoes, bread, butter, and coffee—milk for Jennifer. Since the ladies made up the majority, they dominated the conversation, telling about their various shopping excursions that morning. Miss Steen remarked that she had seen Mr. Creed entering Watson's.

"As a matter of fact," said Creed, pleased to join them in their light chatter, "I also went clothes shopping this morning. I bought a coat, hat, shirt, and some accessories. I may purchase a pair of trousers this afternoon."

"Oh, you're going back to Main Street this afternoon, Mr. Creed?" asked Jennifer anxiously.

"Well, yes, I have to go," said Creed. "I have to get my horse and see if my saddle is finished being repaired."

"I think what Jennifer is asking you, Mr. Creed," said Mrs. Nance, "is whether she might join you. Isn't that right, dear?"

The girl blushed a very rosy red.

"Oh?" blurted Creed, blanching a bit.

"You see, Mr. Creed," said Mrs. Chapman, "Jennifer attends school here in Van Buren because there is no regular school near her parents' farm up on Cedar Creek. She lives here during the school term and goes home when school is not in session. Jennifer's family usually comes to town on Saturday morning, and she goes to market with them while they're here. But sometimes they don't come into town on Saturday for one reason or another, like today because the town is so crowded with outsiders come here for the court. When those times arise, Miss Steen or Mrs. Nance or I take Jennifer shopping with us. None of us realized that her family wasn't coming today, so we didn't take her with us this morning."

"And each of us is previously engaged this afternoon," said Mrs. Nance.

"I was planning to have Sukey Ann accompany Jennifer," said Mrs. Chapman, "but she's only been down from the mountain a few days, if you know what I mean."

"Yes, I think I do," said Creed.

"It wouldn't do for two young girls to be on the streets of Van Buren . . . unaccompanied . . . with so many strangers in town," said Mrs. Chapman.

"I agree," said Creed.

"I can assure you, Mr. Creed," said Mrs. Chapman, "that Jennifer is a perfect lady."

"I've already noticed that about her, ma'am," said Creed. "I'd be delighted to have her and Miss Rogers accompany me this afternoon. That is, if they don't mind visiting a blacksmith shop and a saddlery as well."

"Oh, I won't mind at all," said Jennifer eagerly.

"And as for Sukey Ann," said Mrs. Chapman, "I'm sure she won't be any trouble for you, Mr. Creed."

"I'm sure they'll both be well-behaved young ladies," said Creed.

"Very good, sir," said the landlady. "Then it's settled. You will have them back here before dark, won't you?"

"Certainly," said the Texan. "Before dark."

Most men would have been thoroughly bored chaperoning two young girls for an afternoon of browsing and shopping through a town's business district, but not Creed. He rather enjoyed observing Sukey Ann as she explored what was a whole new world for her, and he received a similar pleasure watching Jennifer lead the serving girl through the maze of stores. He kept them in sight as they examined item after item, and they stayed close to him as he chose a pair of trousers to go with his new coat. With the autumn sun approaching the horizon, the trio found their way to Horatio Ford's blacksmith shop on Water Street.

Sweat glistened and dripped copiously from Ford's sinewy bare arms as he worked on the hoof of a chestnut mare just inside his shop. A bandanna around his head kept the perspiration out of his icy gray eyes.

"Is my horse ready, Mr. Ford?" asked Creed, standing in the doorway flanked by the two girls.

Without looking up, Ford grunted as he dug the hook of the hoof pick into the hoof one more time before answering. "Yes, sir, he is," said the smith as soon as he straightened up. "The bill comes to four dollars and twenty-five cents, Mr. Creed."

Creed gave him a half eagle, saying, "Take it out of this."

Ford smiled greedily at the gold coin as he accepted it. "I'll be right back with your change," he said. He placed the hoof pick on the work bench and went to get the change for Creed.

Creed walked through the barn looking for Nimbus. Jennifer followed behind him. Sukey Ann stayed behind near the smith's work bench. The Texan and the schoolgirl found the Appaloosa in a stall midway to the end of the barn.

Ford joined Creed and Jennifer. "You ought to put that stallion out to pasture, Mr. Creed," said the smith. "He looks like he'd sire some real good horseflesh."

"He's already been put out to pasture once," said Creed, recalling how he'd put Nimbus in with his stepfather's mares last spring while he gathered cattle on the range for the trail drive to New Mexico Territory. "He did his business, then he begged me to take him with me when I hit the trail again."

"Well, for a stallion, I have to say he's real gentle," said Ford. "Just the same, you can never tell when a stallion's gonna turn on you and demand to have his own way. Especially when there's a right nice filly flirting her stuff his way."

"I've had a rough moment or two with him over the years," said Creed, "but for the most part, he's been a real good horse. Reliable. Raring to go when I've needed him on my side."

"Well, here's your change, sir," said Ford, handing over three quarters to the Texan. "If you need anything else while you're here in Van Buren, don't hesitate to bring him here. He was a pleasure to work with."

"I'll do that, Mr. Ford."

Creed took Nimbus by the halter and led him from the barn. Jennifer walked beside the Texan, and Sukey Ann fell in behind her.

"Now where did I put that hoof pick?" Ford muttered as they left.

From the blacksmith shop, Creed and the girls went up the street to the saddle shop, where the Texan paid the saddle maker for a job well-done and picked up his refurbished saddle.

"This is a beautiful stallion, Mr. Creed," said Sukey Ann as Creed saddled Nimbus.

"Thank you, Miss Rogers," said Creed. "I'm proud of him. Nimbus has been with me since the day he was born."

"Nimbus is such an unusual name for a horse," said Jennifer. "How did you come to name him that?"

Creed chuckled, finished saddling the stallion, looked up at the sky, and said, "You see that cloud up there, the one with the gray bottom on it?" He pointed with the index finger of his left hand.

"Yes, I see," said Jennifer, squinting at the sky.

"I see it, too," said Sukey Ann.

"Do you see how the white part sort of looks like a crown or a halo on the gray part?"

"Yes," said both girls.

"That's called a nimbus," said Creed. "My granddaddy once said that ghosts appear out of clouds that are something like that, and I thought that was pretty scary until the day my Nimbus was born."

"How's that?" asked Sukey Ann, now looking at Creed.

"Well, the day he was born it was cold and drizzly and there was fog everywhere. We knew his mama was about to foal, but she was out in the pasture, and we couldn't find her in the fog. We heard her whinny real hard, and we knew she must be giving birth about then. Then she was quiet, and we lost track of her again. Then my little brother saw her standing in a hollow. There was fog all around her, but it was low to the ground. As we got close to her, we heard something in the grass. We stopped and listened, and in a few seconds, there he was. Her colt. He popped up out of that fog just like my granddaddy said a ghost comes out of a nimbus, and that's why I named him Nimbus."

"That's such a romantic story, Mr. Creed," said Jennifer, now all aglow with infatuation.

"Well, I don't know about it being romantic," said Creed.

"Me neither," said Sukey Ann sardonically, "but it's a pretty good yarn just the same."

"I take it you don't believe me," said Creed.

"If you say it's true, then that's good enough for me," said Sukey Ann. "I've heard taller tales, I s'pose."

"Well, I believe every word of it," said Jennifer.

Creed scanned the sky and said, "It's time to head home, ladies. Shall we go?" He started to walk toward Main Street.

"Can I ride your horse back to Miz Chapman's?" asked Sukey Ann, not moving.

"Sure, why not?" said Creed, stopping. "You can both ride him if you like. Together."

"No, I want to ride him," said Sukey Ann. "You know? Just me and the horse?"

Creed chuckled and said, "You're serious, aren't you?"

"Of course, I'm serious," said Sukey Ann. "What do you think I am, Mr. Creed? Some kind of sissy like that Mr. Peterson who thinks you're sweeter than molasses on hotcakes on Sunday morning?"

"Why, Sukey Ann!" gasped Jennifer.

Creed was too flabbergasted by this pronouncement to respond with anything except a flinch.

"Well, it's true, Jennifer," said Sukey Ann. "Mr. Peterson is one of them sissy boys." She studied the shocked expression on Jennifer's face. "Do you mean to tell me that you don't know what that is?" She looked at Creed and saw the storm brewing in his eyes. "You didn't know it either, Mr. Creed?" She burst out laughing. "Now ain't you something?" Her laughter grew louder and annoying.

"I don't see anything to laugh at here," said Creed.

"Well, I sure as hell do," said Sukey Ann.

"Sukey Ann!" gasped Jennifer. "Such language!"

"Aw, come on, Jennifer," said Sukey Ann. "You were born on a farm, and you got brothers and a pappy. Don't tell me you ain't never heard none of them cuss before."

"Yes, I have, but they're men."

"And your mama ain't never said a cuss word in her whole life?" queried Sukey Ann.

Jennifer wanted to defend her mother's honor, but she knew that her mother had spoken more than one epithet in her lifetime. She could only look at her feet in response to the question.

"That's what I thought," said Sukey Ann.

"Miss Rogers, there's no need to embarrass Miss Jennifer like that," said Creed.

Sukey Ann frowned and said, "Yeah, you're right about that. I'm sorry, Jennifer. I didn't mean nothing by that."

Jennifer looked up at Sukey Ann and said, "Yes, I know. Thank you, Sukey Ann. Shall we go now?" She started to walk toward Main Street.

"Well, now that that's settled," said Sukey Ann, allowing Jennifer to get several feet in front of her and Creed, "how about me riding your horse, Mr. Creed?"

"No," said Creed firmly with finality. He started to follow Jennifer.

"What?" groused Sukey Ann, grabbing Creed by the arm and stopping him. "Don't tell me you're all mad about me saying that about Mr. Peterson being sweet on you. I ain't believing a man like you could get mad about something like that."

"A man like me, Miss Rogers? Now what does that mean?"

After making sure that Jennifer was nearly out of earshot, Sukey Ann smiled at the Texan lasciviously, leaned closer so that Jennifer couldn't possibly hear, and said, "That means you're the kind of man who makes a prissy girl like Jennifer swoon when he's being manly and who makes a real woman like me start to burning inside when he's being the same way. If you know what I mean."

"Yes, I know what you mean," said Creed evenly.

"Good," said Sukey Ann with a triumphant smile. "Then can I ride your horse now?"

"No," said Creed. He leaned closer to her and said, "You might not be enough woman to ride this horse, Miss Rogers, and I wouldn't want you to get hurt."

"I appreciate your concern, Mr. Creed," said Sukey Ann, "but I can take care of myself."

"I'm sure you can," said Creed, "but you still can't ride my horse." He took two quick steps after Jennifer and added, "Come along now. We can't be late for supper."

And they weren't.

12

Sunday was a difficult day for the Texan.

Creed spent the morning in worship, attending the Presbyterian Church with Mrs. Nance, Miss Steen, Jennifer, Sukey Ann, and Mrs. Chapman. Much to Creed's chagrin and Sukey Ann's giggles, Nelson Peterson traipsed along with them, placing himself as close to Creed as possible during the long walk through town to and from the Union church building at Washington and Water Streets, and sitting beside the Texan during the service.

In the afternoon, Creed repaired to the barn to care for his horse and trappings and to get away from Peterson. He succeeded in the first but failed in the second purpose. While Creed brushed the Appaloosa thoroughly, the bank teller entered the barn and stationed himself against a stanchion where he could watch Creed closely.

Annoyed, the Texan finally asked, "Is there something that you want, Mr. Peterson?"

"I'm sorry," he said. "Am I bothering you?"

Creed noted the potential for hurt in the fellow's eyes, and he felt sorry for him because he had to do what he had to do. "As a matter of fact, yes, you are bothering me, Mr. Peterson," said the Texan. "You've been following me around like some sort of lovesick puppy, and I wish you'd stop it."

Peterson stiffened as he tried to hold down the pain building inside him. He swallowed hard and said, "I just want to be ... friends ... with you, Mr. Creed."

"Well, I don't want to be *friends* with you," said Creed. "Look, I know what you are, Mr. Peterson. I'm not your kind, and I don't like all the attention you're giving me." Then thinking to soften the blow, he added, "It's flattering that you should think so highly of me, but ..." He let his voice trail off.

Tears welled in Peterson's eyes. "I didn't mean nothing by it," he said softly, choking ever so slightly on the words. He swallowed hard again. "It's just that ... I ... *like* ... you, Mr. Creed, and I want to ... be near you."

Just then, Sukey Ann walked through the doorway, carrying a teakettle filled with boiling water. She stopped, mouth agape, shifting her disbelieving eyes back and forth between the two men.

Damn! thought Creed. Why'd she have to show up now?

"Did I hear him right?" chortled Sukey Ann at Creed. She looked at Peterson. "Did you say you *like* him? Did I hear that right?"

"As a matter of fact, you did," said Peterson boldly, his tears suddenly dried up.

Sukey Ann burst out laughing.

"You don't mean that," said Creed.

"Yes, I do," said Peterson.

"Sure, he does," said Sukey Ann. "Or should I say she?" She laughed all the more.

"Laugh if you will," said Peterson, "that doesn't change a thing. I'm still . . . very *fond* . . . of Mr. Creed." He swallowed hard and added, "Yes, I'm very fond of you, Mr. Creed."

"No, you're not, Mr. Peterson," said Creed.

"Yes, he is." Sukey Ann giggled. "Can't you tell?"

Creed lost his temper and threw the brush over her head intentionally. He jabbed a finger at her and said, "You stay out of this, Miss Rogers. This is not your business."

"All right, I'll keep quiet," said Sukey Ann, now frightened and serious about the moment.

"No, you will leave," said the Texan. "Pour that water into that bucket over there, then leave."

Sukey Ann snickered and said, "Are you sure you want to be left alone with him? I mean, what if he makes a—"

"Just pour the water in the bucket and get out, Miss Rogers," said Creed sternly.

"All right. If you say so." She poured the water into the bucket and left without saying another word.

Creed suspected that the girl hadn't gone far, that she was only outside the door eavesdropping, but he didn't want to take the time now to make her go farther away. He had to contend with Peterson first.

"Mr. Creed, I meant what I said."

"All right, you meant it, but that doesn't change a thing either. I'm not that kind, Mr. Peterson. I like girls. I've got a sweetheart back in Texas, and I'm gonna marry her because I love her."

"But she's in Texas," said Peterson, "and I'm right here and now." He took a step toward the Texan.

Creed aimed a finger at Peterson and said, "Don't come any closer, Mr. Peterson."

The bank teller backed away and said, "Haven't you ever had feelings for another man or another boy when you were growing up?"

"Sure, but not the kind of feelings you're talking about," said Creed. "I loved my father, my grandfathers, my brother, and even my best friend, Jess Tate. But I didn't love them like I love my sweetheart back in Texas or a girl I knew up in Kentucky during the war. I love my sister and my mother, too, but I don't love them in the same way that I love my sweetheart." He shook his finger at Peterson. "I don't love men that way, and I don't want any man to love me that way. Is that understood, Mr. Peterson?"

Peterson's head drooped as he said, "Yes, I understand." He heaved a sigh and added, "I'll leave you be, Mr. Creed."

Creed sighed with relief, but another thought came to mind. "You might think about leaving town, too. You can bet that Miss Rogers is gonna tell everybody around that you're a . . . a . . . a sissy boy, and once that gets around, you can bet your last dollar that the men of this town won't let you live here in peace."

"You're right," said Peterson. His aspect brightened, and he added, "You sound like you care about what happens to me. Do you?"

"Let's just say that I don't like seeing anybody get hurt, and we'll leave it at that. All right?"

Peterson sniffled and wiped his red eyes on his sleeve. Happier now, he said, "Sure, we'll leave it at that. Thank you for the advice. I suppose you're right. I'd better think about moving on from here. Maybe to some city."

"That's right," said Creed. "Why don't you try New Orleans? I ran into a few"—he cleared his throat—"fellows like you down there at the end of the war. You might feel better being around them."

"Yes, I think I would," said Peterson.

"Tell me something, would you please, Mr. Peterson?"

"Sure, anything."

"How long have been . . . like this?"

Peterson shrugged and said, "I don't know. Since I was a boy, I guess. Why do you ask?"

"I just thought you were taking all this a little easy, is all."

Peterson smiled and said, "You're not the first man to turn me away, but I have to admit that you've been the nicest about it. A couple of the others beat me, and one even threatened to kill me if I ever came near him again. That was over to Fort Smith. I haven't been back there since then."

"Good idea," said Creed. "It's best to stay away from men who would do you harm."

"Yes, you're so right." He offered to shake hands. "Well, thank you again, Mr. Creed."

Reluctantly, Creed accommodated him, and as soon as they released the grip, he said, "Now would you leave me alone to finish my chores here?"

"Sure," said Peterson, and he left.

Creed retrieved the brush that he'd thrown over Sukey Ann's head, but he didn't go back to brushing Nimbus. Instead, he took the saddle blanket, rubbed it with a bar of lye soap, then soaked it in the bucket of hot water to get the horse's sweat out of it.

Just as he went back to brushing the stallion, Sukey Ann came into the barn again.

"What do you want?" grumbled Creed.

"You shouldn't have been so nice to him," she said. "Now he thinks it's all right to be a sissy boy."

"That's his business," said Creed. "Not mine."

"But he said he liked you."

"And I told him that I don't care for men in that way."

"But you care for women in that way?"

"One woman," said Creed. "My sweetheart back in Texas."

"Yeah, I heard you tell him that," said Sukey Ann, "but would you say that to me if I was to tell you that I wouldn't mind it much if you was to take me up in that loft for a little tumble in the hay?"

"Yes, I'd say the same thing to you, Miss Rogers. I have a sweetheart waiting for me back in Texas. I promised her that we'd marry one day, and I promised her that I'd stay true to her."

"That's all well and good," said Sukey Ann, moving closer to the Texan, "but what she don't never find out won't never hurt her, will it?"

"That's just it," said Creed. "I'll know, and if I was to go back on my word, I wouldn't be able to look myself in the eye again."

"You got that much honor, Mr. Creed?"

"I like to think so." He stopped stroking the Appaloosa and stared hard at the girl. "Look, Miss Rogers. I think you're just teasing me and yourself about this. You no more want to climb that ladder with me than the man in the moon wants more green cheese."

"You're wrong about that, Mr. Creed," she cooed. "I really do want to go up that ladder with you."

"But we're not gonna do it."

"Well, maybe not now."

"Not now," said Creed. "Not ever. I told you already, Miss Rogers. I got a sweetheart back in Texas, and she's the only gal for me."

Sukey Ann shook her head slowly and said, " 'Tis a pity. I could have showed you a real good time in that loft."

"Maybe. Maybe not. Either way, we'll never find out, now will we?"

She shrugged and said, "I don't know about never. We'll just have to see, won't we?" And with that, she left him to finish his chores.

What a day! he thought. First Peterson, now her. Who's gonna be next? He sighed and returned to his work.

Creed rinsed the blanket several times to make certain that he washed all the lye from the material, then he hung it over the barnyard fence to dry. His last task was applying lanolin soap to the saddle to keep it soft and pliable for the next time that he needed it. He finished that chore just in time to clean up for supper.

Jennifer brought him a towel to dry his hands and face at the pump. "Did you know that Mr. Peterson is thinking about leaving Van Buren?" she said.

"I thought he might," said Creed, taking the towel and hanging it on the pump handle.

"We saw him come out to the barn after you. Did you say something to him to make him want to leave?"

"I told him he might be happier in a bigger city like New Orleans." He dipped a bucket of water from the trough, splashed some onto his face, lathered his hands, and washed his face. He rinsed the soap off his face and hands in the bucket, then dried off with the towel.

"Why did you tell him that?" she asked.

"About going to New Orleans?"

"Yes."

"Maybe you should ask Mr. Peterson that question."

"Does it have something to do with what Sukey Ann said yesterday down by the blacksmith shop? About Mr. Peterson being a sissy boy, I mean?"

Creed nodded and said, "Yes, that's it."

"Oh, I see."

"You shouldn't think harshly of Mr. Peterson, Miss Jennifer. He's just . . . different, I guess, for the lack of a better word."

"Well, I'm certainly glad you're not different like him," she said, eyes twinkling with adoration for the handsome Texan.

"That makes three of us, Miss Jennifer," said Creed.

"Three of us?" queried the girl.

"Sure. You, me, and my sweetheart back in Texas. Her name is Texada, and we're gonna be married one of these days." Seeing the downcast look on Jennifer's face, he thought to make it easier on her by saying, "You know, you remind me of her a little. Her hair's about the same color as yours, and she's got blue eyes, too, although Texada's have a little more violet in them than yours do. She's got freckles, too. Just a few, on her nose and below each eye. Her hair doesn't curl like yours. In fact, I don't think it ever had a curl to it. Not as long as I can recollect, anyway, and that covers a long time because I've known Texada since we were kids. You know, Miss Jennifer, I'm sure glad I met you."

Her eyes brightened as she said, "You are?"

Creed's head bobbed, and he said, "Yep. Knowing you has made missing Texada a little easier to bear. You know, I haven't seen her since last year. I've been away from home that long."

"Oh, that's so sad. A whole year?"

"A little more than that now."

"Oh, you poor man! And your sweetheart. She must miss you terribly."

"That's what she tells me in her letters."

"You write letters to each other? Oh, that's so romantic. Do you write often?"

"I try to."

"Oh, I wish I had someone to write to," said the girl dreamily.

"You do?"

"Oh, yes, I do."

Creed had a thought. "I think I know somebody who wouldn't mind writing to you."

"A man like you?"

"Well, he's not a man yet. He's just about your age, and he's already done some things that other boys can only dream about doing."

"What's his name?" she asked eagerly.

"His name is Elbie Doak, and he lives in the Chickasaw Nation with some friends of mine who run a mission at Cherokee Town."

"Oh, that sounds exciting. Tell me more about him."

"I've got a better idea. Why not let him tell you? After supper, I'll help you write a letter to him. How would that be?"

"That would be wonderful!"

I thought it might, Creed told himself.

13

The Court of the United States of America for the Western District of Arkansas opened for the fall term at 9:00 A.M., Monday, November 5, 1866, at the Crawford County Courthouse in Van Buren, Arkansas. Nearly a hundred men, all standing, crowded into the visitors section. Among them Slate Creed from Lavaca County, Texas, wearing the new outift that he purchased two days earlier.

The court crier banged a staff on the floor, announced the entrance of Judge Sangster, and instructed everyone to rise. Sangster took his place behind the bench and told everybody to be seated. "Court is now in session," said Sangster. He rapped his gavel on the bar to punctuate his statement. "Call the first case, Mr. Ogden."

John Ogden stood up at the prosecutor's table and said, "The United States of America versus Thomas Brown. The charge is treason. John B. Ogden appearing for the prosecution, Your Honor."

Two men rose from the defense table, and one said, "Benjamin Brown, appearing with the defendant, Your Honor."

"Read the charge, Mr. Ogden," said Sangster.

"Your Honor, the defense waives the reading of the charge," said Brown.

"Then how do you plead, Mr. Brown?" asked the judge.

"Your Honor," said the defense attorney, "my client has received a pardon from the President of the United States for his part in the recent conflict, and I would ask the court to dismiss the charge of treason without prejudice."

"What say you, Mr. Ogden?"

"The government is aware of Mr. Brown's pardon, Your Honor," said Ogden, "and it is willing to enter a *nolle prosequi* finding into the record and to allow the charge of treason to be dismissed without prejudice."

"Then so ordered," said Sangster. "Case dismissed." He banged the gavel. "Next case, Mr. Ogden."

94

Thomas Brown left the defense table, and another man took his place beside Ben Brown, the lawyer.

Ogden announced, "The United States of America versus Joel Foster. The charge is treason."

And so it went throughout the morning. Sangster called for the case; Ogden read the plaintiff, defendant, and charge; appearances were stated; the defense asked the court for dismissal because the defendant had a presidential pardon; and the prosecutor agreed to dismiss without prejudice. The process took less than three minutes per case, and by the time Sangster called for a dinner break at eleven-thirty, fifty-two former Confederates had the black cloud of treason removed from their pasts. The only break in the monotony of the simple procedures was an occasional change in defense attorneys. After Ben Brown came Hugh Thomason, then Buckmaster, who was followed by three more defense counsels who did exactly as each predecessor had. As each case was dismissed, the number of men in attendance diminished in kind.

Creed caught Ogden's eye at the recess and took the opportunity to speak to the prosecutor. "Are there many more of these cases?" asked the Texan.

"Just about every man in here today has one of these hanging over his head," said Ogden. "We have to deal with them one at a time."

"But every one of them has been dismissed. Why go to all the trouble of bringing them into court if that's all you're gonna do with them?"

"Two purposes, Mr. Creed. The first one is obvious. These men wish to remove the charge of treason from their lives for serving the Confederacy, and once the judge dismisses the charge the government can't come back at these men at a later date and charge them all over again. The second reason is the government will have a record by which it can determine who has been pardoned and who hasn't. This makes those men who haven't applied for their pardons hasten their efforts in that direction. Once everybody has been pardoned we can all put the war behind us once and for all time."

"I see," said Creed. Damn! he thought, I wish my problem was that easy to handle. "Will there be many more of these this afternoon? I mean, none of these cases are on the trial list posted outside."

"I suspect that we won't be getting to those trials until tomorrow morning at the earliest, Mr. Creed. I would hazard to guess that your acquaintance, Dick Barth, won't have his case heard until tomorrow afternoon at the earliest. Probably not until Wednesday morning."

"I see. The man testifying against him, Willie Vann, has he shown up yet?"

Ogden frowned and said, "No, not yet, and I'm beginning to get concerned about it. I can ask the court for one delay because the witness hasn't shown, but the defense will ask for a dismissal for the same reason, and Judge Sangster might have to throw out the case and set Barth free."

"I see," said Creed. "Well, I guess I'll come back tomorrow and see what happens."

"You do that, Mr. Creed," said Ogden.

As he descended the stairs from the courtroom, the Texan recognized Buckmaster's voice rising from the jailer's space in the basement. He would have ignored the lawyer and gone about his own business, but he heard Buckmaster mention a name: Rogers. Sukey Ann? wondered Creed. He paused at the main floor to listen.

" . . . to see Sinker Wilson this afternoon. How about you letting her in to see him? Out here where it don't smell so bad."

"I don't know, Mr. Buckmaster," said Blodgett.

"Here's a little something to make it worth your trouble, Jake."

"Well, thank you kindly, Mr. Buckmaster," said Blodgett. "I'll take care of the little lady when she comes by. You can count on it."

"Very good, Jake. I'll tell her to bring you some cake or something."

"That would be nice, Mr. Buckmaster. See you later."

Not wishing to be caught eavesdropping on the lawyer's conversation, Creed hurried down the hall to the marshal's office and ducked inside just as Buckmaster reached the middle landing. Lucky for Creed that the attorney was a short man and couldn't see down the corridor until he'd taken two steps up the next flight or Buckmaster's suspicions that the Texan had overheard his conversation with Blodgett might have been raised.

"Mr. Creed," said Marshal Hays, "how good to see you again, sir."

"It's good to see you, too, Marshal," said Creed.

"How are you doing at Mrs. Chapman's?" asked Hays. "I heard you had some trouble with that little squirt, Tom Buckmaster, your first night there."

"A little row over nothing really," said Creed.

Buckmaster entered the office. "Did I hear my name mentioned?" he asked, a Cheshire cat smile on his face.

"The marshal was just asking me about our . . . little dispute the other night," said Creed.

"Oh, that," said Buckmaster with surprising affability. "A mere flare of tempers over a point of law. Nothing to it really, Marshal. Right, Mr. Creed?"

"That's just what Mr. Creed was saying," said Hays.

"Precisely," said the attorney. "Over and forgotten as far as I'm concerned."

Although he didn't believe Buckmaster could be so forgiving and forgetting, Creed said, "Yes, of course, sir. It's a thing of the past."

"Yes, a thing of the past. I quite agree, sir." He pulled his watch from its pocket in his vest, popped the lid, and read the time aloud, "Eleven forty-four. We'd better hurry along, Mr. Creed, or we'll incur the wrath of our hostess. And let me tell you, that lady can be very unpleasant when she's cross."

"Yes, I suppose she can be." The Texan tipped his hat to Hays. "It was good seeing you again, Marshal. Until another time."

"Anytime, Mr. Creed. The door's always open."

Creed and Buckmaster walked back to the boardinghouse, arriving there just in time to hear Mrs. Chapman ring the dinner bell. They hurried into the dining room and took places opposite each other. Mrs. Nance and Mrs. Chapman joined them within a few minutes, but no others came; it was a school day, which meant Jennifer and Miss Steen would be having lunch in the classroom and the other gentlemen would be eating on their jobs.

After Mrs. Nance said grace, Sukey Ann served them hot cream of mushroom soup, bread, and cheese. When she entered the room with the food, she glanced at Creed with a sly smile and a wink that made him look away, hoping that neither Mrs. Chapman nor Mrs. Nance had noticed Sukey Ann's flirtation. To Buckmaster, she looked questioningly and received a slight nod in return, which put a Mona Lisa smile on her lips.

What are these two up to? wondered Creed. They must know each other. Am I the only one who sees it? He looked at Mrs. Chapman who appeared to be oblivious to anything clandestine beneath her roof. A check of Mrs. Nance's face revealed the same attitude. Neither woman appeared to have an inkling of anything suspicious between Buckmaster and Sukey Ann. Maybe I'm just crazy, he thought.

A few minutes into the meal the doorbell rang, and Mrs. Chapman sent Sukey Ann to answer it. The serving girl returned to the dining room in a minute. "There's a boy with a telegram for Mr. Creed," she said.

Creed wiped his mouth with the checked napkin and said, "Please excuse me, ladies?"

"Certainly, sir," said Mrs. Chapman.

The Texan left the table and went to the front door where he took the telegram from the messenger boy and gave him a dime for the service. He opened the envelope and read:

> Slate Creed
> Chapman Boardinghouse
> Van Buren, Arkansas
>   Message received. Do nothing. Will arrive Van Buren
> Wednesday P.M. steamboat La Belle. See you then.
> Burch
> Nashville, Tennessee

I wonder why he's coming here, thought Creed as he read the message a second time. Maybe he thinks he can do something to persuade Barth to testify in my behalf. Or if not persuade him, then maybe force him to do it by some other legal means. The Texan shrugged. I guess I'll just have to wait and see when he gets here. He folded the telegram, replaced it in the envelope, put it in an inside pocket of his coat, and returned to the dinner table.

Sukey Ann stood just behind the kitchen door, peering and listening through the crack to the conversation in the dining room.

"I hope it wasn't bad news, Mr. Creed," said the landlady.

"No, actually, it was good news," said Creed. "A friend of mine is coming here from Nashville. He'll be arriving Wednesday by steamboat."

"Is he a cattleman like you?" asked Mrs. Nance.

"No, ma'am, he's a lawyer."

"A lawyer, you say?" queried Buckmaster, his interest aroused.

"That's right," said Creed.

"From Nashville, you say?" asked Buckmaster, his curiosity growing.

"Yes, from Nashville."

"I've known a few attorneys in Nashville. What's his name?"

"You've probably never heard of him, but his name is John Burch."

Buckmaster swallowed hard, almost as if he were choking, and said, "Colonel . . . John . . . C. . . . Burch?"

"Yes, that's him," said the Texan, surprised by the diminutive lawyer's reaction. "Then you have heard of him?"

Buckmaster cleared his throat and said, "Only by reputation." A light sweat broke out on the attorney's forehead. He reached inside his coat for a handkerchief.

"He was a newspaperman before the war," said Creed, addressing the ladies, "but now he's an attorney. He served under General Nathan Bedford Forrest during the war."

This last fact delighted Mrs. Chapman. "A Southern officer and a gentleman, Mr. Creed?" she queried.

"One of the finest, ma'am. I didn't know Colonel Burch personally until after the war, but I had the honor of meeting him while I was a company commander under General Forrest."

"You served with Forrest?" asked Buckmaster, trying to hide his obvious agitation.

"Yes, sir, I did."

"Well, sir, I am impressed," said the attorney, now near to frothing with excitement.

"So am I," said Mrs. Chapman as she squirmed slightly in her seat. "Did you say you were a company commander, Mr. Creed?" she asked the question like a banker checking a prospective loan customer's assets.

"Yes, ma'am."

"Then you were a captain? Am I right?"

"Yes, ma'am."

"But I thought you were from Texas, Mr. Creed," said Buckmaster. "How did you come to serve as a company commander under Forrest being from Texas?"

"It's a long story, Mr. Buckmaster. Let me just say that I was captured at Shiloh, and by the time I could escape and find my way back to our lines, my outfit was no place to be found, so I joined the first one available, and that one was commanded by Colonel John Hunt Morgan. When Colonel Morgan was captured up north, my company managed to escape the Yankees, and we found our way back to Kentucky where we joined General Forrest's command."

"It sounds like you had some real adventures during the war," said Buckmaster.

"I wouldn't call them adventures, sir," said Creed. "I was just doing my duty."

"As a Southerner, of course," said Mrs. Chapman.

"No, ma'am. It was duty to my family." Seeing that she was a bit offended by his response, he added, "At first, I was excited about joining up because it was what everybody else I knew was doing. Then my grandfather explained that either my brother or me had to join the Confederate Army, while the other one stayed loyal to the Union. It was our duty to protect the family estate." Seeing that his listeners didn't quite understand, he elaborated, "You see, that's the way it's been done in our family for centuries. We're Scots, and whenever there was a rebellion against the English crown, one male member of the family always stayed loyal to the crown just in case the rebellion failed. That way, the family lands stayed in the family."

"So you joined the losing side," said Buckmaster, "and your brother stayed loyal to the Union?"

"That's right."

"So he kept the family lands?"

"He did until he was killed by outlaws last year down to Louisiana when we were trailing a herd of cattle to New Orleans. Now my sister and her husband own the old plantation."

"And you own nothing?" asked Buckmaster.

"I wouldn't put it exactly that way, sir. I have some cattle to my name, and I own part of my stepfather's ranch. I've also got an interest in another ranch and the herds running on it."

"I knew you were a man of means the first time I saw you, Mr. Creed," said Mrs. Chapman. "And a gentleman of the South as well." She squirmed again.

So did Sukey Ann behind the door. Handsome, manly, and a gentleman of means as well, she thought. I got to get closer to this man and see what else he has to offer a woman like me.

14

Creed returned to the courthouse with Buckmaster for the afternoon session of the federal court. Not that the Texan was interested in the proceedings, although he let on to Buckmaster that he was. Actually, he was only curious about the identity of the woman who would be coming to the jail to visit Sinker Wilson because he suspected that she would be Sukey Ann Rogers. Of course, he had no idea why Sukey Ann would be visiting Wilson, and he didn't really care. His interest was purely an exercise in deductive reasoning stimulated by the looks that Buckmaster and Sukey Ann had been exchanging ever since she showed up at Mrs. Chapman's boardinghouse.

The courtroom gallery was half as full in the afternoon as it was in the morning. That and the time were the only changes from the morning session. The court crier made the same announcement; Judge Sangster entered the room, sat down, and banged his gavel the same way; he ordered Ogden to call the first case of the post meridiem session; and the prosecutor called out the case with the only change being the name of the defendant. Even Ben Brown represented the first accused traitor. So it went through four cases, then Buckmaster replaced Brown as the defense attorney.

Creed edged his way to the rear of the courtroom when Buckmaster removed to the defense table. He stationed himself at the top of the stairs where he could look down the well and see anybody coming or going from the basement. He gave the appearance of being interested in the court's proceedings, only casually glancing down the stairs when someone used them. His vigilance finally paid off just as Buckmaster began his last case. He saw a skirt the same color as the one that Sukey Ann had been wearing when she served dinner at the boardinghouse. The Texan left his post and descended the stairs to the first floor. He was too late to catch a better look at the woman; she was already in the basement. Creed eased halfway down the first flight of steps and listened.

"Can I help you, miss?" asked Blodgett.

"Mr. Buckmaster sent me," said Sukey Ann. "He said you might like some cake."

"Why, thank you, miss," said Blodgett. "I'll just set it here on the table." A pause. "Now Mr. Buckmaster said something to me about you wanting to visit with Sinker Wilson."

"Yes, sir," said Sukey Ann. "He's my cousin, and I was just wanting to see if there might be anything I could do for him while he's here in jail."

Her cousin? wondered Creed. That would explain a few things, but not everything.

"Well, that's right kind of you, miss," said Blodgett. "You wait in there," he pointed to the caged room beneath the stairs, "and I'll fetch him for you."

Creed heard footsteps on the stairs above him. Thinking that it could be Buckmaster coming from the courtroom and not wishing to raise the lawyer's suspicions, the Texan hurried up to the main floor, climbed the first step to the second level, looked up, and saw Buckmaster coming toward him. He stopped, smiled, and said, "Finished already, Mr. Buckmaster?"

"Not a whole lot of lawyering to these cases," said the attorney, halting six steps above Creed and leaving him only a head higher than the taller man.

"No, I suppose not. Do you reckon that's the only kind of cases the court will be hearing this afternoon?"

"That's the only kind on the docket for today. The real cases begin tomorrow morning." He grinned. "I've got a few of them, starting with your friend Barth."

"Acquaintance," corrected the Texan. "I don't know Dick Barth all that well."

"Yes, of course. Well, I'm through here for today. Would you care to join me for a libation at one of the town's many fine saloons?"

"Thank you for the invitation, sir, but I have to decline at this time. I have other business to finish before taking any leisure."

"Yes, of course. Well then, I'll see you at Mrs. Chapman's for supper. Good afternoon, Mr. Creed." He took the last six steps to the first floor hall, marched down the corridor confidently, and left the building.

After making certain that Buckmaster was gone, Creed returned to his listening post on the first flight of stairs to the basement. Unable to overhear Sukey Ann's conversation with her cousin—their voices were too hushed—he descended a few more steps.

Still no success. He eased down to the middle landing. At last, he could hear them.

"Buckmaster says I ain't got much chance of getting off this time," said Wilson. "Says these Unionists running things now ain't gonna let the likes of me get away with nothing no more."

"I know, Sinker," said Sukey Ann. "That's why I brought you this."

A pause followed.

"Yeah, this oughta work," said Wilson. "Thanks, girl. I'm beholden to you."

"Don't use it lessen you have to, Sinker."

"Don't you worry none about that. I know what I gotta do here. You just go on back home now and leave the rest to me and Buckmaster. I'll be along soon enough. I won't be missing Christmas on the mountain. You can take that to Sunday meeting, girl. Now go on and git." The voice got louder. "Jake, we're all done here. You can let us out now."

Creed took his cue from Wilson and returned to the main floor. He looked up the stairs, wondering if he should return to the courtroom to stay out of Sukey Ann's sight or if he should try to exit the building before she came up from the basement. He opted for the stairs, taking them two at a time to the middle landing where he stopped to watch the first flight leading to the basement just to make certain that Sukey Ann had been the girl visiting Sinker Wilson in the jail. In the next minute, his assumption was confirmed as Sukey Ann emerged from the basement, peering cautiously in all directions except up. Just the same, Creed took no chances; he moved onto the second flight of stairs to the courtroom to be completely out of her sight. He waited a full two minutes before peeking around the corner and down the long hall toward the front door of the building. No sign of Sukey Ann. He heaved a sigh, descended the stairs to the main floor, and casually walked toward the exit.

Sukey Ann and Buckmaster know each other, thought Creed as he sauntered along Main Street, but they don't want anybody to know it. Why? Because she's Sinker Wilson's cousin? She gave him something. What was it? A gun? A knife? A club? Is Wilson planning to break out of jail? So what? Why do I care about him? My only concern here is Dick Barth. But Buckmaster is Barth's lawyer. Is that it? Yes, that's it. He wouldn't talk to me about Barth. Why not? Legal ethics? Could be. Could be more than that. Maybe I should discuss this with Marshal Hays and Mr.

Ogden. They might know more about what's going on here than I do, and if they don't, then maybe I can help them prevent a jailbreak by Wilson. Yes, I should go talk to the marshal and the prosecutor.

Creed did an about-face and hurried back to the courthouse. He took the steps two at a time, entered the building, and went straight to the marshal's office. Nobody there. He went up to the courtroom. Several men continued to wait to have their cases dismissed. Creed counted them. Thirty-one. He looked at the clock: 2:42. He estimated Ogden would be busy until at least four o'clock, probably four-thirty. What to do? Sit there and wait? Go downstairs to the marshal's office and wait for Hays to return? Go back to the boardinghouse and come back to the courthouse at four o'clock to see Ogden? Leave a message for Ogden with somebody? Leave a message for Hays in his office? Yes, that's it, he thought. Downstairs he went.

In the marshal's office, Creed found a pencil and paper on the lawman's desk. Carefully, he wrote:

Marshal Hays,
   I have reason to believe that one of your prisoners is planning a jailbreak with the help of his lawyer and a girl staying at Mrs. Chapman's boardinghouse. Please send me word that you have returned to your office, and I will come to meet you.

Regards,
Slate Creed

After proofing the note, Creed tucked it into the corner of the ink blotter and left the courthouse for his room at Mrs. Chapman's to await word from Hays.

As he walked up Main Street, Creed passed Watson's Apparel Shop and caught a glimpse of Buckmaster through the window. The lawyer smiled and waved at him. The Texan returned the gesture and continued walking toward the corner with Strokes Street. He turned east at the intersection and strolled the last two blocks to the boardinghouse where he found Mrs. Chapman sitting in her rocker on the porch with Sukey Ann standing in front of her telling her something very dramatic as well as very important judging from the look on the landlady's face.

" . . . so I'll be leaving in the morning," said Sukey Ann in conclusion.

"Well, this does come as a great surprise, Sukey Ann," said Mrs. Chapman. "I thought you wanted to earn enough money to feed your family for the winter."

"Yes'm, I did, but I did me some ciphering last night, and I come to the sum of things that I ain't gonna make nearly enough money to feed my folks working for my room and board and twenty-five cents a day."

Mrs. Chapman noticed Creed coming up the walk to the house. She nodded at him but continued to converse with Sukey Ann. "I told you that we'd find you another situation in town, Sukey Ann," she said. "You really should be patient until we've exhausted all possibilities."

The Texan saw the concern on Mrs. Chapman's face, and he stopped at the first step to listen.

"Yes'm, I know you said that, but I don't figure anybody else is gonna pay me any more than you would. So why should I waste my time here? I can get back to the mountain before we get any snow and help my brothers cord wood for selling down in the towns, and I'm gonna use the money you're paying me to buy them some powder and ball for their rifles so as they can hunt some deer and bear for meat and hides that we can sell in the towns, too. Maybe we can make a few dollars that way and get by till we can get a decent crop in the ground next spring. Anyways, that's what I'm thinking."

"Well, I can't say that I agree with your decision, Sukey Ann," said Mrs. Chapman, "but I won't stand in your way either. I'll have your pay for you right after breakfast in the morning."

"Thank you, ma'am. I'll go help Roberta with supper now." She curtsied politely and entered the house through the front door without acknowledging Creed behind her.

Creed stepped onto the porch and said, "I take it Sukey Ann is leaving."

"Yes, that's right," said Mrs. Chapman. "First thing tomorrow. I don't think she's doing the right thing, but it's her decision to make, not mine." She shook her head slowly. "These mountain folk. I don't understand them at all. They just don't fit in with city people, I guess."

Creed mused over the lady's implication that Van Buren was a city. Certainly for Arkansas, it was, but he'd been to New Orleans and Nashville. Now those were cities. Busy, noisy, teeming, never sleeping, growing constantly. Even Denver was larger than Van

Buren, but more than that, Denver had the cosmopolitan atmosphere of a city whereas Van Buren possessed the provincial flavor of its locality, which, to Creed's thinking, enhanced rather than diminished the river town's charm. Big was not necessarily better in his view.

"No, I guess not," said the Texan. "Mountain folk, you say, Mrs. Chapman? Is Bentonville up in the mountains?"

"No, it's up in Benton County on the other side of the mountain," she replied. "In fact, it's almost to Missouri. Benton County borders on Missouri to the north and the Cherokee Nation to the west. Between Benton County and the mountain is Washington County. Now that's not quite correct. The line between Washington County and Crawford County runs along the ridges of the mountain, so some of the mountain is in Crawford County and some in Washington. Does that answer your question, Mr. Creed?"

Not really, thought the Texan, but he smiled and said, "Yes, thank you, ma'am." He glanced at the door, then back at the landlady. "Mountain folk. Yes, I have to agree with you, Mrs. Chapman. They are a strange breed." And so are lawyers, he thought. A mountain girl and a lawyer in cahoots. Yeah, it figures.

15

Creed received no messages and no visitors the remainder of that day and night. In fact, he spent a quiet evening in Mrs. Chapman's library, reading the Bible, something he did whenever he felt the need to seek wisdom and guidance.

When he was much younger and both of his grandfathers lived at Glengarry Plantation, Creed would often turn to Grandfather Hawk McConnell, the old Choctaw warrior, for advice, and after Grandfather Hawk moved north to the Choctaw Nation, the Texan would seek out Grandfather Dougald Slater to help him deal with the ways of the world. On those few occasions when neither of the older men was available to him, he would ask his mother for guidance, and she would always tell him to "seek your answers in the word of the Lord, Cletus, and you'll find all the wisdom that you'll ever need." Being youthful, he would sigh with frustration, but he would follow his mother's advice and read his Bible.

On this occasion, Creed turned to the Proverbs of Solomon, that wise old king of Israel. Often he had found the solution to a puzzling problem hidden in this book of the Bible. As he read, two verses caught his attention: 12:20 "Deceit is in the heart of them that imagine evil; but to the counselors of peace is joy." And: 12:22 "Lying lips are abomination to the Lord; but they that deal truly are His delight."

The word "deceit" reverberated in his brain. Buckmaster and Sukey Ann. What deceit are they up to? he asked himself. And lying lips! Dick Barth and those other lying cowards. If not for them, I wouldn't be here wasting the best days of my life. I'd be home with Texada, raising cattle, horses, and children. I'd be happy and free and . . . The bile of anger spewed forth, rising to his throat, choking him to tears. "Damn them for what they've done to me!" he said softly through the mist clouding his vision. He wiped his eyes with the thumb and index finger of his right hand as Grandpa Hawk's words echoed in his head: "Never let your enemies see into your heart." He sniffled, swallowed hard, sighed, and set anew his resolve to find justice for himself.

The next morning at breakfast Mrs. Chapman made the formal announcement that Sukey Ann was leaving to return to her family on the mountain. Buckmaster took up a collection among the residents to buy the serving girl a ticket on the stagecoach to Jesse Branson's store in Natural Dam, the closest settlement to Sukey Ann's home in the Boston Mountains. He turned the money over to Mrs. Chapman, excused himself, then left for the courthouse. The other boarders departed to their daily posts of employment, leaving Creed with the landlady and Sukey Ann.

Mrs. Chapman cleared her throat and said, "Mr. Creed, I have other duties that demand my attention this morning. Could I possibly prevail upon you to escort Sukey Ann to the stagecoach depot at Mr. Brodie's hotel?"

"I'd be glad to do it," said Creed.

"I don't need no help getting on the stagecoach," said Sukey Ann. "I can take care of myself just fine."

"I'm sure you can, dear," said Mrs. Chapman, "but someone should see you off. It's the polite thing to do,"

"It is?" queried Sukey Ann.

"Yes, dear, it is."

"Well, in that case, I guess it'll be all right," said Sukey Ann, eyeing Creed. "I'll get my things."

"I still say she's making a mistake going back now," said Mrs. Chapman, looking after the girl, "but it's her decision." She turned to Creed and added, "Thank you, Mr. Creed. I'll feel much better about her leaving knowing that she got on the stagecoach safely."

"Yes, ma'am," said Creed. "Glad to help."

Sukey Ann returned carrying the burlap bag containing her few meager belongings. "I'm ready," she said. "Thank you for taking me in, Miz Chapman. The food was good, and the bed was warm and comfy. Bless your heart, ma'am."

"Thank you, Sukey Ann. May God go with you."

"Thank you, ma'am."

Creed offered to take the bag from Sukey Ann, but she refused to let it go. "I can carry my own stuff," she said defiantly.

"Now how would it look for a gentleman like Mr. Creed to let a young lady carry her own bag?" said Mrs. Chapman. "It just wouldn't be proper, Sukey Ann."

"I'm from the mountain, Miz Chapman," said the girl. "I ain't never put on airs before, and I ain't gonna start now. I'll carry my own bag."

"Suit yourself," said Creed. "It doesn't make any difference to me."

"Good-bye, Miz Chapman."

"Good-bye, Sukey Ann."

Creed tipped his hat to the landlady, then followed Sukey Ann out the front door and down the steps to the street. Without conversation, they walked along Strokes Street to Main, turned south, and continued on to the Brodie Hotel. The stagecoach office was located next door to the hostelry. Creed took Sukey Ann inside and helped her buy a ticket on the stagecoach that would be arriving from Fort Smith within the hour and would be leaving as soon as the passengers and freight were loaded. The fare didn't cost as much as Buckmaster collected for it, so Creed told her to keep the difference: a dollar and thirty cents. Sukey Ann didn't argue the point. She sat down on the bench out in front of the depot to wait, and the Texan decided to join her.

"There's no need for you to wait around with me," she said. "I can get on the stagecoach just fine by myself."

"I'm sure you can," said Creed, "but I gave my word to Mrs. Chapman that I'd see you off."

"Well, you've done that. Now you can just go on about your own business."

"Until you're on that stagecoach, you are my business, Miss Rogers."

"Suit yourself. It's your time you're wasting. Not mine."

As they waited, Creed entertained thoughts of asking Sukey Ann about her relationships with Buckmaster and Sinker Wilson, but he made no inquiries of that nature, figuring she wouldn't give him any straight answers. Besides, what business was it of his? Hadn't he already left a note for the marshal saying that he suspected Buckmaster and Sukey Ann might be helping Wilson to break out of jail? And what about that? Sukey Ann was leaving town now. Why? To be out of harm's way if anything should go awry? Probably. Just put her on the stagecoach, then put her out of your mind, he told himself.

The Concord coach of the Fort Smith & Fayetteville Stagecoach Line crossed the river on the ferry, debarked at the landing, rattled up the foot of Main Street, and came around the corner to stop in front of the hotel.

Sukey Ann and Creed stood up and walked over to the coach. The backup driver jumped down and opened the door. Two male passengers climbed out and stepped down to the boardwalk. The

first driver threw down carpetbag valises to the men who picked
them up and entered the hotel. The express agent came out of
his office and called out for passengers to board the coach now.
Nobody except Sukey Ann came forward. The backup driver
checked her ticket, then without warning he grabbed her bag
from her hands and threw it up to the first driver.

"Oof!" grunted the first driver. He glared down at Sukey Ann.
"What have you got in here, miss? An anvil?" He squeezed the
burlap sack. "Feels like a horse pistol."

Sukey Ann pinched up her face and snapped, "Of course it's
a gun, you damn fool! You don't think I'd go anywhere without
something to protect myself, do you?"

"Who you calling a damn fool, girl?"

"You, you old fart." She held out her hand. "Now give me back
my bag. If I'd wanted it to ride up there, I would have climbed up
there with it."

The first driver threw it back to her.

She caught it, turned to Creed, and said, "If you ever come up
the mountain, handsome, come by our place and I'll cook you
up some possum and black-eyed peas." She nudged him with
an elbow. "And bring that horse of yours. I'd still like to ride
him." She smiled and winked, then turned and climbed into the
Concord. Once she was situated in the seat and the door was
closed behind her, she leaned out the window and said, "Our
place is up to Cat Hollow. Just ask anybody up that way for the
Rogers's farm. They'll tell you where to find us. Just remember
Cat Hollow."

The backup driver closed the coach door and climbed up to the
driver's seat. The first driver snapped the reins over the team,
and the coach lurched forward. A few seconds later the Concord
turned the corner on Washington Street and headed toward the
mountain.

Cat Hollow, thought Creed. It figures that she'd be from a place
with a name like that.

16

As the dust stirred up by the departing coach settled on the street again, Creed sauntered over to the courthouse with the intent of calling on Marshal Hays before attending the morning session of the court. He entered the county building, turned aside to the marshal's office, but soon discovered it to be vacant and the note that he'd left the day before to be absent. He must have gotten it, thought Creed. That puts the matter in his hands now. Might as well go watch the proceedings in the courtroom.

Hays was sitting in a chair behind the prosecutor's table when Creed entered the gallery. The Texan removed his hat, thought about approaching the lawman to ask about the note, but didn't because his attention was drawn elsewhere. He spied a familiar face from his recent past.

It belonged to William Vann, the freedman that Creed had met in the Cherokee Nation that spring. A tall man, a little taller than Creed, Vann was muscular, although he was narrow at the hips and shoulders. He had a broad, prominent nose set between fairly high cheekbones. His strong jaw distracted the onlooker from his thick lips. From the deep, dark chocolate tone of his complexion and the rich, chestnut color of his eyes, Creed guessed correctly that this ex-slave had no whites or Indians in his ancestry, that Vann was a true son of Africa.

Vann and another former slave stood in the rear of the courtroom observing the legal proceedings. Neither noticed Creed until the Texan sidled up to them, but even then, the two farmers paid him no mind.

"Mr. Vann?" whispered Creed.

Vann shuddered with a start at the mention of his name. His eyes showed fear as they shifted in Creed's direction, failing to recognize the Texan immediately. "Does I know you, sir?" he asked softly.

"Yes, sir, you do," said Creed.

Vann stared hard at the Texan for a second, then his memory came to the fore. "Mr. Creed?" he queried.

111

"I'm pleased that you remember me, Mr. Vann," said Creed, smiling and offering to shake hands with the freedman.

Vann flashed a great grin and accepted Creed's greeting, shaking the Texan's hand vigorously. With his free elbow, he nudged his friend and whispered, "Lije, lookey here. It's Mr. Creed. The Mr. Creed I told you about last spring. Had that Choctaw boy with him. Little Bee Doak. Remember?"

"Sure, I remembers," whispered Vann's companion.

"Mr. Creed, this here is Lije Rider," said Vann softly.

Creed extended his hand to Rider and said, "How do you do, Mr. Rider?"

Having been born and raised a slave on the plantation of a mixed-blood Cherokee family, Rider was unaccustomed to being treated with voluntary respect by men of non-African ancestry; therefore, he hesitated to shake hands with Creed. Tall, muscular, thin at the waist, broad at the shoulders; wide, flat nose; almond eyes; coffee complexion; Rider, like Vann, seemed to have no Europeans or Indians in his ancestry.

"Go ahead, Lije," said Vann. "Mr. Creed ain't like other men. He don't see the color of your skin."

"It's all right," said Creed. "If I was a freedman, I wouldn't trust anybody that looked like me either."

"No, sir," said Vann. "That ain't right, Lije. I done told you Mr. Creed is different. Now go on and shake the man's hand."

"I meant no offense, Mr. Creed," said Lije as he took Creed's hand and shook it.

"None taken, Mr. Rider."

"You can call me Lije, Mr. Creed."

"I will if you'll call me Slate."

Rider smiled for the first time and said, "Yes, sir, Mr. Slate."

Creed shook his head and said, "No, not Mr. Slate. Just Slate. And I don't have to be called sir either."

"If you's gonna call him Lije," said Vann, "then you best start calling me Willie."

"Only if you call me Slate."

Vann grinned and said, "It's a bargain, Slate."

Judge Sangster banged his gavel extra loud to silence everybody in the room. "You coloreds back there," he said, aiming the hammer at Vann and Rider. "Hold it down, or I'll have the bailiff remove you from my courtroom." He shifted his view to the Texan. "Good morning, Mr. Creed. I didn't see you come in."

"Good morning, Your Honor," said the Texan. "My apologies, sir, but I am the cause of the disturbance. I was renewing an old acquaintance."

"Well, that's fine, Mr. Creed," said Sangster, "but would you mind doing it outside my courtroom?"

"Certainly, Your Honor," said Creed. He nodded his acquiescence to the bench, then motioned with his head for Vann and Rider to follow him downstairs.

A murmur of surprised voices accompanied the two freedmen and Creed as they descended the stairs to the first floor hallway. They stopped a few feet from the stairway.

"What is you doing here, Slate?" asked Vann. "What happened to Little Bee? Did you find his Uncle Hum?"

Creed smiled and waved a hand to halt Vann from asking any more questions. "First off," he said, "it's a small world we live in, Willie. It seems that Dick Barth, the man who shot your horse and pistol-whipped you, is a man that I know and—"

Vann frowned and interrupted Creed, saying, "You ain't come to testify for him, is you, Slate?"

Creed shook his head and said, "No, nothing like that, As I was about to say, Dick Barth has caused me some grief as well."

"He has?" queried Vann,

"He sure has," said Creed, Over the next few minutes, the Texan explained how Barth, Marshall Quade, Dick Spencer, Jack Blackburn, Jasper Johnson, and Jonas Burr took part in a raid on a military supply column after receiving their paroles in New Orleans and how, after being caught a few months later, they swore that he had been their leader and for that he had been convicted of their crime and sentenced to hang for it. "I escaped before they could hang me," he said, "and ever since, I've been looking for those men to make them tell the truth so I can get my name cleared and go about my life. I found one of them, Marsh Quade, and he confessed that I didn't have anything to do with that raid. But he was killed before we could return to Texas. I did get him to sign a confession, though. Just the same, his confession isn't any good without a living witness to say the same thing. So when I heard that Barth was here in jail, I came to see if I couldn't do something to get him to testify on my behalf and help me clear my name."

"Have you talked to him?" asked Vann.

"Yes, I have, and he says he won't help me. For the life of me, I don't know how I could make him help me. My lawyer is arriving here tomorrow. Maybe he'll have an idea of what can be done to make Barth confess the truth."

"You ain't expecting me to drop my case against Barth, is you, Slate?" asked Vann. "Because if you is, well, I don't think I can let him off. Not without him paying me for that horse he killed."

"That white trash bastard need to go to jail for what he done to you, Willie," said Rider.

"I agree," said Creed. "Barth needs to be put in jail for what he did to you and for what he did to me."

Vann smiled and said, "I's glad to hear you say that, Slate. I sure do want to make that white trash bastard pay for what he did to me." As an afterthought, he added, "And for what he did to you, too."

"Well, I'm glad to hear you say that, Willie, because a thought just occurred to me. Maybe you could hold off testifying against Barth until my lawyer arrives here and we have a chance to discuss matters with him. Colonel Burch might be able to talk some sense into Barth and get him to tell the truth about that business down in Mississippi. I think he'd have a better chance of that before Barth goes to trial."

"I sees what you're thinking, Slate. Sure, I could put off testifying, but I don't think that's up to me to decide."

"No, I don't think so either. I think we have to go talk to Mr. Ogden about that."

"Then we best get to it," said Vann.

"Yes, of course," said Creed, "but we can't tell him why I want the case held up."

"We can't?" queried Vann.

"Mr. Ogden might not be as understanding as you are, Willie. After all, he is a federal prosecutor."

17

Judge Sangster called for a short recess at half past ten so he could make a visit to the privy. This gave Creed and Vann the chance to talk to Ogden about a postponement for Barth's trial. They spoke to him at the prosecutor's table.

"I'm not sure I understand why you want this delay," said Ogden. "I thought Barth was only an acquaintance of yours, Mr. Creed."

"He is," said Creed, "but my attorney is arriving here tomorrow, and I would like him to confer with Barth before he goes to trial. So I was hoping you might reschedule his trial for Thursday."

"Have you spoken to Mr. Buckmaster about this?" asked Ogden. "He is Barth's attorney, you know."

"Yes, I know," said Creed, "but to answer your question, no, I haven't spoken to him about putting off Barth's trial. Should I?"

"Well, he may not wish to delay the trial," said Ogden, "and Barth is his client. I think it would only be appropriate that you speak with him first before having your attorney talk to Barth."

"Yes, of course," said Creed. "But if Mr. Buckmaster is agreeable to a delay, does that mean you'll go along with it?"

"It makes no difference to me what order the cases fall," said the prosecutor, "as long as delaying a trial doesn't jeopardize a conviction."

"Don't worry, sir," said Vann. "Me and Lije will be right here to testify on Thursday. We ain't going nowheres till we has our say in court."

"Very good," said Ogden. "Go ahead, Mr. Creed. Ask Buckmaster for a postponement, and if he agrees, I'll rearrange the schedule so that Barth goes to trial on Thursday."

Creed turned to Vann and Rider and said, "I'll speak with Buckmaster about putting off Barth's trial."

"We'll come with you, Slate," said Vann.

"That's not a good idea," said Creed. "Buckmaster is still living in the past, if you know what I mean."

"You mean he don't cotton to freedmen?" said Vann.

"That's about the size of it, Willie," said Creed.

"Then you best speak to him alone," said Vann. "I might wants to say something to him that would spoil things if I was along. Lije and me will wait here for you, Slate."

"Good enough," said Creed. He patted Vann on the shoulder. "I'll be back soon, my friend."

Creed hurried downstairs to the lawyers' room and found the door closed. Hearing voices within, he knocked on the frame, silencing the conversation inside. He heard footsteps, then the door opened. He recognized the man before him as Benjamin Brown, one of the county's more prominent attorneys.

"May I help you, sir?" asked Brown.

"I'm looking for Mr. Thomas Buckmaster," said Creed. "Would he be in there?"

"Who wants to know?" asked Brown.

Buckmaster recognized Creed's voice. "It's all right, Ben," he said. "I know Mr. Creed personally. You can let him in."

Creed looked beyond Brown to Buckmaster who was sitting at a long table strewn with law books. Making eye contact with the diminutive lawyer, he said, "I'd like to speak to you in private, Mr. Buckmaster, if I could."

"Certainly, Mr. Creed," said Buckmaster. He stood up, slipped by Brown into the hall, and closed the door behind him. "What can I do for you, Mr. Creed?" he asked pleasantly.

"It's about Dick Barth, Mr. Buckmaster," said the Texan. "As you already know, my attorney, Colonel John Burch, is arriving in town tomorrow, and I'd like him to speak with Barth before he goes to trial."

"That won't be possible if Barth goes to trial this afternoon," said Buckmaster.

"Yes, I know. So I'm wondering if you wouldn't mind a postponement until Thursday."

"A postponement?"

"Yes, sir. I've already talked to Mr. Ogden about it, and he's agreed to change the trial schedule if you'll agree to it, too."

Buckmaster folded his right arm across his stomach, pinched his lower lip between the index finger and thumb of his left hand, stared off at nothing in particular, and hummed softly as he gave Creed's request some thought before answering. "A postponement," he muttered. "Hmm." He released his lip, smiled, and said, "I don't see that it would harm anything. But why do you want Colonel Burch to talk to Barth before he goes to trial?

You aren't trying to get Barth to change lawyers, are you?"

"No, sir, nothing like that. It has to do with a matter back home."

"Would you mind elaborating on that, Mr. Creed?"

"Yes, I would mind, but if I don't tell you, you'll just ask Barth about it, and although he won't tell you willingly, I know that you're clever enough to get it out of him anyway. So I guess I'll have to tell you." As succinctly as he could, the Texan repeated most of the tale that he had told so often in the last year. "So now you know why I want Colonel Burch to talk to Barth before he goes to trial. With any luck, he'll get Barth to agree to tell the truth, and Clete Slater can stop running from the law."

"You must think an awful lot of this Slater to go to such lengths for him," said the attorney.

Creed smiled, looked the lawyer straight in the eye, and said evenly, "You're right about that, Mr. Buckmaster. Me and Clete Slater? It's almost as if we were the same man with two different names."

"No doubt, no doubt. All right, Mr. Creed. I'll agree to a postponement, but rescheduling for Thursday won't work for me. Ogden will have to make it a week from this coming Friday."

"A week from this coming Friday?"

"Yes, I'm too busy between now and then. Tell him next Friday or not at all."

"I'll do it right now. The judge called a recess, and he might not be back yet."

"No, wait," said Buckmaster. "I'll tell him myself." He noted the displeasure on Creed's face. "Come along if you like. It's not that I distrust you, Mr. Creed. It's just that I know John Ogden. He'll believe me before he believes you."

"Fair enough," said the Texan. "Lead the way."

Creed followed Buckmaster up the stairs to the courtroom. The judge was still absent, but Ogden was present. As they passed Vann and Rider who were again standing in the rear of the gallery, the Texan winked at them to indicate that all was going well.

"So you found him," said Ogden, looking at Buckmaster first, then Creed. Looking back at the shorter man, he asked, "Did you agree to the postponement, Buckmaster?"

"Yes, on one condition."

"And that is?"

"That you reschedule for Friday next week instead of Thursday this week. My case load is too big to squeeze Barth into Thursday."

"That's not a problem for me, Buckmaster. How about you, Mr. Creed? Is Friday next week all right with you?"

"It suits me fine, Mr. Ogden."

"But how about your friends back there?" asked Ogden, nodding toward Vann and Rider. "How does it suit them? Do they have enough money to stay in Van Buren until then?"

"I don't know," said Creed, looking at Vann and Rider who were watching him closely. "I hadn't thought about that."

I did, thought Buckmaster as he glared at the two freedmen. He remained silent on that subject, but he did say, "Well, that's the way it has to be, Ogden. Friday next week or as originally scheduled. Let me know which way the acorn falls. I'll be downstairs in the law library until my first case comes up."

"I'll send you word," said Ogden as Buckmaster left them.

Before Creed and Ogden could discuss the matter further, the court crier entered the room and announced the return of Judge Sangster.

"I'll have to talk to you later, Mr. Creed," said Ogden quickly. "See me at the next recess."

Creed waited for the judge to be seated and to call the court to order again before he wandered to the rear of the room and motioned with his head for Vann and Rider to follow him downstairs. They didn't speak until they were in the first floor hall, and then Creed said, "Ogden and Buckmaster agreed to postpone Barth's trial, but instead of Thursday, Buckmaster wants it set for Friday next week."

"Friday next week?" queried Vann. "That's more than a whole week away, Slate. We can't be away from our families that long."

"That's right," said Rider. "We can't be away from our families that long, Slate."

Creed studied their faces. They were lying, and he knew it, and he knew why. They don't have the money to stay here that long, he thought, and they're too proud to admit it. How do I let them know that I know their real reason for being unable to remain in Van Buren that long without insulting them? Damn! What do I say to make them stay until Friday next week?

"If you go," said Creed, "Barth will get off free."

"We can't let that happen, Slate," said Vann, "so I guess there won't be no putting off Barth's trial." Seeing disappointment in

Creed's eyes, he added, "We sure is sorry about this, Slate."

"No, it's all right," said Creed. He looked at the floor dejected by this unanticipated turn.

"You see," said Vann, "it's like this, Slate. I needs to get something from the court for the horse that Barth done killed, and if we don't testify against him and he gets off, I ain't gonna get nothing for that horse."

An idea struck Creed. "I'll buy that horse from you," he said quickly.

Rider laughed and said, "You can't buy no dead horse, Slate, but if you's set on doing it, I got a dead cow for sale." He laughed again.

Vann wasn't laughing. He understood what Creed was trying to do here. "I paid seventy-five dollars for that horse," he said. "Mr. Ogden said the judge would order Barth's horse and belongings sold to pay his court costs and fine, and he'd give me whatever was left over up to that much to pay for my horse. Mr. Ogden also said it ain't too likely that there's gonna be much left over for me."

"Then I'll buy that dead horse for seventy-five dollars," said Creed, "and . . . your promise that you'll stay here and testify against Barth next week."

"That sounds real good for me, Slate," said Vann, "but Lije here needs to be testifying with me. Mr. Ogden said so. Especially if that other white trash cowboy comes to testify for Barth."

"Other cowboy?" queried Creed.

"That's right," said Rider. "The other one. The one called Johnson. Mr. Ogden said he might come to testify for Barth, and if he do, then the judge might not believe us because we's colored and they's white and . . ."

Creed didn't hear much more of what Rider was saying. Only one thought occupied his mind: Jasper Johnson might show up in Van Buren to testify for Barth. Now wouldn't that be perfect? he thought.

18

Creed bought Rider's deceased cow for twenty-five dollars as well as Vann's dead horse for seventy-five dollars, and both freedmen swore on their mothers' gray hair that they'd stick around Van Buren until Dick Barth could be tried for his crime.

With that business out of the way, the Texan sat back and watched the court proceedings, the trial of a petty thief who was caught stealing chickens and a breeder sow from an Indian in the Choctaw Nation. The jury came back within ten minutes with a guilty verdict. The judge fined the convicted thief twenty-five dollars for the stolen and eaten animals, the money to be paid to the Indian farmer, and sentenced the thief to thirty days in jail which he'd already served while awaiting trial.

At the noon recess, Creed sought out Ogden and told him that Vann and Rider would be available to testify on Friday next week.

"Fine," said Ogden. "I'll reschedule Barth's trial on that day."

Creed thanked him, then he told Vann and Rider that everything was set.

Now to find out if Jasper Johnson is coming to town, thought the Texan.

Creed went downstairs to see Marshal Hays in his office, but once again, he found the room vacant. Where could he be now? he thought, The answer to his question came to him almost as soon as he asked it. "The best fried catfish in town," he said with a smile. He left the courthouse and hurried over to the Brodie Hotel where he found Hays just sitting down at the last vacant table in the crowded restaurant. "Mind if I join you, Marshal?" asked the Texan.

"Not at all, Mr. Creed," said Hays. "I'm expecting Judge Sangster and John Ogden, but you don't mind eating with them, do you?"

"It's an honor to be in such company, Marshal," said Creed as he slid a chair from beneath the table and sat down.

"Tell me, sir," said Hays, "how are you finding your stay in

120

Van Buren? I trust your accommodations at Mrs. Chapman's are suitable."

"Very comfortable. Good bed and excellent food. I should be there now eating lunch, but I wanted to speak to you."

"Oh? Something pressing?"

"Well, it's not as important as what I wrote in my note, I suppose," said Creed.

"Note?"

The Texan peered quizzically at Hays and said, "Yes, sir. I left a message on your desk yesterday while you were out of your office."

Hays shook his head slowly and said, "I don't believe I saw a note from you on my desk when I came into my office this morning. What did it say?"

Before Creed could reply, Sangster and Ogden entered the dining room. They came straight to the table and exchanged pleasantries with the Texan before being seated.

"Mr. Creed was just telling me that he left a note on my desk yesterday," said Hays, "but I didn't find any note when I came in this morning."

"Is that right?" asked Ogden.

"You don't think it might have been blown off your desk by a sudden draft, do you?" asked Sangster.

"The disappearance of the note isn't the primary concern here, Judge," said Hays. "Mr. Creed was just about to tell me what he wrote in the message when you came in."

"Yes, of course," said Sangster. "The content of the note. What did it say, Mr. Creed?"

Creed was incredulous. Lawyers, he thought. The first dog to chase his own tail must have been owned by a man in the legal profession. He didn't express the sentiment, but he did say, "I'm not sure I can say in front of you, Judge."

"Oh? And why not?" asked Sangster. "Does it involve a defendant in an upcoming case in the federal court?"

"Yes, sir, it does," said Creed.

"Then you're right, sir. I shouldn't hear this."

Ellen Brodie came up to the table. "Good afternoon, gentlemen," she said. "How are things going in court, Judge?"

"Moving right along, Ellen," said Sangster.

"Well, don't move them along too fast," she said, "or all these folks who came to town for that murder trial might leave before they get a chance to spend their money here."

"I'll keep that in mind," said Sangster.

"What's on the menu for today?" asked Ogden.

"Besides catching a whole parcel of catfish," said Ellen, "Rafe butchered a hog this morning, so we got pork chops frying in the skillet."

Each man ordered the chops, corn bread, black-eyed peas, and coffee, and the waitress left them alone again.

"Back to this note of yours, Mr. Creed," said Hays. "Is it urgent that I should know what was in it?"

"Well, it was yesterday, Marshal," said the Texan, "but today I'm not so sure. In fact, I could be way out on a limb with what I wrote."

"Why don't you let me decide that?" asked Hays.

"All right, I will," said Creed. "Should we step outside for a minute?"

"That would be a good idea," said Sangster. "Go ahead, Sam. You might go, too, John, since it concerns one of your cases."

Creed, Hays, and Ogden left the table and went out to the lobby.

"On the day that you took me over to Mrs. Chapman's," said Creed, "a girl from the mountains came to work for Mrs. Chapman. Her name is Sukey Ann Rogers. She said she's from a place called Cat Hollow."

"I know it," said Hays. "It's just this side of the ridge from Devil's Den. It's not exactly a good neighborhood. Most of the folks up that way make their living hunting, trapping, and stealing. Sinker Wilson is from up that way."

"So I guessed," said Creed.

"Does Wilson have something to do with this girl?" asked Hays.

"She told your jailer that she's his cousin," said Creed.

"She told Jake that?" queried Hays. "Why would she—"

"Let me start from the beginning again," interrupted Creed. "Sukey Ann Rogers came to town last Friday and went to work for Mrs. Chapman. At the first meal, I noticed that she and Mr. Buckmaster seemed to—"

"Buckmaster?" interjected Ogden.

"Let him finish, John," said Hays. "Go ahead, Mr. Creed."

The Texan sighed, then continued. "They seemed to be avoiding looking at each other. This went on at every meal. She'd come into the room and look at everybody except Mr. Buckmaster. Then yesterday morning I happened to overhear a conversation between your jailer and Mr. Buckmaster in which he asked the jailer to let a girl in to see Sinker Wilson. I can't say for sure, but I think he paid him some money to let her in. Anyway, I thought this was curious, so I hung around the stairway yesterday afternoon until she came in to see her cousin. I listened to her and Wilson talk in that little visitors' room, and I think she gave him a gun so he can break out of jail."

"You think she gave him a gun?" queried Hays.

"Well, I was sure she gave him a gun at the time, but this morning when I saw her off on the stagecoach—"

"You mean she's left town already?" interrupted Ogden.

"Let him finish, John," said Hays.

"Yes, sir. This morning. I put her on the stagecoach for a place called Natural Dam."

"That's up near Cat Hollow," said Hays.

"Well," said Creed, "she wouldn't let me carry her bag to the depot for her, which I thought was strange; she insisted on carrying it herself. Then while she was getting on the coach, the driver took her bag from her when she wasn't looking, and he complained about how heavy it was. He felt it and said he thought she had a gun in it. She said she did have a gun in it, so now I'm not so sure that she gave Wilson a gun."

"Well, there's only one way to find out for sure," said Hays. "I'm gonna search his cell. Right after lunch. Thank you for this information, Mr. Creed."

"There may be nothing to it, Marshal," said Creed.

"Maybe not," said Hays, "but I'd rather be safe than sorry, if you know what I mean."

"I know exactly what you mean."

"Good. Let's go eat. I see that Ellen brought our meals already."

They returned to the dining room.

"Well, Sam," said Sangster, "was Mr. Creed's note important or not?"

"One of my prisoners might be thinking about breaking out of jail," said Hays.

Sangster laughed and said, "Hell, Sam, they're all thinking about breaking out of jail. What else have prisoners got to think about?"

"This one might have gotten some outside help already," said Hays seriously.

"Then that's a different matter," said Sangster. "What are you gonna do about it?"

"I'm gonna eat my lunch, then I'm gonna go search my jail for a gun."

Sangster looked at Creed, then Ogden, then Hays, but he said nothing.

"It's possible that I could be wrong about this," said Creed.

"Then again, you might be right," said Hays. "We'll just have to see."

"That's right," said Ogden.

They ate their lunch quietly until Creed recalled his initial reason for being there. "Marshal, I came over here to ask you about the other man that was with Dick Barth in the Cherokee Nation," he said.

"The other man?" queried Hays.

"Yes, sir. Jasper Johnson."

"Oh, yes, that fellow. What about him?"

"Well, I was talking with Mr. Vann and Mr. Rider, and they thought Johnson might be coming here to testify for Barth, I was wondering if you might know anything about that."

"No, I don't. Like I said the other day, Johnson came along and saved Barth's butt from Vann and Rider, then they rejoined their cattle drive. My deputy arrested Barth, but he didn't bother with Johnson because Vann and Rider said he didn't have nothing to do with killing Vann's horse and pistol-whipping Vann. As far as I know, Johnson stayed on with the cattle drovers. Leastways, he hasn't come around here to see Barth, and I haven't had any inquiries about Barth from him. How about you, John? Anybody ask you about Barth except Mr. Creed here?"

"Nobody," said Ogden, "except Buckmaster, and he should because he's Barth's lawyer."

"That's right," said Hays.

"Gentlemen," said Sangster, "this conversation is getting into territory that I shouldn't be visiting right now."

"You're right, Judge," said Ogden.

"I can't help you any more than that, Mr. Creed," said Hays. "I haven't heard or seen anything that might connect to this Johnson fellow, but if I do, I'll be sure to let you know about it."

"Same here," said Ogden.

"Thank you, gentlemen," said Creed.

They finished their meal in silence, then Sangster returned to the courthouse alone. Ogden, Hays, and Creed held another short conference on the steps of the hotel.

"I didn't want to say anything about Buckmaster in front of the judge," said Hays, "but if he's been bribing my jailer, I'd sure like something done about that, John."

"Don't you worry," said Ogden. "If Buckmaster's been tampering with your jailer, I'll see that he gets what he's got coming to him."

"Good," said Hays. "Mr. Creed, would you care to come along to the jail with me for the search?"

"Do you think that would be wise, Marshal?"

Hays twisted his mouth in thought, then said, "No, I guess not. I wouldn't want Jake to know it was you who told me about this, especially if nothing comes of it. And it sure wouldn't do for Buckmaster to find out about it. That little bastard can be real mean when he wants to be."

"He's a very dangerous adversary," said Ogden.

So's a rattlesnake, thought Creed.

19

The marshal's search of Wilson's cell turned up nothing; no gun, no knife, not even a spoon for digging in the dirt floor. When Hays questioned the prisoner about his visitor, Wilson admitted that Sukey Ann Rogers was his cousin and that she gave him some cake, just the same as she gave Jake Blodgett, the jailer.

Blodgett supported Wilson's statement. "The only things to pass between Wilson and the girl were words and a piece of that delicious cake."

For some reason, Hays didn't believe Wilson, but he had no way of proving otherwise. As for Blodgett's veracity, the marshal figured Sukey Ann could have passed a howitzer to Wilson and the jailer wouldn't have seen it. The lawman had no choice except to let the matter drop—for the moment. But just to make sure that he didn't miss anything, Hays moved Wilson into Dick Barth's cell, which didn't please either inmate— at first.

"I'm sorry I sent you on a wild-goose chase," said Creed in the marshal's office after Hays told him about finding nothing.

"I might not have found anything," said Hays, "but I don't think it was a wild-goose chase. Wilson's up to something, but now he knows we're on to him. You can bet on that. The girl probably gave him something besides cake, but for the life of me, I can't figure out what it might have been."

"All I know is she said she thought he could use it to help him get out of there," said Creed, "and he thanked her for it. Then she warned him not to use it unless he had to. Now that sounded like a gun to me."

"Me, too," said Hays, "but . . . he didn't have one. Leastways, not that I could find. But I won't worry about it now. I put him in another cell. If he hid the gun in his cell, he won't be able to get to it now." He patted the Texan on the shoulder. "Well, anyway, thank you for your help, Mr. Creed."

"I don't know that I was all that much help, Marshal."

"Better to be safe than sorry, my mother always said." He paused before adding, "Now if you'll excuse me, I have to get back to court."

"I'll go up with you," said Creed.

As they entered the courtroom, Ogden was asking the judge to postpone Dick Barth's trial and Buckmaster was agreeing to the stipulation. Sangster banged his gavel, ordered the motion into the record, and said, "Call the next case, Mr. Ogden."

The prosecutor complied as Buckmaster left the room and Hays took his seat behind the prosecutor's table. Ben Brown stepped forward with the next defendant, a horse thief from the Creek Nation. Sangster called for the charge to be read. Ogden did so. The judge asked the defendant for a plea, and to nobody's surprise, the accused said not guilty. Sangster asked Ogden if he was ready to proceed with the trial, and the prosecutor said he was. The defense said likewise, and the first witness was called. Three more witnesses, and the prosecution rested. Brown called the defendant to testify in his own behalf. He made an unconvincing, halfhearted argument that he was only borrowing the horse with plans to return it when he met up with a stranger who made him an offer for the animal that he couldn't refuse. Shaking his head, Brown threw in the towel, and final arguments were given by the two lawyers. The jury absented themselves from the room for less than ten minutes before bringing in a verdict of guilty. Sangster sentenced the man to a year in the penitentiary at Little Rock, then he called it a day because the next case on the docket was the *United States* v. *Harry Crackley and David Lowe* and he didn't wish to begin a murder trial that late in the day.

Creed left the courtroom with the other spectators, went downstairs, and found Buckmaster standing casually in the hall as if he were waiting for somebody. The Texan soon found out who.

"Going home, Mr. Creed?" asked the lawyer.

"Yes, I am," said the Texan.

"Mind if I walk with you?"

"Not at all."

They left the building together. At the corner of Main and Perry, Buckmaster suggested that they take a different route home. Creed saw no harm in it, so they proceeded along Perry two blocks to Jefferson. When they reached the corner, Buckmaster hailed a gentleman on the stoop of a large brick house across

the street. The lawyer waved and offered a cheery greeting in
French, *"Bonsoir, mon ami,"* and the gentleman returned the
gesture in kind.

"That's Dr. Henri Pernot," said Buckmaster as they turned the
corner onto Jefferson for the final block to the boardinghouse.
"He came to America right after the big trouble in Europe in '48.
He lived in Missouri for a few years while he went to medical
college in St. Louis. He married Mrs. Pernot up in Ste. Genevieve,
Missouri, and they came here to live in '52. Dr. Pernot had a hard
time of it in the beginning because he was a foreigner. You know
how American folks feel about most foreigners who speak with
funny accents. Well, it wasn't any different with Dr. Pernot, but
despite the basic prejudice of folks in these parts, he worked hard
to prove that he could fit in around here. He did everything he
could to become part of this community by not doing anything
to cause anybody any trouble. He stuck to his own business, and
he went along with the majority of folks on things. When the war
came, he served the South as chief surgeon for the Confederate
hospital here in Van Buren. When the Yankees took Van Buren,
they threatened to shoot him if he didn't get out of town, so he
went down to Fort Washita to serve the Confederacy there. He
came back when the war was over and picked up his practice
again. He's a Mason and an Odd Fellow . . . and a member of
other . . . distinguished . . . organizations." He eyed Creed as if
the Texan should know exactly what he meant by the latter
inference.

They came to the walk leading up to the steps of the
boardinghouse, and Buckmaster halted. Creed took his cue and
stopped with him.

"I tell you all this about Dr. Pernot for a good reason, Mr.
Creed," said Buckmaster. "I would hope that you might learn
from his example."

"His example?" queried Creed.

"Yes, his example of minding his own business and not causing
trouble for folks who were here before him."

"I see," said Creed, thinking, *The little runt knows that I told
Marshal Hays about Sukey Ann visiting Sinker Wilson in the jail.*
"Well, I'll try to keep that in mind, Mr. Buckmaster."

"Please do, Mr. Creed. I'd hate to see a fellow . . . former
Confederate fall into evil."

Now that's a threat if I ever heard one, thought Creed. "I agree
wholeheartedly," he said.

"Very good," said Buckmaster, his demeanor stern but friendly. "Shall we go in now?"

"After you, sir."

Creed followed Buckmaster inside the house and up the stairs where they parted company, each man going to his own room.

The Texan pulled off his coat and hung it and his hat on the pegs in the wall. He sat on the cushioned ladder-back chair and pulled off his boots. Less fettered now, he stretched out on the bed and gave serious consideration to the conversation that he'd just had with Buckmaster.

The little runt threatened me, he thought. That was very clear. But why? Just because his client is planning a jailbreak and I put the marshal wise to it? He wouldn't threaten me *after* doing that. That's like closing the corral gate after the horse has run out to the north pasture. No, he's telling me to mind my own business because there's more than just a jailbreak at stake here. Maybe he got wind of my little business transactions with Willie Vann and Lige Rider. Lawyers do hate to lose cases even when their clients are guilty as sin. That could be it, but I doubt it. He didn't have a whole lot of trouble with Barth's trial before I asked him for the postponement. No, it's probably nothing to do with Barth's trial. But if that isn't it, then what is it? Is something else in the works here? If there is, what on earth could it be?

Before he could come up with any possible answers to that question, he fell asleep and dreamt of Texada and home. They were living at Double Star Ranch, and he had just come in from the range. Texada rang the supper bell to call him to the table. He felt an urgency to get there, then he realized that the clanging wasn't in his dream.

Mrs. Chapman ringing the dinner bell roused him awake. More than an hour had passed since he'd come home with Buckmaster. He rubbed the sleep from his eyes, pulled on his boots, and hurried downstairs to supper.

Between bites of chicken and dumplings, Peterson announced that he had given notice that he would be leaving his employment at the bank before the end of the month. "I'm going home to visit my folks for Thanksgiving," he said. "They live up near Bentonville."

"That's nice, Mr. Peterson," said Mrs. Chapman.

Buckmaster blanched and held his breath.

Jennifer stifled a giggle.

Smith cleared his throat and muttered, "A commendable idea, my boy. Very commendable."

Landon, Darrell, Mrs. Nance, and Miss Steen smiled and nodded uncomfortably.

Creed noted all the looks and was put off by them. Obviously, he thought, Sukey Ann spread the word about Peterson's preference for the company of men, and these hypocrites can't wait for him to be out of their presence. At least Smith was civil to him.

"I envy you being able to spend the forthcoming holiday with your family, Mr. Peterson," said Creed. "I haven't been home for Christmas or Thanksgiving or even my birthday since '61."

"That's sad," said Peterson. "You're more than welcome to join me and my family for Thanksgiving, Mr. Creed."

Again, Buckmaster blanched and held his breath.

"Ahem. Ahem." Smith seemed to have another frog stuck in his throat.

Everybody else gasped and waited for Creed to respond to the invitation.

"I'm honored that you'd ask," said Creed.

"Then you'll come?"

"No, I'm sorry, but I have to decline. I can't make any plans until my business here is completed, and as soon as it is, provided that it all turns out as expected, I intend to return to Texas as quickly as I can, hopefully in time for the holidays."

Buckmaster released his breath in relief.

"Going home for the holidays, Mr. Creed?" queried Smith, finally able to speak.

"I hope so."

Roberta came into the room carrying a sheet cake. She placed it on the serving cart, removed the bowl that had held the chicken and dumplings, and returned to the kitchen. In another few seconds, she came back with dessert plates and put them down where the main course had been. One by one she removed the dinner plates from each person's setting.

"I had Roberta fix a special cake for Mr. Peterson," said Mrs. Chapman, "seeing that this is something of an occasion. His announcement, I mean."

"Thank you, Mrs. Chapman," said Peterson. "I'm looking at this move as a step to a happier and more prosperous future."

Creed couldn't be certain, but he thought he detected an exchange of looks between Buckmaster and Smith. Of course, Miss Steen and Mrs. Nance did the same, as did Landon and

Darrell. Damn, he thought, I'm starting to see ghost riders in the clouds. He cleared his own throat and said, "I'm sure you're doing the right thing, Mr. Peterson. I, for one, would like to wish you success and good fortune wherever you go."

"Thank you," said Peterson.

"Yes, I concur," said Smith. "Good luck, Nelson."

Although reluctantly done, the rest expressed the same sentiment to the young bank clerk. All ate their dessert, then retired to their various evening interests.

Creed borrowed a book from Mrs. Chapman's library, but he couldn't absorb himself in it. His mind was too occupied with the connection between Sukey Ann Rogers, Buckmaster, and Sinker Wilson. They're up to something, he thought, but what? He fell asleep with that question still troubling him.

20

Word that the murder trial of Harry Crackley and David Lowe would be first on the court docket for Wednesday spread through town like a virus, and every man and woman who could attend the proceedings the next day did.

Creed managed to squeeze himself into the crowd of spectators to catch a glimpse of Crackley and Lowe as well as the witnesses against them. He was very much interested in speaking to the widow of the murder victim. As he scanned the faces in the audience, the Texan recognized some as folks who had been in attendance the previous two days of the court term. Finally, his view fell on a soldier.

Seated in the front row of the gallery was Sergeant Timothy Aloysius McGuire, the same Sergeant McGuire who had helped Creed through a difficulty in North Fork Town earlier that year when he was passing through the Nations on his way home to Texas. A stouthearted Irishman with a droopy black mustache and pugilist's chin, a bit of the brogue still in his accent, and cobalt eyes; that was McGuire.

Recalling the conversation with Hays, Ogden, and Sangster about the Army capturing Crackley and Lowe, Creed figured McGuire was here to testify against those outlaws, especially since beside him sat a young woman, a former slave that Creed guessed to be the widow of Lucius Slater, the freedman who was murdered by that despicable pair of cowboys. McGuire and the widow sat quietly as they waited for the trial to begin.

The court crier entered the room and called for everybody to stand for the judge. As soon as Sangster sat down, the crier announced that court was now in session. Sangster banged his gavel and ordered Ogden to call the first case of the day. The prosecutor obeyed the instruction, and the ball was begun.

Buckmaster stood up for the defendants and entered a not guilty plea for them. Sangster called for opening remarks. Ogden made a statement about murder being a capital crime and how the defendants deserved the death penalty for the foul deed that they had committed. Buckmaster rebutted with a weak argument that they had done nothing that warranted hanging because the victim was merely a Negro. Ogden objected, and Sangster sustained him, warning Buckmaster that Negroes now had the same right to life as whites. As soon as he was done lecturing the defense attorney, Sangster told Ogden to call his first witness.

"The government calls Hester Slater to the stand, Your Honor," said Ogden.

"Objection, Your Honor," said Buckmaster. "Hester Slater is a Negress, and the law specifically forbids Negroes from testifying against white people."

"Overruled," said Sangster. "This is the federal court, Mr. Buckmaster, and the statutes of the state of Arkansas do not apply to this case."

"Yes, Your Honor, I agree," said Buckmaster, "but the federal laws do not permit Negroes to testify against white people either."

"The recent amendment to the Constitution of the United States has changed that practice, sir," said Sangster. "You are overruled."

"Exception, Your Honor," said Buckmaster.

"So noted," said Sangster. "Proceed, Mr. Ogden."

The prosecutor helped Hester to the witness stand amid a great deal of buzzing from the audience. "Don't be afraid," he said in a voice that only she heard.

"No, sir, I won't," she said, feigning bravery.

The bailiff stepped up with a Bible and swore her to tell the truth, the whole truth, and nothing but the truth.

"I will," she said meekly. She sat down on the witness chair and looked out at the noisy gallery. When Sangster pounded his gavel on the desk for quiet, she started visibly, eyes widening, shoulders shaking ever so slightly.

Poor girl, thought Creed. Not another black face in the room. She's petrified.

The former slave was a true daughter of Africa. Skin the color of rich coffee, eyes like black walnuts, large teeth whiter than ivory, thin lips, black hair the texture of steel wool, high cheekbones, medium figure. She wore a homespun cotton dress dyed with butternut juice. The skirt failed to hide her bare feet as she sat primly in the chair with her hands folded in her lap.

Ogden stood close to the witness stand to ask his questions.
"Would you state your name please?" he asked.

"Hester Slater."

"And where do you live, Hester?"

"Near North Fork Town in the Creek Nation."

"Are you married, Hester?"

"I was until those two men killed my man."

"Objection, Your Honor," said Buckmaster.

"On what grounds, Mr. Buckmaster?" asked Sangster.

"On the grounds that Hester Slater is a Negress—"

"Overruled," said Sangster.

"Exception," said Buckmaster.

"So noted," said Sangster. "Proceed, Mr. Ogden."

"Which two men are you referring to, Hester?" asked the
prosecutor.

Hester nodded toward the defendants and said, "Those two over
there."

"Would you point them out please?"

Slowly, she raised her hand, extended a finger, and pointed to
Crackley and Lowe. "That's them," she said.

"Your Honor, I move that the record reflect that the witness
has identified the defendants, Harry Crackley and David Lowe,"
said Ogden.

"Does the defense have any objections, Mr. Buckmaster?"
asked Sangster.

"Yes, Your Honor."

"On what grounds?" asked the judge.

"On the grounds that the witness is a Negress," said Buckmaster.

"Overruled," said Sangster.

"Exception," said Buckmaster.

"So noted," said Sangster, "but this will be the last time, Mr.
Buckmaster, that I will allow you to object on those grounds.
The next time you do it, I will cite you for contempt. Is that
understood, sir?"

"Yes, Your Honor."

The judge turned to the court recorder and said, "Let the
record read that the witness is pointing to the defendants, Harry
Crackley and David Lowe." Looking back at the prosecutor, he
added, "Continue, Mr. Ogden."

"Thank you, Your Honor," said Ogden. "Hester, you have
testified that you were married until the defendants killed your
man. What was your man's name?"

"Lucius Slater."

"Was he a slave in the Creek Nation?" asked Ogden.

"No, sir. Lucius was a freedman."

"Yes, but was he a slave in the Creek Nation before he became a freedman?"

"No, sir. Lucius and me come from Texas after the war. His master set him free when he died two year back, and the new master let him stay on the plantation until the war was over and we was all set free by the Yankee man. That was when Lucius come for me at Massuh Wash's plantation, and we was married and went north to find us a new home."

"And you found one in the Creek Nation?"

"Not at first. We heard bad things about the Nations, so we tried going around them to Kansas. Then we heard the Yankee man was gonna give the Nations to the freedmen, so we went to the Creek Nation to claim a piece of land for our own."

"I see," said Ogden. "And that's where you were living when Harry Crackley and David Lowe came along and killed your man?"

"Yes, sir."

"Would you tell the court what happened that day, Hester?"

"Yes, sir." In detail, Hester told how she saw Crackley and Lowe following her husband toward the house, how they threatened Lucius, how Lucius did everything he could to be nice to the two cowboys, how Crackley shot Lucius in the back, how the outlaw slapped her and started to abuse her, and finally how the soldiers came and saved her and her baby from certain death.

"Thank you, Hester," said Ogden, "I have no more questions of this witness, Your Honor."

"Your witness, Mr. Buckmaster," said Sangster.

"Your Honor, the defense will not countenance this travesty of justice against the white race by questioning a Negress," said the defense attorney.

A few spectators voiced their agreement to Buckmaster's statement, and Sangster-banged his gavel for quiet. "There will be no more outbursts like that again, or I will clear the room," said the judge. "Since the defense has no questions for the witness, the witness is dismissed. Call your next witness, Mr. Ogden."

"You can go back to your seat now," Ogden told Hester gently. Louder, as Hester stood up and returned to her place in the gallery, he said, "The government calls Sergeant Timothy McGuire to the stand, Your Honor."

McGuire stood up, waited for Hester to be seated, patted her reassuringly on the upper arm, then walked to the witness chair. He was sworn to tell the truth by the bailiff, and after saying he would, he sat down.

Ogden proceeded the same way with McGuire as he had with Hester, asking the sergeant to state his name, his rank, and his place of duty. With those formalities completed, he asked McGuire to tell the court about the events of August 3, 1866.

"I was in charge of a detail that was sent down to Boggy Depot to help folks there clean up after a bad storm and a flood. We were returning to our cantonment at North Fork Town when we heard shots being fired. I divided my men, and we went to see what the trouble might be. We discovered those two cowboys there in the cabin of—"

"Which two cowboys?" interjected Ogden.

"Those two right there," said McGuire, pointing at Crackley and Lowe.

"Your Honor, I move that the record reflect that the witness has identified the defendants, Harry Crackley and David Lowe," said Ogden.

"Does the defense have any objections, Mr. Buckmaster?" asked Sangster.

"No objections, Your Honor," said Buckmaster.

The judge turned to the court recorder and said, "Let the record read that the witness is pointing to the defendants, Harry Crackley and David Lowe." Looking back at the prosecutor, he added, "Continue, Mr. Ogden."

"Thank you, Your Honor," said the prosecutor. "Please continue, Sergeant."

"Well, we found those two in the cabin of Lucius Slater," said McGuire. "Lucius Slater was dead already on the floor. The baby was crying, and that one"—he aimed an index finger at Crackley—"had his pants down and was in the process of having his way with Mrs. Slater."

"Your Honor, I move that the record reflect that the witness has identified the defendant, Harry Crackley, as the man having his way with Mrs. Slater," said Ogden.

"Does the defense have any objections, Mr. Buckmaster?" asked Sangster.

"No objections, Your Honor," said Buckmaster.

The judge turned to the court recorder and said, "Let the record read that the witness is pointing to the defendant, Harry

Crackley." Looking back at the prosecutor, he added, "Continue, Mr. Ogden."

"Thank you, Your Honor," said Ogden. "Was Mrs. Slater willingly allowing Harry Crackley to have his way with her?"

"No, sir, she was not," said McGuire firmly.

"Then would you say that Crackley was raping Mrs. Slater?"

"Objection," said Buckmaster. "The question calls for a conclusion by the witness, Your Honor."

"Sustained," said Sangster.

"I'll rephrase the question, Your Honor," said Ogden. "Sergeant, you said Harry Crackley was having his way with Mrs. Slater and that she was an unwilling participant in this act. Is that right?"

"Yes, sir, that's right," said McGuire. "Crackley was raping Mrs. Slater."

"And what did you do about it?"

"I pulled Crackley off Mrs. Slater."

"What condition was Mrs. Slater in when you pulled Crackley from her?"

"The poor woman had been beaten, and she was crying."

"Thank you, Sergeant. No further questions of this witness, Your Honor." Ogden returned to his chair.

"Your witness, Mr. Buckmaster," said the judge.

Buckmaster stood up and said, "Sergeant, what did you do to Mr. Crackley after you interrupted his sport with the nigger woman?"

"Objection, Your Honor," said Ogden angrily. "Calling Mrs. Slater 'the nigger woman' is an uncalled-for slur, and I would ask the court to strike those words from the record."

"Your Honor," said Buckmaster with a snicker, "the fact is the woman is a nigger."

Ogden exploded. "And you're a short little runt!"

Sangster rapped his gavel on the desk. "That will do, Mr. Ogden." He redirected the mallet and his wrath at Buckmaster. "And you, sir, will refrain from referring to the previous witness as 'the nigger woman.' Is that clear, Mr. Buckmaster?"

Confidently, Buckmaster faced Sangster and said, "Your Honor, am I to understand that this court would deny me my right to freedom of speech as guaranteed by the First Amendment to the Constitution of the United States?"

"How dare you invoke the Constitution!" gasped Ogden.

Sangster was speechless.

"I wasn't talking to you, Ogden," said Buckmaster.

Sangster found his tongue. "This court would never deny you or anybody else their rights under the Constitution of the United States, Mr. Buckmaster, but this court does reserve the right to maintain a certain decorum. Therefore, you will refrain from using that phrase, or I will cite you for contempt. Have I made myself clear on that point, Mr. Buckmaster?"

"Yes, Your Honor," said the diminutive lawyer.

"All right then," said Sangster. "Continue with your cross-examination of the witness."

"Yes, sir," said Buckmaster. "Sergeant, what did you do to Mr. Crackley after you interrupted his sport with the previous witness?"

"I beat him within an inch of his life," said McGuire defiantly, "because the bastard deserved it."

Sangster pounded his gavel on the desk, directing the action at McGuire, and said, "Sergeant, you will also watch your tongue in my courtroom. Is that understood?"

"Yes, sir," said McGuire. "I'm sorry, Your Honor."

"You say you beat Mr. Crackley within an inch of his life, Sergeant. Did you do this because you're a nigger lover?"

"Objection, Your Honor," said Ogden.

"Sustained," said Sangster. "You've been warned, Mr. Buckmaster. Once more and I'll halt this trial and put you in jail with your clients."

"I'm sorry, Your Honor. It was merely force of habit. I am still unaccustomed to being the slave of Yankee laws." As a murmur of agreement floated over the gallery, he cleared his throat and turned his attention to McGuire again. "Sergeant, did you beat Mr. Crackley within an inch of his life because you have a fondness for the Negro race?"

"No, sir. I did it because I can't abide a man who forces himself on a helpless woman. No matter what her color is."

"I see," said Buckmaster. "No further questions of this witness, Your Honor."

"You may step down, Sergeant," said the judge. "Call your next witness, Mr. Ogden."

"The government rests, Your Honor," said Ogden.

McGuire returned to his seat beside Hester.

"Mr. Buckmaster, are you ready to present your defense?" asked the judge.

"Yes, Your Honor."

"Then proceed."

"The defense wishes to call Harry Crackley to the stand, Your Honor."

Crackley stood up, walked to the witness chair, and was sworn in by the bailiff.

"Be seated, Mr. Crackley," said Sangster.

"Mr. Crackley," said Buckmaster, "would you please tell the court about the events of August 3, 1866?"

"Yes, sir," said Crackley. "Davy and me had just quit Captain Millett's trail crew because we found out that the cows we was driving were stolen, and we headed off toward North Fork Town, hoping to find a stake to take us back home to Texas. That's when we come across this nigger farmer—"

Sangster interrupted him with a bang of his gavel. "Mr. Crackley, you will not use that word in this courtroom," said the judge.

"I'm sorry, Your Honor," said Crackley, "but I don't know no other way. They's always been niggers to me."

Sangster sighed with exasperation and said, "They are Negroes, Mr. Crackley, and you will call them that. Is that understood?"

"Yes, sir, but I can't promise nigger won't slip out again, Your Honor."

"Just try, Mr. Crackley."

"Yes, sir."

"Go on, Mr. Crackley," said Buckmaster. "You said you came across a colored farmer."

"Yes, that's right, we did. Anyway, this colored boy called us over and invited us up to his house for a bite to eat and a go at his woman for a dollar each."

"That's a lie!" screamed Hester.

Sangster banged his gavel. "You had your say, Mrs. Slater," he said sternly. "Now it's Mr. Crackley's turn. You just sit there and be quiet now."

Hester's head drooped as McGuire tried to ease her fears with a pat on the arm and a few soft words.

"Proceed, Mr. Buckmaster," said the judge.

"Thank you, Your Honor," said the defense attorney. "Mr. Crackley, you say this colored farmer invited you and Mr. Lowe up to his house for a bite to eat and a go at his woman for a dollar each."

"That's right."

"Then what happened?"

"Well, we went up to the house with him, and when we got there, that colored woman there was waiting for us with a shotgun."

"That ain't so!" said Hester.

Sangster struck his gavel on the desk and said, "I warned you, Mrs. Slater. One more word out of you, and I'll put you in jail."

McGuire tried to comfort Hester. "It's all right, Mrs. Slater," he said softly to her.

"But he's lying," said Hester through her tears.

"Yes, I know," said McGuire, "but he'll pay for it just the same as he'll pay for killing your husband."

"Go on, Mr. Crackley," said Sangster.

"Well, she had this shotgun pointed at us, but her man was between us and her. I drew my six-gun to defend myself, and as I was taking aim, the colored boy backed into me and my gun went off and killed him. The woman screamed and dropped the shotgun, and after that, I ain't sure exactly what happened until that bluebelly sergeant started whuppin' on me. The best I can figure is I was so mad that this colored woman had a shotgun aimed at us that I started to do something that I ain't exactly proud of now." He hung his head, feigning shame. "Anyway, as God is my witness, I swear that's how it happened."

"Thank you, Mr. Crackley," said Buckmaster. "Your witness, Mr. Ogden."

"I had planned to ask this witness a few questions, Your Honor," said Ogden, "but after hearing such deceitful testimony, I don't think it would serve justice one iota."

"Objection, Your Honor," said Buckmaster. "The prosecution has no right to call my client a liar."

"Overruled," said Sangster. "Call your next witness, Mr. Buckmaster. You can go back to your seat, Mr. Crackley."

The outlaw returned to the defense table.

"I wish to call David Lowe to the stand, Your Honor."

Lowe came forward and was sworn in.

Buckmaster got right to the point and had Lowe relate his version of the events on August 3, 1866.

"Well, sir, it was mostly like Harry said. That black buck invited us up to his house for some grub and a poke at his whore—"

"Objection, Your Honor," said Ogden.

"Sustained," said Sangster. "Mr. Lowe, you will refrain from calling Mrs. Slater a whore."

"Yes, sir."

"Go on, Mr. Lowe," said Buckmaster.

"Where was I, Mr. Buckmaster?"

"You were invited to the house by the victim."

Lowe seemed puzzled by the word. "The victim?"

"The colored farmer," said Buckmaster.

"Oh, sure, that's right," said Lowe. He looked at the ceiling as if he were trying to remember something. "Oh, yeah, now I recollect," he said, looking at Buckmaster again. "Well, sir, when we got to the house, she had this shotgun, and Harry shot that buck in the back by accident, just like he said."

"Then what happened, Mr. Lowe?" asked Buckmaster.

"Harry, he got madder than a wet hen and started in on that whore—"

"Mr. Lowe," said Sangster, "you were warned not to refer to Mrs. Slater as a whore."

"I'm sorry, Judge. I forgot."

"Go on, Mr. Lowe," said Buckmaster.

"Well, Harry started in on her. He slapped her a time or two, and her dress come off, and I guess Harry got himself all worked up at the sight of her like that. It'd been a long time since either of us had seen a woman, least of all a naked woman. Well, he was just beginning with her when them Yankees came in and jumped us and that big Yank over there started whuppin' Harry real good. I still don't know why he was so worked up at us. We was only gonna poke a nigger."

"Your Honor," pleaded Ogden with exasperation.

Before Sangster could reply, Buckmaster said, "No further questions of this witness, Your Honor. Your witness, Mr. Ogden."

Ogden sighed heavily and said, "No questions, Your Honor."

"You may step down, Mr. Lowe," said Sangster. "Call your next witness, Mr. Buckmaster."

"I have no further witnesses, Your Honor. The defense rests."

Sangster checked his watch and said, "We'll take a recess until this afternoon, gentlemen, at which time, the court will hear final arguments." He pounded his gavel once on the desk. "Court is adjourned until one o'clock this afternoon."

Everybody stood up as the judge left the room.

As the other spectators filed out of the courtroom, Creed stationed himself near the exit, hoping to speak with Sergeant

McGuire and Hester. From her testimony, the Texan concluded that she had been a slave on Washington Foley's plantation and that Lucius had been a slave at Glengarry, although he couldn't remember a slave of that name. He wanted to confirm this conclusion as fact, and he wanted to renew his acquaintance with McGuire.

McGuire saw Creed standing near the door as he and Hester followed the crowd toward the doorway. The face looks familiar, he told himself, but what's the name that goes with it? As he drew closer to the Texan, he recalled the name and the events that had involved both of them the previous spring. Not exactly his fondest memories.

"Mr. Creed, isn't it?" said McGuire.

Creed smiled and said, "I'm honored that you remember me, Sergeant."

"There's not much that I do forget," said McGuire. "Come here for the murder trial?"

"No, I'm here on other business," said Creed, "but when I heard about this trial, I decided to see what it was all about, especially since the victim might have been somebody I knew back in Texas." He let his view fall on Hester. Nodding at her, he added, "My name is Slate Creed, Mrs. Slater. I come from Lavaca County, Texas."

Hester gasped and covered her mouth.

"You say you might have known Mrs. Slater's husband?" queried McGuire.

"I'm related to the Slaters of Glengarry Plantation," said Creed, "and they had several slaves who were set free when Dougald Slater died in '64. One of them might have been Mrs. Slater's husband."

"That's where Lucius come from," said Hester. "Glengarry Plantation, and he was set free when Massuh Dougald died, but he couldn't go no place till the Yankee man come and say it was all right to leave."

"And you came from Washington Foley's plantation?" asked Creed.

"That's right," said Hester. "Did you know Massuh Wash, too?"

"Yes, I did. He was a good man, if I recollect rightly."

"Yes, sir, he was a good massuh, but he was still a massuh."

"I'd like to talk to you about the other people who left Texas with you," said Creed.

Hester looked at McGuire for help in responding to Creed's request. "Why are you so interested in those people?" asked the sergeant.

"It's a long story, Sergeant, but I suppose it won't hurt to tell it to you. I left another former Slater slave in the Chickasaw Nation just a few weeks back who's looking for her family. Her name is Hannah, and she was a house servant at Glengarry Plantation who stayed behind when the others left for Kansas last year. Her mother's name is Dinah, and she's got a brother named Gabriel and a sister named Sheba."

"I knowed them," said Hester. "They was with us folks who went north last year."

"Did they go to the Nations with you and Lucius?"

"No, sir, they went to a place in Kansas."

"Do you know where in Kansas?"

"A place called Lawrence."

"When did you last see Dinah and the others, Hester?"

"Last summer up to Missouri. A place called Carthage. It wasn't much of a place, though. The Kansas Yankee man burned it during the war."

Maybe so, thought Creed, but at least it's a place to start looking for Hannah's family.

21

Creed left McGuire and Hester at the courthouse and walked the three blocks south to the boat landing to inquire about the arrival time of the steamboat *La Belle*. The dock master informed him that the stern-wheeler *La Belle de la Rivière* should be tying up that afternoon "around three o'clock, I expect. Leastways, that's been when she usually ties up here. Give or take an hour."

With that information secured, the Texan returned to Mrs. Chapman's boardinghouse for lunch. Only Mrs. Nance and the lady of the house were present, Buckmaster having sent word that he would be working through the noon hour and would be unable to join them for the midday repast. The ladies asked Creed about the murder trial of Crackley and Lowe, and he related the details to them as best as he could recollect. After eating, he excused himself and returned to the courthouse for the conclusion of the trial.

The court crier announced the return of Judge Sangster, and the judge called the court into session. "Mr. Ogden, are you ready with your final argument?" he asked.

"If it pleases the court," said Ogden, "I would like to recall a witness before proceeding with the government's final argument."

"Which witness and why?" asked Sangster.

"I'd like to recall Sergeant McGuire, Your Honor, to ask him about the shotgun that the defendants claim Mrs. Slater threatened them with."

"Objection, Your Honor," said Buckmaster. "The government's counsel had plenty of opportunity to ask the witness about the shotgun the first time around, and besides, he's already concluded his case against my clients."

"The defendants brought the shotgun into the picture, Your Honor," argued Ogden.

"Overruled," said Sangster. "Recall Sergeant McGuire."

Ogden obeyed the judge's order, and McGuire took the stand. "I remind you, Sergeant," said the prosecutor, "that you're still under oath to tell the truth."

"I understand, sir," said McGuire.

144

"Sergeant, the defendants have testified that Mrs. Slater threatened them with a shotgun," said Ogden. "Did you see a shotgun in the Slater house when you were there?"

"No, sir. In fact, we didn't find any firearms in the house except those belonging to the defendants."

"Then you're saying that you and your men did a search for weapons in the Slater house? Is that correct?"

"Yes, sir, that's correct."

"Your witness, Mr. Buckmaster."

"I have no questions for the witness," said Buckmaster.

"You are excused, Sergeant," said Sangster. "Do you have any other witnesses that you'd like to recall, Mr. Ogden?"

"No, Your Honor. The government rests."

"Mr. Buckmaster, would you like to recall a witness?" asked the judge.

"No, Your Honor. The defense is prepared to make its final argument now."

"Very good," said Sangster. "Proceed, Mr. Ogden."

Ogden approached the jury and made his argument. "I won't drag this out, gentlemen. The evidence and testimony are quite clear in this matter before you. Harry Crackley and David Lowe shot and killed Lucius Slater, a freedman residing in the Creek Nation, and then they attempted to rape Mrs. Slater. These lawless acts must not be allowed to go unpunished; therefore, it is your duty to bring in a verdict of guilty. Thank you." He sat down.

Buckmaster stood up and walked over to the jury box. "It's like this," he said. "Who are you gonna believe in this case? Two white men who served the Confederacy in the recent war? Or are you gonna believe a Yankee and a colored woman who probably doesn't know the meaning of the word truth." He snorted a laugh. "Heck, everybody knows darkies can't tell the truth. Why should this one be any different?" He paused for effect as a ripple of snickers trickled through the audience. "Well, that's it, gentlemen, It's as simple as the difference between black and white. My clients said it was an accident, that they were only defending themselves against a colored whore with a shotgun. So who are you gonna believe? Two good Southerners or a Yankee and a colored woman? I believe my clients, gents, and you should, too. Do your duty and find these innocent boys not guilty. Thank you, gents." He returned to his seat.

A round of whispers rippled through the audience, most lauding Buckmaster's summation.

"Gentlemen of the jury," said the judge as soon as the court-room was quiet again, "you have heard the evidence in this case and you have heard the arguments of each side for conviction and acquittal. I charge you now to retire to the jury room and make your decision on the guilt or innocence of the defendants. If you should find either or both of the defendants guilty, you must also decide the degree of that guilt. Now retire and do not return to this room until you have reached a verdict."

The jury departed, and Sangster closed the session until such time that the jury should make its decision and return to the courtroom. As soon as the judge was gone, the crowd burst into a buzz of conjecture. Were Crackley and Lowe guilty? Yes. No. Was Crackley guilty and Lowe just an accomplice? Yes. Probably. Should Crackley and Lowe hang for killing a Negro? Definitely not. How long would the jury take to make its decision? An hour. Less. More. An enterprising fellow came up with the idea of wagering on the time and the verdict. His announcement cleared the building as the gambling men in the audience rushed out to place a bet at the nearest pool hall and many of the remainder followed them as spectators.

Although he was as equally curious about the outcome of the trial as the others, Creed had other business to attend, namely meeting Colonel Burch whose steamboat was due around three o'clock. He noted the time on the clock in the courtroom: 1:52. The dock master said give or take an hour, he told himself. Better go down to the landing and wait just in case the boat is early.

This day *La Belle de la Rivière* tied up at the Van Buren dock a half hour before its scheduled arrival time. Standing at the rail of the upper deck was Colonel John C. Burch. Balding, bearded, blue eyes, he was impeccably attired in a black suit and a silk plug hat which he removed and waved in salute to Creed.

During the war, Burch served on General Nathan Bedford Forrest's staff, which was where Creed came to know of him. After the cessation of the conflict, he returned to the legal profession in Nashville, where Creed met him while he was searching for Marsh Quade in Tennessee. Upon learning of Creed's quest to clear his real name, the lawyer offered his services and political connections to the Texan, and Creed accepted them without question. Burch aided the fugitive from the Army's injustice with a letter of introduction that saved his life in Missouri and assisted him in finding Quade in Colorado. Now they were meeting again for the first time since

Creed left Nashville in February. Over the intervening months, they had remained in contact through the mails, and both looked forward to the reunion.

"How are you, my boy?" asked Burch as he shook Creed's hand vigorously when they faced each other at the end of the gangplank.

"I'm fine, sir, and you?"

"Couldn't be better." He released Creed's hand. "I'm so glad to see you, Slate. My, what a year you've had!"

"Yes, I suppose so," said Creed as several memories sped past his mind's eye in a long blur.

"From Tennessee to Missouri to Texas to Colorado and now here to Arkansas. You do get around, Slate."

"Yes, sir." Creed didn't know why, but he felt the cold fingers of sadness on his soul. They sent a shiver through him and conjured up tragic images within his brain. Dark visions of a murdered clergyman in Missouri, a dying mother in the Cherokee Nation, a hotheaded youth in Texas, the funeral of an enemy turned friend in Colorado, the drowning of a friend turned enemy in Kansas. A pall of sorrow shaded the Texan's eyes for a brief instant.

Burch missed the look on Creed's face. "Such adventures you've had, my boy. You must tell me about them in great detail."

"Certainly," said Creed, regaining control of his emotions, "but not until you tell me why you came here to meet me."

"That's simple, Slate. Marshall Quade's confession and Dick Barth."

Creed's brow furrowed. "I don't understand, sir."

"Didn't I write you to keep Quade's confession in a safe place?"

"Yes, sir, you did."

"Well, I've come to take it to that safe place until the time comes when I can present it to the right authorities who can remove the blemish from your name. Do you still have the document?"

"Yes, sir."

"Good. You can turn it over to me in due time before I begin my return trip to Nashville Friday morning."

"You're returning to Nashville so soon?" he asked.

"I must," said Burch. "Too many cases to clear off before the holidays."

"Of course," said the Texan. "Well, I don't know if there's a hotel room available for you, Colonel. The town is pretty full up because of the court term."

"So I thought it would be. That's why I'll be staying on the boat. It will be docked here the entire time, and I'm returning on it to Little Rock."

"Good idea."

"Now what about Dick Barth? You wired that he was here awaiting trial and that he was unwilling to help."

"Yes, sir, that's right." In short order, Creed related everything he knew about Barth's crime and the upcoming trial, and in conclusion, he said, "I visited him in the jail and asked him to confess that he and the others lied about me taking part in their crime, and he so much as told me to go to hell."

Burch nodded grimly. "I suspected as much from your telegram. Tell me everything he said. You wrote that Quade told you that this Colonel Peck is responsible for these men putting their guilt on your shoulders. Did Barth confirm this?"

"No, it never came up in the conversation," said Creed.

"Well then, we'll just have to speak to Mr. Barth about it, won't we? Is he still in the jail here?"

"Yes, he is."

"Has his trial come up yet?"

"No. After I received your telegram that you were coming here, I managed to have his trial postponed until next week to make certain that he'd be here when you arrived."

"Does he have representation?"

"Yes, a lawyer named Buckmaster."

"Buckmaster? Thomas Buckmaster from Benton County?"

"Yes, sir. Do you know him?"

Burch's left eye twitched. "Uh, no, I don't know him, but I have heard the name. Is he a good lawyer?"

"He seems to know his business," Creed remembered Buckmaster's reaction to the mention of Burch's name. Odd, he thought. He behaved the same way as the colonel. "He said that he's heard of you, too. How did he put it? He knew your full name, and he said he knew you by reputation. From how he choked and broke into a sweat, I'd have to say your reputation must know no limits."

"Surely, you flatter me, Slate," said Burch, forcing a chuckle through his words.

"Well, maybe so," said Creed. "But the man was impressed when I told him you were my attorney."

The colonel cleared his throat and said, "Indeed, but let's get back to Barth. I would like to visit him as soon as possible to see if I can't persuade him to testify in your behalf or at least to make a confession the equal of Marshall Quade's. Which way to the jail?"

"I'm not sure we can get into the jail to see him right away, Colonel. The marshal here is pretty busy with court, and trying to get a word with him can be difficult. Of course, we might be able to catch him right now if the jury hasn't come back yet."

"The jury?" queried Burch.

"Yes, sir. There's a murder trial going on right now, and the jury went into deliberation just a little while ago. If they're still out, we might be able to speak with Marshal Hays right away and get permission to visit Barth in jail."

"Well, what are we waiting for then?"

They hastened to the courthouse. Along the way, Creed explained that Buckmaster was defending the two cowboys who were accused of killing one of his grandfather's former slaves and of attempting to rape the victim's widow after the murder. They arrived just in time to join the crowd of spectators returning to the gallery to hear the verdict of the jury. The judge, bailiff, prosecutor, defense counsel, defendants, et al., were in their places when Creed and Burch found standing space in the rear of the room. Sangster rapped his gavel on the desk and said, "Gentlemen of the jury, have you reached a verdict?"

Josiah Harrell, the foreman, stood up and said, "Yes, we have, Your Honor."

"The defendants will rise and face the jury," said Sangster.

Buckmaster stood up with his clients and faced the jury to hear the verdict.

Harrell held up a piece of paper and read from it. "We, the jury, find the defendant, Harry Crackley, guilty of murdering Lucius Slater in the Creek Nation." A murmur of disbelief rose from the audience. "We find the defendant, Harry Crackley, guilty of attempting to rape Hester Slater in the Creek Nation." More murmuring. "We find the defendant, David Lowe, not guilty of murdering Lucius Slater in the Creek Nation."

The crowd noise grew so substantially that Sangster was forced to bang his gavel to quiet the spectators. "Please continue, Mr. Harrell," said the judge.

"We find the defendant, David Lowe, not guilty of attempting to rape Hester Slater in the Creek Nation," said Harrell.

Crackley slammed his fists on the table and screamed, "He was only a nigger! You can't convict a white man of murdering a nigger! It ain't right! He was only a nigger! A nigger, I tell you!"

Sangster banged his gavel repeatedly. "Quiet down, you!" he yelled at Crackley. "Quiet down!"

"Calm down, Harry," said Buckmaster.

Hays stood up behind the defense table, his hand on the butt of a Remington revolver.

Crackley turned and saw McGuire and Hester sitting in the first row of gallery seats. "You son of a bitchin' bluebelly bastard!" he screamed as he picked up his chair to throw it at McGuire.

"No, Harry!" said Buckmaster, raising his hands to defend himself more than to stop Crackley.

Hester screamed and cringed against the sergeant.

Hays drew his gun and whipped it against Crackley's jaw just as the outlaw brought the chair over his head.

Crackley's bead snapped sideways, and he stumbled backward against the table, dropping the chair beyond it.

"You can't do that to Harry!" yelled Lowe. He grabbed Hays by the right wrist, bringing the Remington to bare directly at his heart. He made a fist to strike the marshal and drew it back, turning sideways to the lawman.

Hays cocked the revolver instinctively, and when he saw Lowe preparing to hit him, he jerked the trigger.

BANG! The ball exploded from the barrel of the gun and ricocheted off Lowe's sternum, falling harmlessly afterward to the floor; but the flame set fire to the outlaw's coat and shirt. "Ai-ah!" he yelped. He beat at the burning cloth. "I'm on fire, Harry!"

Crackley attacked Hays from behind, wrapping his left arm around the marshal's throat and using his right hand to grab the lawman's gun arm. They struggled.

Ogden and the court bailiff came to the marshal's rescue, pulling at Crackley from opposite directions until Hays was free of the outlaw. They fell on the villain, the three of them in a heap atop the defense table.

Hays cracked Lowe on the head, dropping him into an unconscious pile on the floor. He spun around, cocked his weapon, and put the muzzle to Crackley's nose. "That'll be enough, you son of a bitch!" he bellowed.

Crackley gave up.

Ogden and the bailiff released the outlaw and moved away from him ever so slowly.

"Kill him!" screamed Hester. "Kill that white trash bastard! Kill him like he killed my Lucius!"

As much as he wanted to do it, Hays held off. He would have no blood on his hands this day.

22

Order was restored in the court, and Sangster adjourned the session until the next day when he would pass sentence on Crackley. Hays and the bailiff escorted Crackley downstairs to the basement jail, while Dr. Pernot was summoned to tend to Lowe's injuries. The marshal chose not to arrest Lowe for his part in the courtroom melee, figuring "the poor stupid bastard is hurt enough already, what with a ball creasing his chest, his clothes set afire, and his skull cracked open like a bad melon. Pretty nasty burn he's got there."

Pernot concurred with the lawman's diagnosis. Lowe's burns were first, second, and third degree. "He will be some long time healing from this," said the physician.

As soon as a majority of the spectators vacated the courtroom, Creed led Burch along the gallery aisle with the intention of introducing the Tennessean to Ogden and Buckmaster, but before they reached the railing, they came face-to-face with McGuire and Hester who were leaving the courtroom. All eyes shifted back and forth from person to person. An awkward instance. Creed felt uneasy about the meeting because he suspected Burch might take offense if he were introduced to the soldier and freedwoman. Quickly, he turned to the Nashville lawyer and said, "Would you excuse me for a moment, Colonel, while I have a word with Sergeant McGuire and Mrs. Slater?"

"Certainly," said Burch, "but if I may . . ." He took Hester's hand and with true Southern chivalry said, "I am Colonel John Burch from Nashville, Mrs. Slater. Mr. Creed told me about the loss of your husband, and I would like to extend my sympathies to you, if I may."

Flabbergasted, she muttered, "Thank you, sir. That's very kind of you."

Burch nodded, released her hand, glanced at McGuire, and said, "Sergeant."

McGuire snapped to attention and said, "Yes, sir."

The colonel stepped aside to wait for Creed.

152

Now what? wondered Creed. The colonel snubbed McGuire.
Do I apologize for him? No, that would embarrass the colonel. A
quick look at the sergeant said everything. McGuire understands.
Officer and enlisted. That was all there was to it.

The Texan focused on Hester and said, "Don't let any of this
worry you, Mrs. Slater. Crackley will get his due."

"He might," said Hester, "but what about the other one? He's
going free."

"I don't know what to say about that," said Creed, "except that
God will punish him if he deserves it."

"I hope you're right, Mr. Creed," said McGuire. "I suppose
only time will tell."

"That's right," said the Texan.

"Will we see you at the sentencing tomorrow, Mr. Creed?"
asked McGuire.

"Most likely."

They said farewells, then moved toward the exit.

Creed introduced Burch to Ogden. The prosecutor shook the
Tennessean's hand, engaged in a rapid exchange of greetings,
then promptly asked to be excused because he had work to do.

Buckmaster was next.

"How do you do, Mr. Buckmaster?" said Burch.

"The pleasure is all mine, Colonel Burch," said the diminutive
lawyer. "I understand you've come all the way from Nashville to
question a client of mine about a matter that occurred last year in
Mississippi."

Burch looked askance at Creed, then said, "Yes, that's right."

"I haven't had the opportunity to discuss the subject with
Barth," said Buckmaster, "but no matter. You just go ahead
and talk to him all you want, and if there's anything that I
can do to help, just call on me. I'd be glad to be of service,
sir."

"Thank you, Mr. Buckmaster," said Burch. "I'll keep that in
mind."

"Please do," said Buckmaster. "Well, I must be going now."

"We'll walk down with you," said Creed.

"Will you be staying in Van Buren for very long, Colonel?"
asked Buckmaster as they moved toward the exit.

"No, I'll be leaving on Friday aboard the steamboat that brought
me here."

"Too bad. I would hope to have the chance to discuss politics
with you."

"Perhaps this evening, Mr. Buckmaster. After supper. If you don't mind coming down to the docks, that is."

They arrived at the main floor hall.

"It would be a pleasure, Colonel," said Buckmaster. "Until then?"

"Until then," said Burch.

Buckmaster left.

Creed and Burch only had to wait a few seconds before Hays ascended the stairway from the jail. They approached him immediately. Creed introduced Burch to Hays, and in the next breath, he asked permission for them to speak with Barth.

"Why?" asked Hays, eyeing Burch warily.

"Dick Barth was involved in a raid against a federal supply caravan last year in Mississippi," explained Burch, "and after he was caught with several other men who were also involved, they implicated an innocent man as being their leader. That man is my client. I've come here in order to convince Barth to recant his statement that my client was involved."

"Who is your client?" asked Hays, eyeing Creed.

"That's privileged information," said Burch.

"I can tell you his name, Marshal," said Creed. "It's Cletus Slater. He's from Lavaca County, Texas, the same as I am. He was convicted of Barth's crime and sentenced to hang, but he escaped."

"How do you know he's innocent?" asked Hays.

"Because I was with Slater in Texas when the raid in Mississippi took place," said Creed.

"Didn't you testify for this Slater that you were with him when it happened?" asked Hays.

"Yes, I did, but the Army court wouldn't believe me."

"I see," said Hays. "Why didn't you tell me all this before?"

"I fought for the Confederacy, Marshal, and since the war's end, I've had a lot of trouble with . . . Unionists. With you being a federal officer and all, I wasn't sure of what to expect from you."

"You mean you didn't trust me, is that it?"

"I guess you could put it that way."

"I suppose I can't blame you none there. All right, I'll let you see Barth again. Come on. I'll take you down myself."

"Thank you, Marshal," said Burch.

Creed and Burch followed Hays down the stairs to the basement. The foul odor of the place must have offended Burch's senses, but he said nothing about it. He studied the jailer's space with a practiced eye. The marshal ordered Blodgett to get Barth from his cell and bring him to the caged visitors' space in the stairwell. "I won't stay around, gentlemen," said Hays. "I have work to do in my office." He tipped his hat to them and left.

Creed and Burch entered the visitation room and waited for the jailer to bring Barth to them. Fearful that the prisoner would balk if he saw Creed before he was locked into the cage with them, the Texan stood in the darkest corner of the room. Burch stationed himself in the opposite corner.

Blodgett brought Barth to the room. "Give me a holler when you're done with him, Colonel," he said. The jailer locked the door behind the prisoner. "I'll be down the hall checking on the other residents of this here hotel." He broke into a sadistic laugh and drifted away toward the cell block.

"Who are you?" asked Barth, squinting at Burch because the light in the hall and stairwell was brighter than the dimness of his cell.

"I am John C. Burch, Mr. Barth." He noticed that Barth's hands and sleeves were covered with a chalky dust, wondered why, but made no speculation at this time.

"He called you Colonel. Where's your uniform, Yank?"

"Confederate officers are no longer allowed to wear their uniforms."

"Oh, I see," said Barth with a touch of joy. "So what can I do for you, Colonel?"

Burch pointed to a chair. "Have a seat, Mr. Barth, and I'll get right to the point of my visit." As Barth sat down with his back to Creed, still unaware that the Texan was present, Burch pulled out the other chair and seated himself. "I am a lawyer from Nashville, and I represent Captain Cletus Slater. I believe you know him."

Barth frowned and said, "Never heard of him."

"I thought you would say as much," said Burch. Turning very stern, he added, "Don't fool with me, Mr. Barth. I won't tolerate it."

"The war's over, Colonel, and I ain't in your damned army no more. You can take your orders and shove them up your ass."

Without warning, Burch reached across the table and slapped Barth's face. Twice. "If we were still in the Confederate Army," he said, "I couldn't do that to you, now could I?"

Creed stiffened as he prepared to jump into the affray that he expected to erupt in the next second. Nothing happened.

Too shocked to react, Barth felt his cheek and whined, "You ain't got no right to—"

Burch slapped him again and said, "Do I have your attention yet, Mr. Barth?"

Barth cowered from him and said, "Yes, sir."

"Good. Now let's get down to business. You have caused a great deal of trouble for a gentleman who served his country well during the recent war."

"I wasn't the only one," said Barth.

"True, there were others, but the others aren't here. You are, and so am I. I came here because you don't seem to understand the problems that you've caused Captain Slater, and I would hope that I might convince you to right the wrong that you've done to him."

"I ain't gonna do that, Colonel."

"That's what he told me you would say. Well, Mr. Barth, you have two choices here. One is very good, and the other one can be very bad for you."

Worry spread over Barth's face. "What are you talking about, mister?"

"It's very simple, Mr. Barth. You can tell the Yankees that Captain Slater had nothing to do with that raid in Mississippi last year or you can go to prison."

Relief relaxed Barth's face as he laughed and said, "That's a good one, Colonel. You had me goin' there for a second. I ain't goin' to prison. As soon as I have my trial, they're gonna let me go, and I'll be walking out of here."

"What makes you think they'll find you innocent, Mr. Barth? From what I understand, they've got two witnesses against you."

"Sure, they do," snorted Barth, "but they're both niggers. Who's gonna believe a couple of niggers over the word of a white man?"

"I see," said Burch, nodding. "Are you aware of the outcome of the murder trial that was just concluded in the courtroom upstairs?"

"Sure, what about it?"

"The jury that heard the case believed a colored woman that her husband was murdered by a white man and that the same white man tried to rape her."

"So what's that got to do with me? I didn't kill nobody. Not even a nigger."

"But you did beat a colored man and kill his horse, didn't you?"

"So what if I did? No white jury is gonna convict me for that. I'm white, too, Colonel."

"I'm afraid that won't help you this time, Mr. Barth. The gentlemen running this court aren't working under the same rules that we Southerners have employed for the past two and a half centuries. These men believe coloreds have rights under the law, just the same as we do, and when those rights are violated, they will punish the violator."

"Bullshit!"

"You can continue to take that attitude, if you like, Mr. Barth, but it will avail you nothing. The witnesses are set to testify against you, and the jury will convict you on their testimony. The judge will then sentence you to a long stay in prison."

"Bullshit!" said Barth as he turned sideways in the chair. His eyes had finally adjusted to the brighter light of the caged room, and he saw Creed's feet. He jumped up and away from the Texan. "Who's that?"

Creed stepped forward and said, "It's only me, Dick."

"What's going on here?" demanded Barth. He jumped up and moved to the locked door. He shook it and yelled, "Jake, get me out of here! Do you hear me, Jake? I want out of here!"

"You quiet down in there, Dick Barth," said Blodgett from the cell block hallway. "You ain't coming out of there till the colonel says to let you out. Now behave yourself."

"He's right, Mr. Barth," said Burch. "In fact, he's very right. You're not going to get out of this jail except to go to prison, and I promise you this. You won't get out of there . . . alive. That is, you won't unless you decide to do right by Captain Slater."

Before Barth could make any kind of reply, several footsteps thudded on the stairs above them. Instinctively, the trio of men looked up, although they had no way of seeing through the wooden stairs to view the persons making the noise.

Blodgett heard the newcomers descending the stairway, and he emerged from the cell block hall to meet them as they reached the basement. "Afternoon, Sheriff," he said. "What have you got there?"

"Bank robber," said Whitesides.

Creed peered through the bars of the visitors' cage with disbelief. Standing beside Sheriff Whitesides was Nelson Peterson.

23

As head cashier and chief clerk at the bank, Leo Smith took it upon himself to audit Peterson's account books because Peterson planned to leave town. Smith soon discovered several discrepancies in the ledgers and more than a thousand dollars missing from the bank's vault. He reported these facts at a hastily called meeting of the board of directors which included several of Van Buren's leading businessmen, and he was instructed to swear out a warrant against Peterson, charging him with theft of the bank's funds. Smith expressed his reluctance to do so, stating that Peterson had always been a good employee and that possibly the decision to have the assistant cashier arrested should be delayed until another audit could be done by a member or two of the board. Possibly, concurred the board, but wasn't Peterson due to leave town the next day and wasn't that too soon before an audit could be done by anybody? Well, yes, admitted Smith. Then have the man arrested was the order. Smith obeyed.

Creed had a hard time believing that a fellow of such mild manners as Peterson could be a bank robber. He interrupted the interview with Barth to ask Sheriff Whitesides if he could speak with the accused teller. The lawman saw no harm in it and gave his permission. Creed spoke to Peterson in the cell block hall.

"I didn't do it, Mr. Creed," said Peterson, tears streaming down his cheeks. "They say I took over a thousand dollars from the bank. I didn't take a dime, I swear. Please help me, Mr. Creed. I don't know what to do here. I've never been in a place like this, and I'm scared."

"Take it easy, Nelson," said Creed softly. "If you're innocent, then you'll get out of here and everything will be all right. Have you got a lawyer yet?"

"No, sir, I don't. Could you get one for me?"

"I'll see what I can do. In the meantime, do you need anything else?"

"I don't know," said Peterson.

"Well, if you think of anything, let me know. I'll tell Jake to watch out for you."

"Thank you, Mr. Creed. You're a good man."

"Well, that remains to be seen." He patted Peterson on the shoulder and added, "Remember, if you need anything, just tell Jake to send word to me over to Mrs. Chapman's. In the meantime, I'll see about getting you a good lawyer."

Peterson's arrest was the talk of the town. Some wanted to hang Peterson for his crime. Some wanted to hang him simply because he preferred the company of men over that of women. Few wanted him to be given the same rights under the law as other white men were entitled to receive.

Creed counted himself among the latter. No matter what Peterson's "social" preferences happen to be, thought the Texan, he deserves to receive a fair and honest trial. He found support with this argument from Colonel Burch who expressed it to Buckmaster when they met to discuss politics that evening aboard the steamboat *La Belle de la Rivière*.

"You seem to be willing to defend the—how should I put it?— the least popular of those accused of breaking the law," said Burch. "I should think that you would be willing to defend this Peterson fellow."

"Yes, I have been known to take cases that other attorneys consider to be beneath their contempt," said Buckmaster, "but even I have my limits, Colonel."

"Surely, you can find it within yourself to offer your services to this young man," said Burch.

"Especially since you know him already," said Creed.

Buckmaster made no reply, but he did twitch nervously and avoid eye contact with Creed.

"If I were licensed to practice here and had the time," said Burch, "I would volunteer my counsel to the lad."

"Aren't you the man who said that everybody deserves legal representation no matter what they might or might not have done?" argued Creed.

Buckmaster forced a chuckle and said, "You would recall that part of our debate, wouldn't you?" He smiled nervously and shifted in his seat. "All right, I know when I'm licked. I'll defend Peterson, if he wants me. Does that satisfy you gentlemen now?"

Burch and Creed nodded their approvals to each other and to Buckmaster. "Yes, it does," said the colonel.

"Good," said the diminutive lawyer. "Now let's get onto another subject. How did your visit with Barth go today?"

"Not well," said Burch. Displeasure darkened his face, and he shifted his view to the floor as if to hide his thoughts. "The man is quite obstinate. He's certain that he'll be acquitted for beating that Negro in the Indian nations."

"I'm a pretty fair country lawyer, Colonel, but even I can't win his case. I know that he'll be found guilty. White or not, this is 1866, not 1860, and the law is different now. I believe that was demonstrated in court today when the jury found Crackley guilty of murdering a colored man and attempting to rape his wife."

"That's what we tried to tell Barth," said Creed, "but he wouldn't listen to us."

"Do you think he might listen to you?" asked Burch.

"He'd believe me, I'm sure," said Buckmaster, "but so what? Aren't you desirous of having him testify on behalf of this falsely convicted friend of yours, Mr. Creed?"

"Yes, that's right," said the Texan, "but he says he won't do it because he's gonna be found not guilty and walk away from here scot-free."

"That's exactly my point," said Buckmaster. "He'll be found guilty, but that still won't get him to testify in your friend's behalf. Did you offer him anything for his testimony?"

"I didn't get much of a chance to do that," said Burch, "because of all the commotion when Peterson was being locked up in the jail. But if I had been given the opportunity, I would have told him that I could get his sentence commuted and see to it that he gets a pardon for his part in the raid in Mississippi last year."

"Can you do that?" queried Buckmaster.

"Don't forget that President Johnson is from Tennessee, Mr. Buckmaster, and although we aren't exactly on the same end of the political spectrum, I do carry a certain amount of weight within Tennessee's politics. A commuted sentence and a pardon for a petty criminal such as Barth? Johnson won't think twice about signing them."

"I am quite impressed, Colonel," said Buckmaster. "I'll not only present your proposition to Barth, but I'll guarantee that he'll accept it."

"And you, sir, will be amply rewarded for your efforts," said Burch. "You can rest assured of that."

Their conversation turned to the overall political situation in the South. All three men agreed that the states that had formed the Confederacy were only beginning to feel the iron fist of radical Republican revenge; however, they disagreed on how Southerners should deal with this looming threat to their freedom. Creed favored patience and cooperation with the Unionists and the elevation of the freedmen through education and economic opportunity. Burch agreed with Creed as long as the Negroes remained docile, that is, they didn't think themselves the new masters of the South. Buckmaster opposed the idea of equality for Negroes, and he resented having it forced on white Southerners by Northerners with a desire to reap the spoils of war. Creed abhorred the use of violence to oppose the Unionists, Burch said it might be necessary, and Buckmaster supported it as the only solution to maintaining the supremacy of the white race in the South. The discussion came to a close well past nine o'clock when Creed noted the hour and Buckmaster said that he needed to retire early because he had the first case in the morning and still had some preparation to complete.

As they passed up Main Street from the docks, Creed and Buckmaster noticed that many of the town's saloons were still quite busy, filled with loud, boisterous customers who weren't celebrating a holiday with song and dance but were very noisy all the same. The way they clumped together around a single speaker reminded Creed of another time a few months back when he was in Central City, Colorado Territory. The local citizenry there had become disturbed over the presence of an outlaw in their jail, and they planned to do something about changing his residence to the local cemetery.

"This is most unusual," said Buckmaster. "It's the middle of the week. I know Crackley's and Lowe's murder trial brought extra business to town, but I didn't realize they'd brought in this much business."

They walked on to the courthouse, and much to their surprise, it looked like an armed camp. The whole building was lit up. Marshal Hays stood on the steps holding a rifle. Sheriff Whitesides and a few other men with weapons could be seen through the windows.

"What's going on here?" Buckmaster wondered aloud.

Creed noted the genuine worry and concern in the lawyer's aspect. He's actually afraid of something, thought the Texan. Well, he isn't fearless after all. How about that?

"Why don't we ask Marshal Hays?" suggested Creed.

"Good idea," said Buckmaster.

They turned up the walk to the front door.

"Hold it right there," warned Hays, lowering his rifle in the direction of the newcomers and squinting into the shadows around them. "What do you want here?"

The lawyer halted, stuck out an arm to stop Creed, and said, "It's Tom Buckmaster, Marshal. And Slate Creed. What's going on here?"

Hays lifted his gun and said, "Sorry, Buckmaster, I didn't recognize you in the dark. Can't be too careful at a time like this. Come on ahead if you like."

Creed and Buckmaster moved up the walk to the steps. "What's this all about, Marshal?" asked the lawyer.

"Rumors," said Hays.

"Rumors?" repeated Buckmaster.

"Yep. One going around says there's a band of coloreds over to that shantytown below Fort Smith planning to come over here to drag Crackley out of jail and lynch him. Another says some of the boys around here are planning to hang that queer bank robber the sheriff brought in this afternoon, Another says some of the white men around here don't think it's right that Crackley was found guilty for killing a Negro and they're planning to break him out of here. Now I don't know how much truth is in any of those rumors, but I can't take any chances. I sent word over to Fort Smith for some help here. I expect to see some soldiers any minute now."

"Good idea," said Buckmaster. "What can we do to help until they get here?"

"Are you any good with a gun, Mr. Buckmaster?" asked Hays.

"Well, no, I'm not."

"Then you might as well go home," said the marshal. "I wouldn't want a man in here who might get himself hurt unnecessarily." He focused on the Texan. "Mr. Creed, if you want to stay, I've got an extra shotgun in my office that you can use if it's necessary."

Creed took the first step and said, "I'll stay. Mr. Buckmaster would you please inform Mrs. Chapman that I won't be returning until late?"

"Certainly," said Buckmaster.

Turning back to Hays, Creed said, "Do you want to show me that shotgun, Marshal?"

Before Hays could answer, somebody in the street shouted that a company of soldiers had just landed at the ferry dock. "I guess we won't be needing you after all, Mr. Creed, Thanks all the same."

"I'll wait until the soldiers arrive here at the courthouse," said Creed.

"So will I," said Buckmaster, "and then we can walk home together."

"You're a pretty persuasive fellow, Mr. Buckmaster," said Hays. "Maybe you could talk some sense into these damn fools who want to take the law into their own hands."

"Yes, I suppose I could do that," said Buckmaster tentatively. "But I don't know that I could do it alone." He eyed the tall Texan. "Would you go with me, Mr. Creed?"

"Not without my gun," said Creed. "I know it's against the law in this town to carry a gun, Marshal, but I've had some experience in these matters, and I can tell you that a gun comes in mighty handy when you're trying to make a point about the law."

"I know exactly what you mean, Mr. Creed," said Hays. "You go ahead and get your gun, and don't worry none about the law. I'm authorized to hire temporary deputies when there's an emergency, and I guess this is as much of an emergency as we'll ever see in this town. So consider yourself deputized. Come on, and I'll get you a badge."

A badge, thought Creed. I wonder if he'd be pinning a badge on me if he knew that I'm wanted by the Army. He chuckled aloud.

"What's so funny?" asked Hays.

"Nothing much," said Creed. "I was just thinking about a fellow back home and what he'd think if he saw me wearing a lawman's badge. That's all."

"Surprise him, would it?" asked Hays.

"Yeah, it would," said Creed. Probably scare the hell out of Kindred, he told himself.

24

Company F of the 19th United States Infantry surrounded the Crawford County Courthouse that night in order to preserve order and protect the prisoners in the basement jail. Many citizens of Van Buren vocalized their displeasure at the presence of the soldiers, but they kept a safe distance from the Federals, usually in the security of a saloon.

With Creed to accompany him as something of a bodyguard, Buckmaster did his duty as an officer of the court by moving among the discontented and attempting to persuade them that the law should be allowed to take its course in both cases. Crackley was found guilty by a jury of his peers; that was the law working at its best, he told them. Peterson was only accused of a crime; nothing had been proven yet, which meant he was innocent until his guilt should be established beyond a reasonable doubt, he argued. Buckmaster called up every ounce of eloquence within him as he spoke to each group, and by midnight, he had convinced the overwhelming majority of the disgruntled to go home and sleep off their drink and their aggression. "Tomorrow," he promised, "will bring a new day, and everything will look different and better by the light of our glorious Arkansas sun."

Slate-gray clouds covered the sky at dawn, and just as Roberta began serving breakfast at Mrs. Levi Chapman's Boardinghouse Hotel, a steady downpour commenced outside. A dreary beginning to a day that threatened to be counted among the worst in Van Buren's history.

In spite of the tension of the previous evening, Judge Sangster opened the court session promptly at nine o'clock, announcing that the first business before the court was the sentencing of Harry Crackley.

Creed stood among several other armed deputies who lined the wall behind the judge's bench. Company F lined both walls of the main floor hall to get out of the weather and just in case they were needed upstairs.

Marshal Hays brought Crackley, manacled and shackled, into a courtroom that was jammed to overflowing with hung over spectators. He sat him at the defense table beside the weary, bleary-eyed Buckmaster.

"Harry Crackley," said Sangster, "do you have anything to say to the court before sentence is passed on you?"

Buckmaster rose slowly, then nudged his client to do the same.

Crackley stood up resolutely and said, "You ain't got no right to sentence me to anything. I didn't do nothing wrong. I shot a nigger. So what?"

"That's right, Harry!" said a spectator. "So what?"

Sangster rapped his gavel and said, "Bailiff, throw that man out of here."

"Which one?" queried the bailiff.

Frustrated, the judge said, "Never mind. This court will tolerate no more such outbursts from the gallery."

"Why don't you shut up and let Harry have his say?" said the anonymous spectator.

"Yeah, let Harry talk," chorused several others at the same time.

"Yeah! Yeah!"

"Aw, what's the use?" said Sangster to himself. He leaned back in his chair and threw up his hands. "All right, Crackley. Get on with what you were saying so I can get on with my job."

"Like I was saying, Judge, I shot a nigger. So what? I tried sampling some of that dark meat. So what? I'll bet there's half a dozen men in this town who have killed a nigger or two, and I'll bet there's ten times that many who have had themselves a nigger bitch or two. How about you, Judge? You ever get twixt the legs of a nigger whore?"

Sangster banged his gavel with outrage and shouted, "You've said enough, Harry Crackley."

"What's the matter, Judge?" chortled Crackley. "Did I touch a nerve or something?"

Sangster banged his gavel again and again. "Silence!" he bellowed. "Do you hear me, Crackley? I order you to shut your mouth or I will shut it for you and for good."

"Let him talk," barked several spectators.

Buckmaster turned to Crackley and said in a low voice, "Quiet down, Harry, or he's liable to put a noose around your neck."

"He ain't got the nerve," growled Crackley.

"Let Harry talk," chorused some spectators.

Crackley turned to the gallery and said, "I've had my say, boys. Now it's the judge's turn."

A short murmur of disgust followed, but soon the room was quiet.

"Harry Crackley," said Sangster, "you have been found guilty of murder and of attempted rape. Under the laws of these United States, I hereby sentence you to a minimum of ten years to a maximum of twenty years in the penitentiary at Little Rock."

The crowd erupted in protest. Those in the rear began pushing against the men in front of them until they pressed against the railing that separated the gallery from the bar.

Sangster banged his gavel, but to no avail.

Seeing the sudden surge of angry humanity, Marshal Hays drew his revolver, grabbed Crackley by the coat collar, and pulled him around the defense table toward the judge's bench. Creed and a few of the other deputies who saw the marshal's maneuver drew their weapons and stepped forward to assist Hays.

Buckmaster jumped onto the defense table and faced the mob. "Hold on, boys!" he shouted above the din of discontentment. "Hold on now! Let the law take its course! It's only right, boys!"

Gradually, the collective voice of the protesters subsided, and those men in the back ceased their pushing and shoving those in front of them.

"This isn't over, boys," said Buckmaster. "Not by a long shot. There's all sorts of things to be done yet, starting with my filing an appeal. This isn't over yet. Trust me, boys. There's no need to get worked up here and start something that we'll all be sorry for later. Just back off, boys, and let the law take its course. Justice will be served. I promise you that. Now let the marshal do his job, and let the judge do his, and I'll do mine. And don't forget those soldiers downstairs. If you don't let this go here and now, we'll have those bluebellies to contend with again, and there's not a man here who wants that, is there?" When nobody replied, he answered for them. "Of course not. Now let's let this go, boys. Crackley will get justice. I promise you that. Now why don't you boys go on about your business? I don't think there's gonna be much more to do here today."

Buckmaster was right.

Sangster adjourned the court for the rest of the week and ordered the courtroom cleared.

Hays put his deputies and the bailiff to work moving the crowd out of the building, while he returned Crackley to his cell in the basement jail.

"Got pretty noisy up there, Marshal," said Blodgett. "Anything wrong?"

"Some of our local residents objected to Crackley being given such a stiff sentence," said Hays.

"Stiff sentence?" queried Blodgett. "How stiff?"

"The son of a bitch gave me ten to twenty," said Crackley.

"Shut up, you," said Hays, jabbing Crackley in the spine with the muzzle of his revolver. "Let's get him locked up quick, Jake. I got to get back upstairs and see how things are going."

Blodgett unlocked the cell block door and opened it for the marshal and his prisoner.

Hays pushed Crackley ahead of him into the hallway, and the convict stumbled forward to the door to his cell. He stopped in front of it.

The jailer unlocked the door, entered ahead of Crackley, then waited for the prisoner to step inside. Blodgett removed the shackles from Crackley's ankles and the manacles from his wrists, while Hays stood guard. The jailer took the irons with him when he left the cell. Hays backed out of the cell, and Blodgett locked up behind them.

"I've got extra guards coming down here in a few minutes, Jake."

"Extra guards? What for?"

"There could be trouble later, and I don't want you or the night man to be caught down here all alone."

"What kind of trouble?"

"Could be that some of the boys in town might want to remove a prisoner or two tonight. You never know about these things."

That's right, thought Blodgett. You never know about these things.

25

The rain stopped, and the skies cleared that afternoon. Most folks from out of town departed for their homes in other parts of the county, and Company F returned to Fort Smith. An uneasy quiet settled over Van Buren.

Creed and Colonel Burch discussed visiting Barth in jail once more, but they decided against it because of the turmoil in town. "Let's allow Mr. Buckmaster a chance at Barth first," said Burch. "He might succeed where we failed, and if he should, he knows where to contact me."

"Suppose he does get Barth to recant his story to the Army," said Creed. "Then what happens?"

"That all depends on Barth's situation," said Burch. "If he's in prison, I will either get him released into my custody in order to take him to a military post where his statement can be made to a senior grade officer or I'll find a provost marshal to accompany me to the prison to get his story for the record. I will then present his testimony and Marshall Quade's confession to the Army in Washington to have them review the facts of the case. You may have to come to Washington with me, but we'll cross that bridge when we get to it."

Creed gave Quade's deathbed confession to Burch in the privacy of the colonel's cabin aboard *La Belle de la Rivière.* Burch hid the document in a leather pouch that he stuck inside his travel valise. With that piece of business completed, they left the boat for some fried chicken at Mrs. Chapman's because the lady of the house had asked Creed to bring his distinguished friend to supper with him that evening.

Mrs. Chapman made Burch the center of attention, and the residents asked the lawyer dozens of questions about his role in the war, his home city of Nashville, and his home state of Tennessee. Smith seemed to be the most interested in Nashville as a city of financial opportunity, and Burch assured him that the Tennessee capital would continue to grow as the major rival to Memphis. Landon asked about the stores in Nashville, and Darrell made inquiries about the roads of Tennessee. Miss Steen wished to learn about the educational system in Tennessee, and Jennifer asked about finishing schools for young ladies. Mrs. Nance and Mrs. Chapman concerned themselves with Burch's ancestry, asking how his people came to be in Tennessee, and he replied that they had come there from Virginia at the end of the last century. Buckmaster refrained from posing any questions of Creed's guest because he planned to escort Burch to *La Belle de la Rivière* at the conclusion of the colonel's visit and have a drink with him.

At half past seven, Creed asked to be excused from the polite company because he had agreed to stand two hours of guard duty at the jail starting at eight o'clock. Burch took this as his cue to depart as well. He thanked his hostess and said farewells all around, wishing each of the residents a good night and a good tomorrow.

Creed said goodnight to Burch and Buckmaster in front of the courthouse. He entered the building and reported to Marshal Hays in his office.

"You don't have to stand your watch down in the jail," said Hays. "Tucker John, the regular night jailer, is down there. I only wanted extra deputies in the building in case there's trouble. Most likely nothing will happen, but I'd rather be safe than sorry."

"I don't blame you none there," said Creed. He looked around the office absently for a moment, then turned back to Hays. "I was wondering if I could visit with Mr. Peterson for a few minutes while I'm here."

Hays squinted an accusing eye at Creed and asked, "Why would you want to visit with that queer? You ain't one of them, are you?"

Creed sighed with patience, then said, "No, Marshal, I'm not. I just want to tell him that Mr. Buckmaster has agreed to be his lawyer."

Hays smirked and said, "That figures. Buckmaster is always taking on cases like Peterson's. Some of us have got to thinking that he's as crooked as his clients. We've never had any evidence to support our hunch, of course, but he is a lawyer, and that don't say a whole lot for any man. Now this. Hell, he might be queer, too. Who knows these days what any man is anymore? Well, you go ahead and tell Peterson that Buckmaster is gonna be his lawyer. Just show Tucker your badge, and he'll let you in the cell block when you go down."

Creed nodded and left. Closed minds, he thought as he passed through the hall to the stairs. They're everywhere.

Tucker John looked a lot like Jake Blodgett, making Creed wonder if being ugly was a prerequisite for the job. The jailer unlocked the cell block door and told Creed that Peterson was in the third cell on the right, the one just beyond the space occupied by Dick Barth and Sinker Wilson.

As he sauntered down the hall, Creed thought he heard a scraping noise coming from within Barth's and Wilson's cell. He stopped to listen closer, heard a clink of metal on metal followed by the giggles of both men, put his ear to their door, and rattled it unintentionally, which effectively silenced all sound from within. Whatever they're up to in there, thought Creed, can't be good. I'd better tell the jailer about it when I get done with Peterson. He moved on to Peterson's cell door, slid back the peephole door, and spoke through the opening. "Nelson, are you awake?"

"Mr. Creed, is that you?"

"Yes, it is. I just came by to tell you that Mr. Buckmaster has agreed to be your lawyer."

"Buckmaster?"

Creed noted surprise and fear in Peterson's voice. "Yes," he said. "My attorney, Colonel Burch, asked him to take your case, and he agreed to do it."

"Uh, I don't know about . . . having Mr. Buckmaster as . . . my lawyer, Mr. Creed."

"Why not? Don't you like him?"

"Uh, no, I don't."

"But he's a pretty good lawyer," argued Creed. "I'm sure he can help you."

"He's already helped me enough," said Peterson dryly.

"What?" asked Creed, confused. "He's already helped you enough? Is that what you said?"

"It doesn't make no never mind, Mr. Creed. Just forget I said anything about him. I'm glad to have Mr. Buckmaster for my lawyer. Thank you for your help."

"No, wait a minute here, Nelson. You said that he's already helped you enough. What did you mean by that?"

"I can't tell you," said Peterson. After a short pause, he added, "It won't help me none if I tell you."

All sorts of possibilities flashed through Creed's brain, and all of them had one detail in common. Secrecy. He's hiding something, thought Creed. But what? "Why won't it help you if you tell me?" asked the Texan.

"It just won't," said Peterson.

Creed sensed the anguish in the prisoner's voice. "If you won't tell me," he said, "then who can you tell?"

"Nobody," sobbed Peterson. "I can't tell nobody. It'll only make things worse."

"I want to help you, Nelson," said Creed slowly and with as much sincerity as he could muster. Thinking aloud, he added, "You asked me to get you a lawyer, and I did, but now you object to Mr. Buckmaster. I don't know why, but I do know that you're trying to keep something secret from the whole world, and I can only guess what that might be."

"Don't," said Peterson. "Just leave it alone. Please? Please, Mr. Creed? Just leave it alone?"

"You're in deeper trouble here than just stealing the bank's money, aren't you?"

"No, that's not it."

"Then what is it?"

"It's Buckmaster," blubbered Peterson. "He made me what I am."

Creed was stunned. The possibility that the diminutive lawyer preferred his own gender over women had never entered into the Texan's thinking. He fumbled for words. "Are you telling me that Buckmaster . . . ?"

"Yes," said Peterson. He sniffled a few times, then regained control of his emotions. "Mr. Buckmaster comes from up to Bentonville, the same as I do. He did some law work for my folks when I was about thirteen, I guess, and that's how I came to meet him. The other boys used to pick on me a lot because I was tall and gangly and clumsy. Even when I was little, I was taller and ganglier than the other boys, and I've never been able to do things that other boys can do. I can't even ride a horse without falling off at regular intervals. Mr. Buckmaster was nice to me, and he treated me with kindness, and I guess I sort of took a shine to him. Then he took me for a buggy ride one day, and—"

"I don't want to hear the rest," interjected Creed. "I just don't want to hear it."

"Well, all right," said Peterson. "I suppose that's not the important thing here. It's the other stuff that you need to know." He was calm now, objective even. "I went to work for him in Bentonville for a while, but I didn't like the work. Leastways, that's what I told him when I quit. The truth is I found out that Mr. Buckmaster had a mean side to him, and I didn't much care for it. To keep me in town, he got me a job at the bank as a clerk. That was all right for a while because it got me away from him a lot of the time. Then the war came, and the bank closed up, and I went back to live on the farm with my folks. After the Yankees got control of everything in this region, I went to Fort Smith to work as a clerk for the Army. Remember, I told you about a fellow over there threatening to kill me if I ever came near him again?"

"Yeah, I remember," said Creed.

"Well, I left there and came here to Van Buren. I ran into Mr. Buckmaster outside the courthouse the second day I was here. I didn't have a job yet, and I was staying at the Brodie Hotel. He arranged for me to work at the bank with Mr. Smith, then he took me to Mrs. Chapman's and vouched for me to live there. That was last fall. I've been working and living here ever since."

"All right, you've been living and working here ever since," said Creed. "So what?"

"Well, after you've been in a place for a while, you get to know your way around," said Peterson, "and you see and hear things because you happen to be in the right place at the right time."

"All right, so you've seen and heard things," said Creed, a little annoyed because Peterson seemed to be skirting his point. "So what?"

"So I know that I wasn't Thomas Buckmaster's first or last . . . paramour."

"I don't care about Buckmaster's . . . personal life, Mr. Peterson. In fact, I don't even know why I'm listening to all this. I just came down here to tell you that Buckmaster agreed to be your lawyer, and you tell me all this stuff about you and him. All right, you don't want him for your lawyer. I'll find somebody else for you. Is that what you want?"

"Yes, thank you, Mr. Creed."

"All right. First thing tomorrow I'll start asking around and see what I can do for you."

With his mind completely boggled by Peterson's revelation, Creed hurried to the cell block door and demanded to be let out. When John unlocked the door, the Texan rushed out past the jailer, ran up the stairs two at a time, stopped in the hall to sort out his thoughts, and wound up keeping to himself for most of the remainder of his watch as he searched for answers to the dozens of questions plaguing him.

26

Buckmaster came by the courthouse just as Creed completed his stint at the jail. They met on the front steps.

"How was your watch, Mr. Creed?" asked the lawyer in a most natural manner, although his words were slightly slurred with inebriation.

"Enlightening," said Creed evenly.

"Oh? How so?" Buckmaster's tone expressed surprise but not suspicion.

"I paid a visit to Mr. Peterson."

"Oh? And what did the dear boy have to say?" asked Buckmaster, still not suspecting anything out of the ordinary.

"He told me a lot of things, Buckmaster. Particularly about you."

"About me?" queried the lawyer with the same surprise as he displayed before. "What on earth would he have to say about me?"

"Don't play so innocent with me, Buckmaster. I know what you are now. I didn't care much for you before, and now I think even less of you. I've known your kind before, Buckmaster. Back in Kentucky last January, I had some unsatisfactory business dealings with a man like you. He wasn't a lawyer, but he was still a lying cheat. He also had a preference for boys. I had to kill the dirty bugger before everything could be said and done."

Buckmaster flinched and backed away. "I don't know what you're talking about, sir," he said defensively.

"You disgust me, Buckmaster," said the Texan. He drew his Colt's from his waistband, cocked the hammer, and aimed the muzzle at the lawyer's nose. His anger came to a boil, and he was rapidly losing control of his emotions. "You make me so sick that I feel like blowing a hole right through your head right now."

"Oh, God, no!" cried Buckmaster, his eyes wide with fright, his face drained of color. "Don't shoot me, Mr. Creed! I didn't do—"

"Don't lie about it, you little piece of shit!"

"You don't understand, I tell you. You just don't understand."

"Yes, I do understand," said Creed through gritted teeth. "You abused that poor fellow when he was a boy who didn't know any better, and now he's in jail for stealing money from a bank. Did you teach him to do that, too?"

Buckmaster failed to answer. He sucked hard for air and reached for his throat as if that would help him breathe. It didn't. His eyes rolled up in his head, and he collapsed on the steps.

Seeing Buckmaster in a twisted heap at his feet poured cold water on the fire within Creed. "Aw, hell," he said as he uncocked the revolver and replaced it inside his waistband. He nudged the lawyer with his foot and said, "Get up, Buckmaster. I'm not gonna kill you. Something tells me I should, but I'm not gonna do it. Leastways, not now. Come on. Get up."

Buckmaster twitched convulsively, but he didn't regain consciousness.

Marshal Hays stepped outside at that moment. "What's going on here, Mr. Creed?" he inquired. "I heard voices." He noticed the quivering form sprawled on the lowest steps. "Who's that on the ground?"

"Mr. Buckmaster," said Creed. "He passed out." He nudged the diminutive attorney with his foot again. "Are you all right, Mr. Buckmaster?"

"Passed out?" queried Hays. He jogged down the steps to the fallen man, knelt down beside him, and sniffed his breath. "He's been drinking," he announced. "Probably had too much. That's probably why he passed out. Help me get him up, and we'll take him inside until he can walk on his own again."

Reluctantly, Creed helped Hays. Each took an arm, pulled it around his own neck, lifted Buckmaster easily, and between them carried him into the marshal's office. Hays scanned the room for a place to put the unconscious lawyer and saw only his own chair.

"Maybe we should take him downstairs," suggested the marshal. "He can sleep it off in the jail. There must be a free bed down there for him."

"I don't think he's so drunk that he needs to be locked up," said Creed, feeling a little guilty over scaring the bejesus out of Buckmaster.

"Oh, I won't lock him up," said Hays. "We'll just put him in a cell and let him sleep it off. I'll tell Tucker to let him go home as soon as he wakes up and wants out."

"You're the marshal," said Creed.

They carried Buckmaster down the stairs to the jail.

"Tucker, have you got a vacant cell for Mr. Buckmaster here?" asked Hays. "He's had a little too much to drink and needs a bed for the night."

"Sorry, Marshal," said John, "we're all filled up. Every cell has a prisoner or two. I could put him in with that killer Crackley. He's by himself, and ain't he one of Mr. Buckmaster's clients?"

"That's right, he is," said Hays. "But I got a better idea." A mischievous grin curled the lawman's lips. "Let's put him in with that queer Peterson. He's his lawyer, too. The two of them deserve each other if you ask me."

"That might not be such a good idea," said Creed. "Peterson told me that he doesn't want Buckmaster for his lawyer after all."

"Too bad for both of them then," said Hays. "They're gonna spend the night together." He giggled sadistically. "Come on, Tucker. Open up and let's put him to bed."

"Really, Marshal," said Creed, "I don't think this is such a good idea."

"Well, I do," said Hays with a touch of belligerence, "and my opinion is the only one that counts here. Now let's get him in that cell."

Reluctantly, Creed helped Hays carry Buckmaster to the cell block door which John opened with a great deal of noise.

"Hey, what the hell's goin' on out there?" grumbled Crackley, his voice muffled only slightly by his cell door. "I'm tryin' to get me some sleep here. Knock off the goddamned racket, asshole!"

Several other prisoners' voices made the same protest. Strangely, none of them belonged to Dick Barth or Sinker Wilson.

"You boys just hold it down," John shouted back at them. "We got us a sad case out here. Drunken lawyer."

"Lawyer, eh?" queried Crackley. "Too bad it ain't that judge. I'd sure like to get him in here with me for a while."

"Lucky for you that it isn't Judge Sangster," said Hays. "If he heard you threaten him like that, he'd put you away for the rest of your life for killing that Negro."

"I ain't gone to prison yet, Marshal," said Crackley through his door.

"Yeah, but you're going just the same, Crackley," said Hays. "That partner of yours ought to be going with you, but I guess the jury saw it otherwise."

"Yeah, and you had to shoot him, you son of a bitch."

"I didn't kill him," said Hays. "Besides, he's burned worse than he's shot. He's over to Doc Pernot's right now in a nice soft bed. He's being taken real good care of, Crackley. He'll be fine, and I'll let him come by and see you before we ship you off to Little Rock."

"You'd better," said the convict. "Davy and me have been pards since we was boys. I've been looking after him for a lot of years, and I gotta make sure he's okay."

"Well, you can quit worrying about it, Crackley," said Hays. "Doc Pernot is taking good care of him."

"I'd like to see that for myself."

"Well, that's not gonna happen tonight," said Hays. "Now go back to bed and mind your own business."

John opened the door to Peterson's cell. "Stand away in there, queer," he said to the prisoner. "You got company coming for the night."

The shadow of a tall man rose from the lower bunk and shuffled to the rear of the cell. "Who is it?" asked Peterson, squinting into the light of the hall.

"It's Marshal Hays and me," said Creed.

"Mr. Creed?"

"That's right, Nelson," said Creed.

"Who's that you're bringing in here?" asked Peterson.

"Mr. Buckmaster," said Creed.

"Thomas?" queried Peterson.

"That's right," said Hays. "I figure you two deserve each other. Leastways, for one night." He giggled.

So did John.

Creed and Hays placed Buckmaster on the lower bunk.

"Which way do you want him, Peterson?" asked John. "Faceup or down?" He laughed at the ribald insinuation.

"I don't want him in here with me," said Peterson. "Get him out of here."

"We could put you in with Crackley if you like," said the jailer. "I'm sure he'd *love* your company what with his partner in Dr. Pernot's hospital for the night."

"That's right, Peterson," said Hays. "You'll have Buckmaster here for a cell mate tonight or you'll have Crackley. The choice is yours."

"I guess it'll have to be Mr. Buckmaster," said Peterson slowly.

"Good choice," said Hays.

"Ain't Buckmaster gonna be surprised when he wakes up in the morning?" said John. He laughed.

So did Hays.

Creed didn't. He looked at Peterson and said, "Just take it easy, Nelson. He'll be out of here tomorrow, and I'll see about getting you another lawyer first thing in the morning."

"That's right, Peterson," said Hays. "You just take it easy. You're in enough trouble already." He turned to John. "Lock up good, Tucker. All's quiet in town tonight, so Sheriff Whitesides and I are calling off the extra deputies as of midnight. You'll be on your own after that."

"That suits me just fine, Marshal. I prefer being down here alone anyway. That way I don't have to talk to nobody except Betsy."

"Betsy?" queried Hays.

"My shotgun," said John.

The three lawmen exited Peterson's cell. John locked the door behind them, and they walked back to the jailer's room. John locked the cell block door.

Creed and Hays went upstairs and said goodnight again in front of the sheriff's office. Hays went inside to stand one more watch with the sheriff before calling it a night, and Creed headed home to try to get some sleep and forget about Peterson and Buckmaster and this whole lurid business surrounding them.

27

Instead of climbing into the upper bunk, Peterson curled himself in a corner of his cell much of the night. Staring. Not sleeping. Staring with hate, with fear. Wide awake. Staring at Buckmaster. His mind in a turmoil. Hating the diminutive lawyer, fearing him. Hating Buckmaster enough to want him dead. Fearing him too much to do the deed himself.

Midway through the night, finally feeling the cold, Peterson rose stiffly and walked softly to the bunk bed to retrieve a blanket. Inadvertently, he disturbed Buckmaster, waking the smaller man.

The room was dark. The only light filtered into the cell through the barred basement window, emanating from a street lamp outside and creating shadows within the cell.

"Christ, what stinks?" muttered Buckmaster. He rolled over on the bunk and realized that he wasn't in his soft, cozy bed at Mrs. Chapman's. Panic raked his senses as he gasped, "Where am I?"

"You're in jail, Thomas," said Peterson evenly.

The voice was familiar, but the sound of it didn't strike the right chord in Buckmaster's memory instantly. "Who's there?" he demanded. He lifted up on an elbow and shrank away from the speaker.

"It's me, Thomas. Nelson."

"What are you—?" Then he was struck by Peterson's first words. "Did you say jail?" he queried. He moved closer to Peterson.

"That's right, Thomas. You're in jail. With me."

Buckmaster sat up on the edge of the bunk. His head hurt. "What am I doing in jail? With you?" More panic attacked his mind. "You didn't tell them, did you, Nelson?"

"Tell them what, Thomas?" asked Peterson calmly.

"About us and Smith and the bank. You didn't tell them, did you, my boy?"

"I'm not your boy, Thomas," said Peterson, anger and hate discoloring his tone. "Not anymore, I'm not."

Buckmaster's memory flashed a scene before his mind's eye. He and Creed on the courthouse steps. The Texan said he knew about me, he thought. Knew what? About me and Nelson? About this bank business? Yes, he mentioned something about that. He stood and confronted Peterson. "You told him about us and Smith and the bank, didn't you, Nelson?" he said angrily. "You told him, didn't you? You fool!" He reached out to slap Peterson's face, although he wasn't certain exactly where the taller man was standing.

Peterson sensed more than saw the blow coming toward him from the much shorter man. He raised his left arm to block it. He succeeded. Feeling bold now because he had thwarted his attacker, he grabbed Buckmaster's wrist and twisted it downward. "No, Thomas, you will not strike me," he said through gritted teeth. "Not now, not ever again." He continued to twist the lawyer's arm.

"You're hurting me, Nelson," whined Buckmaster.

"Good! I mean to hurt you. I mean to hurt you a lot. I mean to hurt you as much as you've hurt me all these years." He lashed out with his right hand and slapped Buckmaster across the face. "How's that for starters, Thomas?" He slapped him again, using the back of his right hand. "There's more, Thomas."

"No, Nelson, don't hit me again," cried Buckmaster as he cowered from his assailant.

Peterson ignored the plea. He jerked Buckmaster closer to him and repeated the blows. "Yes, Thomas," he said, his voice becoming demonic, "I'm going to strike you again. I'm going to strike you for every time you've struck me these past eight years." He made a fist and slammed it into the lawyer's cheek.

"No, don't, Nelson!" screamed Buckmaster, He struggled to free himself from Peterson's vice-like grip. "Help me, somebody! Help me!"

Buckmaster's cry for assistance broke through the veil of Morpheus draped over the cell block, rousing Crackley first, then the other prisoners. "What the hell's going on over there?" demanded the killer from Texas. Others made similar protests.

The last to hear the disturbance in Peterson's cell was Tucker John, and he became cognizant of it only after Crackley and the other prisoners began voicing their displeasure at being awakened in the middle of the night. Legs and feet resting on the desk, head lolling against the wall, chair tilted back, he opened his eyes groggily. "Now what the hell is that all about?" he asked nobody in particular. He licked the dryness from his lips and listened for a few seconds before taking his stiff lower limbs from atop the desk and righting his chair. "That son of a bitch Buckmaster must have come awake and found out where he's at and who he's with." He giggled at the thought of the lawyer's surprise. "Better go let the little bastard out of Peterson's cell." He picked up the ring of keys from the desk and stood up. He paused to yawn and stretch before stepping around the desk to unlock the cell block door. Hearing more protests from the inmates, he shouted, "Hold it down, you sons a bitches! You're gonna raise the dead with all that pissin' and moanin'."

Peterson landed several more blows to Buckmaster's face and head, and the lawyer continued to scream for help and make pleas with Peterson to let him go.

John opened the cell block door and stepped inside the hallway just in time to hear Buckmaster cry out, "He's killing me! Somebody help me!" Killing him? wondered John. Goddamned queer! What's he doing to Buckmaster? Buggering the little runt to death? Remembering that Peterson was a good head taller than he was, the jailer was caught up with the fear that he might not be able to handle the prisoner bodily. Better bring Betsy, he thought. He went back to the jailer's room and picked up the shotgun. He broke open the action, checked the twin loads quickly, locked the barrels in place again, and returned to the cell block hall. Realizing that he would need a light to see into Peterson's cell, he hurried to the far end of the hall to retrieve the wall lamp.

"Oh, God, he's killing me!" shrieked Buckmaster.

The other prisoners no longer protested having their sleep interrupted. Now they demanded to know what was happening. Who's being killed? Who's killing him? Some of them thought they recognized Buckmaster's voice, but they couldn't be sure. One called out, "Buckmaster, is that you?" The others picked up the name.

John stood in front of Peterson's cell door. Keys in his left hand, shotgun and lamp in the other. He missed the keyhole on the first try, succeeded on the second, turned the key, and unlocked the door.

Caught up in the fury of his own rage, Peterson was oblivious to the jailer at the door, continuing to slap and punch Buckmaster.

Buckmaster fought desperately to free himself from Peterson's clench and at the same time dodge the blows from the taller man. Blood, sweat, and tears streamed down his left cheek, over his jaw, and down his throat to be absorbed by his shirt and coat. He saw John in the doorway and screamed, "Help me, Tucker, help me! He's killing me!"

"Stand away from him, Peterson!" shouted John.

Peterson ignored the order.

"Shoot him, Tucker!"

John set the lamp on the basement floor and leveled the shotgun at Peterson. "Stand away from him, Peterson!" he shouted. "Stand away or I'll shoot!"

Peterson heard John. He stayed his hand in mid-swing and glared at the jailer. "I'm gonna whip him within an inch of his life like he used to do to me," he said through gritted teeth. He completed the blow.

John heard Peterson's words, and they confused him. He wanted to sort through them before acting, but Buckmaster's frightful, anguished scream denied him the luxury of meditation. "Stand away, Peterson, or I'll shoot!" He cocked the hammers of the shotgun.

Peterson grabbed Buckmaster by the front of his coat and lifted him off the ground.

John pulled the first trigger.

BANG! Betsy belched fire and lead. The balls ripped into and through Buckmaster, some lodging in Peterson's torso. Blood splattered from the lawyer onto the prisoner. Peterson staggered for a second, still clutching the now rigid Buckmaster in his hands. His rage tempered with the pain of injury, he threw the wounded lawyer at John. Eyes bulging with shock and disbelief, Buckmaster collided with the jailer, and they crashed to the hallway floor in a bloody heap of arms and legs thrashing to be free of each other.

"Get him off me!" screamed John.

Peterson stumbled forward to the doorway amid the shouts of the other prisoners demanding to know what was happening. He steadied himself by holding onto the door.

Buckmaster gurgled blood.

John freed himself from the lawyer, rolled to one side, scrambled on his hands and knees to get farther away, bumped into the wall, lost his balance, and came to rest with his back against a cell door. Frightened at the sight of Peterson standing in the doorway to his cell and at the sight of the dying lawyer gasping his last breath on the floor, John cried out, "Stand away, Peterson! Stand away! You hear, boy? Stand away!"

Peterson struggled to comprehend the tragedy that had just transpired. Oh my God! he thought. What's happened here? He stared down at Buckmaster as the lawyer expired his death sigh. Thomas! Thomas! Thomas! "No!" he cried. He dropped to his knees, tears in his eyes, his hands reaching out but not touching the dead man. "No, Thomas, I didn't want this. I didn't want you dead. Not completely dead."

"What the hell's goin' on out there?" shouted Crackley above the other prisoners.

John slid along the wall until he bumped into the cell block door. He pulled himself up with the door. "Get back in your cell, Peterson," he said, his voice quavering with fear. "Get back in there, I tell you."

Peterson's head twisted in John's direction. "He's dead," he sobbed. "He's dead. And you killed him."

"What?" mumbled John. "What's that? I killed him? No, you did it. You did it, Peterson. You put him between us when I fired. You did it. I didn't kill him."

Peterson started to get up. "You killed Thomas, you son of a bitch!" he shouted. "You killed him. You killed my Thomas, you son of a bitch!"

"No, I didn't do it," said John. "You did it. You did it, I tell you." He backed through the doorway to the jailer's room. Seeing Peterson stagger toward him, he grabbed the door, slammed it closed, went to lock it, then realized that the keys were still in the lock of Peterson's cell door. Panic set in. He ran for the stairs, for the upstairs hall, for the front door to the courthouse, for the alarm bell in front of the building.

Peterson made it to the cell block door, opened it, and heard John's footfalls on the stairway. He's going for help, he thought. I'm doomed. He turned around to survey the scene in the hallway. Buckmaster was dead. That much was certain. His cell door was open. The key in the lock. The keys! he thought, He stumbled back along the hall to his door. He removed the key from the lock, then moved down the hall to the next cell. One by one he unlocked them, setting the other prisoners free.

The first pair of inmates to enter the hall saw Buckmaster's body on the floor. "Oh, shit!" they said in unison. "What happened here?" queried the one looking at Peterson. "Never mind that," said the other. "Let's get the hell out," said both. They stepped over the corpse and fled. So did the second pair, and the third.

Peterson unlocked Crackley's door.

The convicted killer threw open the door and stepped into the hall. He saw the bloody body, looked at Peterson, noted his wounds, and said, "He killed you, too, friend." Spying John's shotgun beside Buckmaster, he stooped down, picked it up, broke open the action, noted that one barrel was still loaded, closed the barrels again, then headed for the exit.

Peterson unlocked the remaining doors in sequence and released their inmates until he came to the cell next to his, It was the last. He turned the key in the lock and opened the door, but nobody came out. He pushed the door wide open and peered inside. No Wilson, no Barth, no bars on the window.

28

Clutching the jailer's shotgun, Crackley followed the other inmates up the stairs, down the main floor hall to the front door of the courthouse, and saw John ring the alarm bell as they stepped outside. The thought of stopping and putting a charge of shot into the bastard crossed the killer's mind, but he discarded the idea as being counterproductive to his ultimate goal of finding his lifelong companion David Lowe. Focused on that goal, he started his search by asking the other prisoners where he might find Dr. Pernot's hospital. One of them said to go with him and he would show Crackley where it was.

Dr. Pernot heard the alarm bell, and like nearly every other resident of Van Buren, his initial fear was fire. He donned his trousers, shoes, coat, and hat and stepped outside to learn the reason for the emergency. He had barely reached the sidewalk in front of his house when Crackley and the escapee guiding him came running along Perry Street. The physician didn't recognize either man or the shotgun that Crackley carried at his side, but this didn't concern him as he stopped them to ask, "Where is the fire?"

"Jailbreak!" shouted John above the clanging of the town emergency bell. "Jailbreak! Jailbreak!"

Soon, the word spread throughout Van Buren.

Creed heard the bell, and like most people, his first instinct said a fire was blazing somewhere in town and every available man was needed to fight it. Ready to answer the call, he tumbled out of bed, turned up the lamp, and slipped into his trousers and his boots.

KNOCK-KNOCK-KNOCK!

"Mr. Creed! Mr. Creed!" called Mrs. Chapman. "Are you awake, Mr. Creed?"

"I'm up, Mrs. Chapman," said Creed.

"Hurry, Mr. Creed. There's been a jailbreak."

"A jailbreak?"

"That's right. The word is all over town."

Barth and Wilson, thought Creed. Damn! I forgot to tell the jailer about the noise in their cell. He grabbed his Colt's, checked the loads and caps, shoved the weapon inside his waistband, donned his hat and coat with the deputy's badge still pinned to the lapel, and opened the door.

The other residents stepped into the hall, each of them in various costume from Smith who wore a nightshirt and trousers to Jennifer who had thrown a blue woolen shawl over her nightshirt.

Roberta came down the hall to Mrs. Chapman. "Mr. Buckmaster don't answer his door, Miz Chapman," she said.

"He's not there," said Creed.

"He's not?" queried Mrs. Chapman.

"No, he's in the jail," said the Texan. "He, uh, fainted from too much drinking, and Marshal Hays thought it would be best that he sleep it off in the jail."

"I see," she said calmly. Then it struck her. "Good lord! Mr. Buckmaster is in the jail. So is Mr. Peterson, and there's been a jailbreak. Oh, my!"

"What's this?" muttered Smith. "Buckmaster and Peterson in a jailbreak together? My God!"

Others mumbled similar questions.

"Take it easy, folks," said Creed. "Let me go see for sure what's happened first before we go to jumping to any conclusions about Mr. Buckmaster and Mr. Peterson." He pinpointed his view on Smith and added, "Especially, Mr. Peterson. We shouldn't be too hasty to rush to any judgments here."

Smith winced, and beads of clammy perspiration trickled down his forehead and cheeks.

"Yes, of course, you're right," said Mrs. Chapman.

Scanning the worried faces in the hall, Creed said, "The best thing you folks can do is stay here. If you men have any weapons, get them and everybody come together in one room. Draw the drapes and shades, Mrs. Chapman, and lock all the doors to the outside. Don't let anybody inside until you're sure who they are."

"Yes, of course," said Mrs. Chapman. "Come along, folks. You heard Mr. Creed. Mr. Smith, get that handgun of yours, and everybody come down to the parlor immediately."

"I'm going now, ma'am," said Creed. "Lock the door behind me." He didn't wait for anybody to say good-bye or wish him luck or anything else. He rushed down the stairs and out the front door.

Voices could be heard all through the town. Men shouting, women crying, children shrieking with fear. In the midst of the human cacophony the town alarm bell rang from the courthouse square. Street lamps on every corner provided enough light to create eerie shadows everywhere.

Better go slow, thought Creed as he stopped where Mrs. Chapman's walkway intersected with the sidewalk. I'm a stranger here, and somebody's liable to mistake me for an escaped prisoner and put a load of buckshot in my hide. He looked for signs of a fire but saw none, which confirmed that the emergency was a jailbreak. Barth and Wilson. It must be them. Damn!

Crackley might have been born and raised in Texas, but he knew a foreign accent when he heard one. "Are you Dr. Pernot?" he asked.

"Yes, I am."

Crackley pointed the shotgun that he'd been holding at his side toward Pernot. "Then you're just the man I want to see," said the outlaw.

"Who are you?" demanded Pernot.

"Hey, I ain't sticking around here," said the other escaped man. "Good luck, Crackley."

"Crackley?" blurted Pernot.

"Yeah, that's right, Doc. Where's Davy?"

"Davy?"

"My pard," said Crackley angrily as he put the muzzle of the shotgun up to Pernot's face. "Davy Lowe. Where is he?"

"He's inside in bed," said Pernot, unshaken by the threat of violence.

"Then let's go see him, Doc."

Wearing a blue cotton robe over a pink nightshirt, Mrs. Pernot saw the scene unfolding in front of her house from the second-story bedroom window, and although she didn't recognize Crackley, she did see the weapon in his hands and how he was threatening her husband with it. Memories of their wartime experiences flashed through her mind. The Pernots had been faced with similar situations but with Union soldiers, and all of them required a cool head.

Frightened, her children came into the room. She told her oldest son, Sargeant, to leave by the back door and fetch Marshal Hays as quickly as possible. When her husband and the man with the shotgun started to come toward the house, she ordered the remaining children to stay in her bedroom with the door locked until she told them it was safe to come out again. They obeyed, and she hurried downstairs to wait at the door for the doctor and the stranger to come inside. "Where's the fire, Henri?" she asked calmly when they entered.

"Mr. Creed!"

The Texan responded to his name, recognizing the caller as Marshal Hays. He saw the lawman running along Strokes Street, coming toward him from the east.

"Mr. Creed, there's been a jailbreak," panted Hays. "Are you willing to help?"

Creed opened his coat to show his Colt's and said, "I'm ready. Am I still a deputy?"

Hays sucked in a breath, tapped Creed's chest, and said, "You're a deputy as long as you're wearing that badge. Come on. Let's get over to the courthouse and see what's happened."

They trotted along Strokes to Webster and turned south, Hays yelling, "Marshal Hays here! Stand away!" They made the short block to the courthouse where John was still spreading the alarm with the bell and his voice. Hays ran up to him. "What happened, Tucker?" he asked breathlessly.

John stopped ringing the bell, turned to Hays, and said, "Jailbreak, Marshal."

"Don't you think I know that already, you fool?" snapped Hays. "What happened?"

"Peterson killed Buckmaster."

Creed grabbed John's arm. "What?"

"Peterson . . . killed . . . Buckmaster?" stammered Hays with disbelief.

"I thought you said there was a jailbreak," said Creed.

"There was," said John, frightened by the Texan's size and forceful manner. "Every last son of a bitch we had down there has escaped. Peterson let them go."

"How did he do that?" asked Hays.

"He jumped me when I was trying to stop him from killing Buckmaster. He took my shotgun and keys, killed Buckmaster, and unlocked all the other cells and let everybody go. I saw them all run out while I was ringing the bell to warn the town."

"All of them?" queried Creed. "Including Barth?"

"Yeah, sure," said John with uncertainty.

"We'd better go check," said Hays.

"Yeah," said Creed, suspicious that John was only telling them half the truth.

"Tucker, if any law officers show up," said Hays, "you hold them here. We'll need to organize a posse." He turned to Creed. "Are you ready?"

"Let's go," said the Texan. He followed Hays to the courthouse steps.

"We'd better take it slow here," said Hays. "We don't know who might be in there yet and whether they're armed or not."

Seeing the fear in the lawman's eyes, Creed drew his Colt's and said, "I'll go first, Marshal. You just back my play."

"Yes, of course." The marshal drew his own weapon.

"There ain't no fire, lady," said Crackley. "Just me. Now where's Davy?"

"What's going on here, Henri?" asked Mrs. Pernot.

"This is Mr. Crackley, Emmy," said Pernot. "He has come for his friend Mr. Lowe. Come and help us prepare him to leave."

"Yes, dear," she said. "This way, Mr. Crackley." She led the way to the dimly lit hospital room.

Lowe was sitting up in bed, his torso wrapped with bandages. "What's goin' on out there, ma'am?" he asked, not yet seeing Pernot or Crackley behind her just yet. "I hear somebody ringing a bell. Is there a fire somewheres?"

"There ain't no fire, Davy," said Crackley.

"Harry?"

"Yeah, boy, it's me."

"What are you doing here, Harry? How'd you get out of jail?"

"Never mind all that now, Davy. We got to get out of here before they find out I'm gone. Get your clothes on."

"I can't go nowheres, Harry. I'm hurt too bad."

"Your friend is right, Mr. Crackley," said Pernot. "Mr. Lowe's burns are very bad. The dressings need to be changed every day until the skin has healed over the burn."

"If that be the case," said Crackley, "then maybe we'd better take you with us, Doc, to see that he gets proper care. Have you got a stable out back?"

"Yes," said Pernot.

"How many horses have you got?"

"Four," said the doctor.

"That's plenty. Let's get out there and get them saddled up. How about guns? Have you got any guns in the house?"

"I am a physician," said Pernot proudly. "I save lives. I do not take them."

"Fine. You ain't got no guns in the house. Davy, get your clothes on and come on out back when you're dressed. Ma'am, you rustle us up some grub for the road, and be quick about it. We ain't got much time here. And don't think about goin' for no help. If any law shows up here, I'll kill your husband right off. Is that understood?"

"It goes without saying," said Mrs. Pernot.

"All right, let's go then. Lead the way, Doc."

Pernot led Crackley through the house to the back door, and Mrs. Pernot retired to the kitchen to get the food for them.

Lowe struggled to get into his pants as most movements caused him a lot of pain in the area where he was burned. His boots were easier as was his coat. He didn't bother with his shirt because most of it had been destroyed by the shooting at the courthouse. Taking his hat from the peg on the wall, he walked tenderly down the hall to the back door of the house and outside to the barn.

With both outlaws out of the house the back way now, Mrs. Pernot hurried upstairs to her bedroom. "Open up, children," she said softly. "It's Mother."

The lock clicked, and the door opened.

"Henri, run out the front door and go to the courthouse and find the sheriff or any of the other lawmen and tell them that Harry Crackley has come here to get Mr. Lowe and that they are running away. Do you understand, Henri?"

"Yes, Mother," said the boy.

"Hurry, Henri."

The boy bolted from the room, down the stairs to the front door, and was soon gone into the night.

"The rest of you stay in here," said Mrs. Pernot, "and keep the door locked. Don't let anybody except me or your father in here. Understood?"

"Yes, ma'am," said the oldest girl. "What's going on, Mother?"

"Never mind now, Emmy. Just do as I told you."

"Yes, ma'am." She closed and locked the door again.

• • •

Creed moved slowly up the steps. The door was wide open, allowing him a clear view of the entire hall. Nobody in sight. No, wait. At the far end. On the stairs to the courtroom. Peterson? Yes, it was him. He was sitting on the third step, hunkered over and holding his gut. The Texan entered the building. The marshal's office door was closed, so was the sheriff's. Both were locked. Good, he thought. Nobody broke in to steal any guns. He waved for Hays to follow him. When the marshal came close, Creed asked, "Any of these other offices have guns kept in them, Marshal?"

"No," said Hays. "Just mine and Sheriff Whitesides. The only other gun in the building was the jailer's shotgun." He saw Peterson for the first time. He leveled his revolver in the wounded man's direction. "My God! That's one of them!"

Creed bumped his arm to spoil the man's aim and said, "Don't shoot. It's Peterson, and he's hurt."

"What? How do you know?"

"You didn't fight in the war, did you, Marshal?"

"No, I didn't."

"I did. Trust me. He's hurt bad." The Texan moved ahead and added, "Come on."

Cautiously, Hays followed Creed down the hall.

Peterson heard their footsteps. He lifted his head to look at them. He recognized Creed, and he recognized the guns pointed in his direction. "Go ahead and shoot," he wheezed. "I'm already dead."

"What's that?" asked Hays, holding his ground.

"He's gut-shot, Marshal," said Creed over his shoulder. "He's not gonna hurt us." He moved close to Peterson for a good look at the man's blood-soaked clothing. "Who shot you, Nelson?"

"The jailer."

"You're a liar," said Hays, coming up behind Creed.

"How?" asked Creed.

"He was trying to stop me from killing Thomas."

"Thomas?" queried Creed. "Buckmaster?"

"Yes," said Peterson. He winced with pain. "I was beating him when the jailer opened the door and ordered me to stop. When I didn't, he fired and killed us both. He's downstairs. He died quick. I guess I'm not gonna be so lucky."

"Did you let the other prisoners out of their cells?" asked Creed.

"Yes. All but the cell next to mine. Nobody was in there, and the bars were missing from the window."

"Damn!" swore Creed. "I knew it. I heard them working on the window when I was down there earlier."

"You heard them?" queried Hays. "And you didn't say anything to me or Tucker about it?"

"It slipped my mind, Marshal. I was thinking about other things." He looked down at Peterson. "Like a few of the things Nelson told me."

"I didn't tell you everything, Mr. Creed," rasped Peterson. "I didn't tell you about the bank robbery."

"You said you didn't do it," said Creed.

"I didn't, but I know who did."

"Who?" demanded Hays.

"Mr. Smith."

"Mr. Smith?" queried Creed. "From the boardinghouse?"

"Yes, him."

"Leo Smith?" asked Hays. "The bank cashier?"

"Yes, sir. He stole the money with Thomas. They were in it together. I found out, confronted them with it, and they threatened to expose me for . . . what I am if I told on them. I got scared and went along with them, and they promised to give me some of the money. I didn't know that they were planning to put the blame on me for their crime."

Creed knew well how that felt.

"Is that why you were beating Buckmaster?" asked Hays.

Peterson looked at Creed, his eyes asking if he should tell the truth or not. Finding no answer in the Texan's face, he said, "Yes."

Mrs. Pernot returned to the kitchen to finish putting some food in a basket for the outlaws to take with them. She turned up the lamp with the hope that a neighbor or a passerby might see what was happening in her house and might bring help.

The back door opened, and Crackley poked his head inside. He was unarmed now. "What's holding up that grub, lady?" he groused.

Mrs. Pernot put a cloth over the basket and said, "It's all ready now. I'll bring it out."

"Just hand it to me, and go back to bed." He saw the worried look on her face, and for a brief instant, the little bit of decency still in him came to the fore. "if all goes well, ma'am, your

husband will be coming back to you in the morning and this
will all seem like a bad dream." He took the basket from her.
"Now go on and git."

Calling on her wartime experiences as a guide, she didn't
hesitate to obey him. She hurried down the hall to the staircase,
looked back to make certain that Crackley had gone out the back
door, and once she was satisfied that he had, continued on up the
stairs to her bedroom. She knocked softly and said, "Emmy, it's
Mother. Let me in."

The lock clicked, and the door opened.

Mrs. Pernot brushed past her children to go to the front window.
She spread the drapes apart and peered out at the street below.

"Marshal!" shouted John from the end of the hall. "It's Crackley.
One of the Pernot boys says he's over to Dr. Pernot's hospital right
now trying to get Lowe out of there. You'd better come quick."

Creed and Hays exchanged looks, and the Texan spoke first.
"Let me go, Marshal," he said. "I think I'm better able to deal
with his kind than you are. Don't you agree?"

"Yes, I do," said Hays. "Go ahead. And take some of the boys
with you."

"No, thank you. They'll only get in the way."

"Do you know where Dr. Pernot's hospital is at?"

"Yes, I do."

"Good luck."

Creed left the courthouse, spoke briefly to the Pernot boy, then
headed east along Perry Street. Dr. Pernot's house was only a
block away.

A tall man stood on the sidewalk facing the house. Mrs. Pernot
didn't know him, but she knew that he was a lawman when light
from the street lamp reflected off the badge pinned to the lapel
of his coat.

"Thank God," she muttered beneath her breath. She went back
to the door, stopped, turned back to her daughter, and said, "Lock
the door again, Emmy." Without waiting to see if the girl obeyed
her, she went downstairs again to the front door.

Creed missed seeing Mrs. Pernot as she looked at him through
the second-story bedroom window, but he couldn't fail to see her
when she opened the front door and stepped onto the porch. He
didn't know her any more than she knew him, but he surmised that
she was Dr. Pernot's wife and started up the walk to speak to her.

"Are you a deputy?" she asked him when he reached the porch steps.

"Yes, ma'am. Are you Mrs. Pernot?"

"Yes, I am. Did my son find you?"

"Yes, ma'am. He told me that one of the prisoners from the jail came here to get his friend from the hospital."

"That's right. Crackley, the killer. He took Mr. Lowe and my husband out to the barn in back of the house. They're saddling horses right now as we speak."

"Go back in the house, Mrs. Pernot. Your husband will be along shortly."

These were bold words from a stranger, but the steel in his eyes said he would make that promise come true. She obeyed him.

Creed drew his Colt's and hurried around the house on its Jefferson Street side. With the eye of a military man, he surveyed the scene.

The barn's double doors faced the street. The only cover for Creed was the house, but it was too far away from the stable for him to use the Colt's effectively.

Damn! he thought. Only one thing to do here.

Knowing that Crackley and Lowe had only one exit from the barn, the Texan stationed himself directly in their path and waited. He heard the crossbar being lifted on the inside of the door. Only seconds now.

The doors opened wide. The interior of the barn glowed with the light of a kerosene lantern. Three mounted men. Pernot, Lowe, and Crackley, in that order, on a chestnut mare, roan gelding, and roan mare, respectively. Crackley had the shotgun. They started to exit the horses from the stable at a walk, none of them able to see the deputy waiting for them in the dark driveway.

Creed turned sideways, leveled the Colt's at Crackley, cocked the hammer, and waited another second for the riders to come a few feet closer.

Lowe's gelding took this moment to defecate.

"Hold it right there, Crackley," said Creed.

"Who's there?" demanded the outlaw.

Lowe's horse started, reared, and threw him to the ground behind it.

Pernot knew what to do. Without hesitation, he hunkered down on his mare's neck, kicked her in the ribs, and burst ahead past Creed.

Frightened, Crackley stared into the darkness ahead of him, but he couldn't see much of anything, which only put more fear into him. He cocked the hammers on the shotgun and brought it to bear in the Texan's direction.

Creed knew that the slow hand usually wound up on a dead body. He squeezed off a round.

The ball shattered the bottom two inches of Crackley's sternum, rocking him backward. The outlaw's trigger finger contracted around the triggers, firing the shotgun harmlessly into the air. The force of the blast spilled him from the mare beneath him. He landed on his back, the crash driving the wind from his lungs. Gasping, he rolled onto his side. His head lolled for a second, then fell into the dung from Lowe's gelding.

Lowe gathered his few wits about him when he saw Crackley on the ground. "Harry!" he screamed with anguish. He scrambled on all fours to get to his friend.

Crackley spit blood as he tried to get air into his lungs. His body stiffened with convulsions.

Creed walked slowly toward the fallen outlaws, gun at the ready for more action, if necessary.

Lowe reached Crackley. "Harry!" he cried. He cradled Crackley's head against his chest oblivious to the horse manure that he was rubbing into his own wounds. "Harry!"

Crackley's eyes bulged at Lowe with a plea for help. He gasped for air, blood gurgling into his lungs. The convulsions shook his body repeatedly for a few seconds until his eyes rolled up into his head and his death sigh bubbled from his collapsed chest. He was dead.

"Harry! Harry! Harry!" Tears fell copiously from Lowe's eyes. "Harry," he sobbed. He looked up at Creed. "Help him, mister. Will you help him for me? Please?"

Creed shook his head and said, "I already have."

EPILOGUE

A norther blew into Arkansas at daylight that Friday morning whipping a cold rain ahead of it. The day bit deeply into the body and even deeper into the soul.

Van Buren took stock of itself. Buckmaster and Crackley were dead. Peterson was dying of his wounds; his death being only a matter of hours away. All of the other prisoners, with two glaring exceptions, were recaptured and back in their cells without anybody else being injured. The pair still missing was Dick Barth and Sinker Wilson. So were two horses from John Austin's stable.

Marshal Hays made a quick inspection of the cell where Barth and Wilson had been held until the night before. The investigation revealed that they had chiseled the mortar away from the bars in the window and had squeezed through the opening to freedom sometime between Creed's visit to Peterson in the evening and the incident that led to the general jailbreak in the middle of the night. Hays discovered the hoof pick that they'd used to do the deed on the ground outside the courthouse window.

"They've got a good six to ten hours head start on us," said Hays, "and with this weather like it is, we don't have a snowball's chance in hell of tracking them. I doubt there's an Indian across the line in the Nations who could track them in this rain."

That was the general consensus among the lawmen. The only man of a differing view was Creed. "I'd like to go after them right now," he said, "before they can get too far away from here."

"Do you know which direction they took?" asked Hays.

"I can't be positive, but it's my guess that they went north. Isn't that the direction of the Boston Mountains?"

"That's correct," said Hays, "but the Boston Mountains are pretty big. There's nooks and hollows everywhere, and they could have gone up any one of them and be hiding there for months, and we'd never know it unless we were to stumble on the exact right one. I'm sorry, Mr. Creed, but you're shit out of luck if you think you can just ride out of town and find those boys today or

195

tomorrow or the next day or next week or next month. Sinker
Wilson knows those mountains better than most. He could live up
there for a year, maybe two, without anybody ever getting close
to him. Face it, Mr. Creed, Wilson and Barth are long gone, and
that's all there is to it."

Creed was unwilling to give up so easily. "How about if I go
after them alone, Marshal?" he said.

"No, sir," said Hays. "Not unless you keep that badge you're
wearing right now."

"Would you let me do that?"

"You'd be on your own. You'd have to pay your own expenses,
and you wouldn't get paid any wages till you came back here and
only then if you bring in the lawbreakers. Is that understood?"

"Perfectly," said Creed.

"Then good luck to you. You're gonna need it."

If Creed had only known then how much luck he would be
needing, he might have just gone back to Texas and forgotten
about looking for Barth ever again.

AFTERMATH

Leo Smith was never arrested for his part in robbing the bank. Marshal Hays and Creed revealed Peterson's confession and witness that Smith and Buckmaster had been the actual thieves, but the grand jury refused to accept the word of a dead homosexual. Just the same, Smith slipped out of town late on the night before Christmas for parts unknown.

David Lowe's burns became infected by the horse manure that had rubbed off Harry Crackley's face, and he died in Dr. Pernot's hospital nine days later.

Colonel Burch said farewell to Creed on the dock at Van Buren, and he returned to Nashville to resume the legal fight to clear Creed's real name of the black mark put upon it by Jack Blackburn, Dick Barth, Jasper Johnson, Dick Spencer, and Jonas Burr. It would be a long struggle.